MORE MIRACLE THAN BIRD

Copyright © 2020 Alice Miller

Published by Tin House, Portland, Oregon

Distributed by W. W. Norton and Company.

Library of Congress Cataloging-in-Publication Data

Names: Miller, Alice, 1982- author.
Title: More miracle than bird / Alice Miller.
Description: Portland, Oregon : Tin House, [2020]
Identifiers: LCCN 2020001507 | ISBN 9781947793767 (hardcover) | ISBN
  9781947793866 (ebook)
Subjects: GSAFD: Occult fiction. | Love stories.
Classification: LCC PR9639.4.M57 M67 2020 | DDC 823/.92--dc23
LC record available at https://lccn.loc.gov/2020001507

First US Edition 2020
Printed in the USA
Interior design by Diane Chonette
www.tinhouse.com

MORE MIRACLE THAN BIRD

ALICE MILLER

 TIN HOUSE / Portland, Oregon

for Peter Miller and Sue Oakley

Once out of nature I shall never take
My bodily form from any natural thing,
But such a form as Grecian goldsmiths make
Of hammered gold and gold enamelling
To keep a drowsy Emperor awake;
Or set upon a golden bough to sing
To lords and ladies of Byzantium
Of what is past, or passing, or to come.

—W. B. YEATS, "Sailing to Byzantium"

ONE

WINTER 1916

Georgie was waiting outside in the empty hallway, aware that she was early, but at the sound of a scream she pushed the heavy door open.

She stopped in the doorway and did not cover her ears.

She had entered an enormous room with a high ceiling and long scarlet curtains, and a parquet floor lined with white beds filled with men. One of the men was sitting up, his eyes shut, mouth wide.

No one else in the room seemed to hear him. One man was reading a newspaper, one sipping a glass of water. They had not noticed her come in, either. She could not say how long she stood in the doorway, but at some point the screaming stopped. The man reading the newspaper flipped over to the next page. For a moment, the silence was worse. She moved out of the doorway.

"You'll get used to it," someone said near her. A low voice, from the bed nearest the door, where a young man was watching her. His feet were exposed below the sheet, and his toes were purple and red, rotted open, raw. All his toenails black. She tried not to stare. He noticed and smiled.

"Trench foot. You'll get used to that too."

Georgie looked away. Other men in the room were noticing her now, and she could feel their eyes on her.

The young man was reaching forward to drape the sheet over his raw feet, wincing as the cotton brushed his toes.

"The matron'll be along any moment. She's a good sort."

Georgie concentrated on keeping her face entirely neutral. The truth was, she'd walked here in a haze of self-congratulations. She thought she'd come up with a masterful plan: by getting a job at the hospital, she'd escaped her mother; she had her own—yes, modest, but her *own*—room provided for her; and she was in London where Dorothy Shakespear and Willy Yeats were, where she could see them as often as she wished. Not only that, but—this was always somewhat of an afterthought—she would be helping with the war. She didn't believe in the war, but it wasn't the soldiers' fault that they'd been gulped down by it.

But how was it that during those weeks of training, of making beds and mopping floors, she hadn't imagined that the ward would be like this—these lines of anonymous white-sheeted beds filled with half-oblivious, damaged creatures? One of the best small hospitals, they had said. For officers only. Not a single death. Had she expected the men not to scream, not to have grotesque, rotting feet? Had she expected them to nod to her as she dutifully changed their pillowcases?

"Hyde-Lees. You're early." Stated without emotion. The matron, Mrs. Thwaite, had arrived on the ward. She had the sort of gaze that took everything in at once—travelling, assessing, judging. Her eyes swept over Georgie.

"We are very protective of our officers," she said, as she started to walk down the centre of the room to the far end, with the expectation that Georgie would follow. The matron demonstrated the sort of posture that made you question your own.

"I've heard very good things," Georgie managed to say.

"Of course. Our officers are first priority and last priority. If you neglect them in any way, we cannot be expected to keep you on."

Georgie nervously eyed the men. Willy had not been impressed to hear she was working at a war hospital. "You're giving up all that time?" he'd said. She had responded stiffly that she preferred to think of it as *giving* time, rather than giving *up* time, but he was not convinced. Never mind. In time he would figure out why she was really here.

"Colonel Fraser," the matron was saying, walking down the line of beds, gesturing sharply to each man as they went past. This man was sleeping with his lips turned inwards, as though he were trying to suck his face in through his mouth. "Captain Christie" had curled his hand over the stained yellow bandage that covered his eye. "Captain Emery-May" was covered from head to toe with a blanket. "Lieutenant Gray," staring at the wall, his face pale orange with dry scales, was the young man who had been screaming. They kept on towards the door. "Second Lieutenant Pike" was the man with the rotting feet, and on the other side of the room, an older man, "Major Hammond." Although this last man was asleep, the matron pinched the edge of the white bedsheet, gently lifting it, to reveal the wound down the major's side.

It was a test for Georgie. The wound resembled a crude dotted map of Norway, long, lumpy, filled with blood, tissue, and ooze, and interspersed with fine white stitches, where, the matron reported, the doctor had extracted the shrapnel. It was clear to Georgie that these words were fictions; *extract* was far too clean a word when you were talking of meat and bone. As Georgie looked down, the major shifted in his sleep, and his wound winced—a sac of mustard-coloured pus drooped, threatened to fall on the sheet. Georgie did not take her eyes from it, clenching her fist hard against her hip.

Mrs. Thwaite turned to Georgie and offered a cool smile.

"All right, Hyde-Lees?" She didn't wait for an answer. "You can begin with the floors: start in the upstairs hallway, then the stairs, back through the kitchen. Upstairs there is one bed that needs to be stripped and made. Then mop the ward." She pointed to a mop and an empty bucket with a rope handle, and headed out to the other room.

Georgie took the bucket and went straight to the basin. She tried not to picture the man's skin, the bubbled texture where tissue and blood mixed. She took the bucket upstairs and mopped as if it were a noble pursuit, as if she herself were fighting a war.

———— • ————

When she returned after mopping the entire upstairs, there were no other hospital staff on the ward. She slid the mop along the floor, ignoring the new twinge in her back. She couldn't imagine doing this again tomorrow. She was trying to concentrate only on the mop and not think of anything else. Still, she was wondering how she could manage to get out of this, how she could slink away with no one noticing. But when she glanced at the clock, she saw her shift was almost over.

"First day's the worst," Second Lieutenant Pike called to her. She stopped beside his bed. Unlike the others, he was unshaven. From here she could see the individual hairs of his stubble. His skin stretched as he smiled. She held the mop in one hand.

"It's not so bad," she said.

"Come on, it's horrid. Divine plan's gone a bit awry, I reckon."

"I'm not the best person to talk to about divine plans."

"Why, you don't believe in them? Me neither. Why make these feet just to mangle them?"

The matron had come back into the room. Georgie exhaled, glanced at the clock once more, and returned the mop to the bucket. The matron was coming towards her.

"Hyde-Lees," she said, "what are you doing?"

"My shift is over, ma'am."

"And I suppose that means you are free to prostrate yourself over the second lieutenant?"

Georgie took a step back. "I beg your pardon?"

"In my hospital, you may not *lean* over the men. You may not *dangle* over them."

"I did nothing of the sort."

Second Lieutenant Pike had overheard them. "It was my fault. I was chittering."

Across the room, Major Hammond laughed.

"Oh come on, Matron. She's sweet on our Tom! Plenty of rotten fish in the sea, but none—like—Pike." Some of the men who had woken from the noise, or were already awake, were laughing. Someone gave a low whistle.

"Want to get under his bloody sheets?" another called. "Naught more attractive than a man who can't run from your clutches."

The second lieutenant was smiling a watery smile. Major Hammond was laughing with his mouth wide open, an overloud laugh that did not contain amusement. Georgie kept her back rigid and tried not to look at the faces of the men, either chuckling or comatose, as she walked between the beds towards the washroom.

"Not much to look at though, is she," one of the men said as she passed.

"Well," said another, "fine for wartime." When she got to the washroom and shut the door, she could still hear one of the men: "We were called up, not to fight the Hun but to woo and screw the girls of England!" More laughter, and one of the men started to sing a song that Georgie didn't know.

She heard Mrs. Thwaite yell above them, "All right, gentlemen!" and one man's laugh rang out like a howl. Georgie scrubbed her hands—pressing them together to stop them shaking—changed her clothes, and headed out onto the street.

TWO

Outside, the air was a gift, crowding her face. It had nothing to do with decay. A last streak of sun was creaking down behind the buildings, and soon it would be dark. She started to walk towards the dormitory. Still, she could hear that jeering, see the major's bubbling wound, the matron's cut-glass stare. For a moment she thought of writing to her mother, of admitting she'd been wrong to come. Already she yearned for the silence and privacy of her bedroom, of the small library on the first floor of her mother's house.

But she wouldn't write. She would go back to her room and arrange the contents of her two leather suitcases on the few provided shelves and rest until her next shift at the hospital. Tomorrow she would write to Willy and to Dorothy and announce she was settled in London, and next week she would go to a meeting of the Hermetic Order of the Golden Dawn, without having to lie to her mother about where she was going.

She'd glimpsed this kind of freedom at the first soirée that her mother had taken her to, back before the war, in 1908 when she had turned sixteen. The soirée was what she would come to know as the usual affair at Olivia Shakespear's; in the large drawing room, clusters of people chatted and sipped, and Jelly d'Aranyi played Schumann on the violin, and a servant walked around refilling glasses of what Olivia whispered was rather middling claret that someone had gifted her and she was trying to get rid of. Discussions ranged from Schopenhauer to Schubert, tarot and Tattwa, to the most thrilling moments at recent séances. Olivia had attended a session only last month where an ancient Egyptian soul had spoken, declaring that the current age was nearly over and another was about to begin.

Georgie had been taught to call her parents by their first names—never "Mother" but always "Nelly"—and in this room she saw a different Nelly from the one she knew. Nelly had clearly spent many evenings in that drawing room, and Georgie was startled to watch her integrate herself so effortlessly, talk without self-consciousness, and laugh with an ease that Georgie had rarely heard at home. Nelly introduced her to the pianist Walter Rummel, whom Georgie had seen play at concerts, and the poet W. B. Yeats—known to all as W. B.—whose poems Georgie knew and admired, and with whom she had a brief conversation about the Renaissance philosopher and occultist Giovanni Pico della Mirandola. Georgie even shyly mentioned that she had started to translate the early works of Pico from Latin, and she could have sworn that W. B. had looked impressed.

But the person Nelly most wanted her to meet was Olivia's daughter, Dorothy. When Georgie saw Dorothy across the room, chatting assuredly to two young men, she was doubtful that they would be friends. Dorothy was already twenty-three, and very pretty in an unreal way, like those drawings of jaunty women from Harrods advertisements. She wore a dark blue dress which, while not especially revealing, hung on her body and clung to every lovely angle of her, as if the dress itself had a kind of nonchalance. The guests around her, whether they faced her or not, all seemed aware of each dip of her head, each arching of her fine, white neck. Georgie was surprised to see her slide that neck to the side and fix her eyes right on her.

"Are you Georgie? Nelly said you were coming." Dorothy was smiling at her with white, even teeth that made Georgie nervous. The young men reluctantly made room so she could join them in the circle.

"I suppose that makes you Nelly's daughter," one of the men said.

"I suppose it does, but thankfully I'm many other things besides."

The man laughed but hardly managed to pry his eyes from Dorothy. He was handsome in a bland way and spoke with the hint of squeezed colonial vowels. He held an unlit cigar, but one of his fingers was twitching, and his laughter sounded as if he were on the verge of spitting, as if he were holding marbles in his mouth. Georgie waited for Dorothy to introduce them.

Instead, she said, "Excuse us. I need to show Georgie something." Without another word, she was gone. Georgie hesitated a moment—meeting the bewildered eyes of the men—before following Dorothy as she slipped out of the drawing room and down the hall. At the end of the hall, Dorothy turned into another room, and once Georgie went in, Dorothy closed the door behind them.

She flicked a match and lit a thin white candle on the table, illuminating the library, with shelves full of books up to the ceiling and a narrow ladder leaning beside the window. Georgie looked around and back at Dorothy.

"Alone at last," Dorothy said.

"That man's in love with you," Georgie said, realizing it herself. "They both are."

"They're infatuated. It's not the same."

"How do you know?"

"Who cares. Freddie can't stop telling me all about it. It's horrendous."

"I can imagine," said Georgie, who couldn't.

"Drink?" Dorothy pulled from a shelf a heavy cut-glass decanter of brandy and two tumblers, the kind Georgie's father drank from. Georgie nodded. She was rather overwhelmed by Dorothy's ease, and she tried to unstiffen her own body as she found herself a place in a large leather chair. She could still hear the blur of chatter in the drawing room.

Dorothy poured. "Do you paint?"

"Terribly," Georgie said, "but cheerfully."

"Good," Dorothy said, who handed her a drink and, after offering a cigarette to Georgie, who declined, lit one for herself. Georgie took a cautious sip of the brandy. She knew she would have to go home for dinner—it was still only early evening—and she wondered what Nelly would say if she were visibly drunk.

"Are the parties always like this?" Georgie said, watching Dorothy sit on another armchair and draw her knees up to her chest like a girl. Georgie had recognised other people out in the drawing room—the painter Rothenstein, the actress Florence Farr.

"Always." Dorothy glanced back towards the drawing room, as if the chatter were carrying on purely to irritate her. "Freddie, whom you didn't quite meet, is on the road to being a typical Oxford man."

Georgie nodded. "I think I'd prefer to *be* an Oxford man than to marry one," she said, taking a larger sip this time. "I am a translator."

"You are? That's something, I suppose." Dorothy was still frowning as she balanced her cigarette between two slim fingers. "But all those Oxford types are the same; I plan to do things a little differently. I'm on the lookout for something"—she tapped her fingernail on the lip of her glass—"though to be honest I'm not sure what yet." She smiled. "Do you go in much for the occultish things, the séances and all that?"

"Do you?" Georgie had only read about séances. She liked the idea of speaking to the dead, but at the same time she found something embarrassing in the expectation they would answer.

"I've been to some, all dull. But I've heard about an occult order, a sort of society, one of those secrets everyone's talking about. Very exclusive. I'm trying to get an invitation. You could come with me, if it was of interest? It will probably be codswallop but maybe entertaining codswallop. I won't be asking Freddie or Herb to come, I know that much."

"I'd like that." Georgie watched Dorothy, who at the mention of Freddie and Herbert looked thoroughly bored—but the bored expression of long-gowned, glamorous Dorothy Shakespear was exquisite. At that moment Georgie had the feeling that if the dead would speak to anyone, it would be Dorothy Shakespear.

"I'll let you know," Dorothy said. "Also, some of us are going to Florence next month. A painting trip. Painting and rambling. And drinking. If you want to join."

Georgie felt a trickle of excitement, before she realised, of course, she couldn't do anything of the kind.

"I have to go back to school."

"Surely Italy is a better education than St. James's?"

"Of course," Georgie said, putting her drink down on the table, "but . . ." The sentence that had been forming on her lips fell away, and she found herself staring at the lazy trail of smoke from Dorothy's cigarette as it rose, weaving in and out of itself. There was no way that Nelly would let her quit school. But the longer Georgie sat drinking brandy with Dorothy, as their conversation ambled between the Futurists and Debussy and those new silk dresses which fell straight to your ankle, the more convinced she became that Dorothy's approach was the right one. Surely Georgie's life could also be different.

That night she'd gone back with her mother for dinner at Drayton Gardens. It was probably the brandy, but in the car she thought her pulse was so loud that her mother would hear it. When they got home there was a pause while Nelly went to talk to Georgie's father upstairs, but when Georgie arrived at the dinner table, both her parents were already sitting in their places. Lucy brought in the soup, and both Nelly and Gilbert seemed to pay the soup more attention than usual. Were her parents responding to her? she wondered. Could they sense this change inside her, this determination? They each had a glass of wine, which Georgie pretended not to notice; the presence of alcohol in the house had become a source of anxiety, so that no one looked at or spoke about it. How timid this behaviour seemed to her, almost dishonest. Georgie was filled with bravery and brandy. She glanced over to see Lucy retreat to the other room. She raised her spoon above her bowl and paused.

"I have decided to leave St. James's," she said. "Dorothy and the others are going to the Continent, and I plan to go with them."

Her mother held a crust of bread halfway between her lips and her plate. "Oh, darling. You can't leave." It had been Nelly's idea to commit Georgie to St. James's School for Girls in West Malvern.

"I spend all day learning nothing of use, and I have hardly any time when I come home to study *real things*." Her older brother, Harold, was in his last year at Eton, and he too disliked school, but at least he was studying history and theology. St. James's taught classes on sewing and cookery and deportment, to a horde of girls who seemed somehow satisfied with this as an education.

"Dorothy loved it there."

"Maybe so"—and if she had, she certainly hadn't mentioned it—"but *I don't*." It occurred to Georgie only now that Nelly would have much preferred a daughter like Dorothy: charming, easy, gifted at telling people what they wanted to hear.

Her father had taken a large spoonful of soup and now tore a chunk of bread in his fingers.

"Are you sure you want to leave?"

"I wish I liked it more," Georgie said, "but I can't stop criticising it."

He smiled. "You get that from me."

"You think she doesn't get it from me?" Nelly's smile was tight. "It's only another year to stay on. And the school is very well regarded."

"I don't see the point in staying," Georgie said. "What's the use? It would cost less to have me at home."

Nelly shook her head slowly. "There are different kinds of cost."

Gilbert reached forward for his glass and took a gulp of wine. "You would have done far better at Eton and Oxford than Harold or I will ever do." No one contradicted him. The greatest achievement of Gilbert's education was being part of the winning team in the Oxford Fours boat race. He never took a degree. But no one would consider sending Georgie, a young woman, to Oxford.

"It doesn't matter anyway," Georgie said, gathering momentum, "I'm going to Italy with Dorothy. I've decided."

"All right, pup, we hear you," Gilbert said. "We can talk about it. But the thing is we have our own news, actually. Your mother is kicking me out of the house again."

"Gilbert."

"It's true. She's requested I leave for a few weeks. Leave her to her soirées and her lectures."

"That is *not* what we discussed," Nelly said. She put her spoon down and sat very still. The last time Nelly had sent him away, it was to a home for inebriates in Twickenham. It had taken months of Georgie's pleading before she had let him come back. They hadn't mentioned it afterwards.

"It is, really," Gilbert said cheerfully, finishing his glass and looking around casually to see if Lucy might refill it. Georgie delivered soup to her mouth, then spent some seconds coaxing herself to swallow. "But I love your mother, and I give her what she wants, insofar as in my awfully limited capacity I am able. I've decided to go down to Suffolk and catch up with an old military chum."

Georgie swallowed. She knew that there was a lot more to what was being said, but right now she didn't want to consider it. She tried to glide past these words, past the looks that her parents were exchanging, and said with confidence, "And I will leave St. James's."

Her mother glanced at the two of them, placed her spoon back down on the tablecloth, and, like a defeated ruler, rose from her chair.

"Very well," she said. "You both must do as you like."

——— • ———

Georgie heard a knock on her door a few hours later, when she was sitting on her bed reading her Latin primer. She was continuing with her translation of Pico della Mirandola; after she'd mentioned it at the soirée, it seemed more urgent than before. Wouldn't a project like this be worth leaving school for? Or would she find it too lonely? It could take years. The door pushed open, and her father leaned his long frame against the doorway before coming in and sitting beside her on the bed.

"Are you here to talk me out of it?"

He smoothed the bedcover with his thick fingers, and she could feel his breath, warm air, claret, smoke. "I'm here to make sure you're sure. I'm only concerned that, without school, you wouldn't have enough structure."

She put the primer face down beside her on the bed. It was easier to be honest with him than with her mother. "I'm not completely sure. But I think I'm sure. I want to go to Italy. I have some translation projects. That might be enough." She paused. There was the possibility, of course, that it wouldn't be. That perhaps she would struggle. "Do you think it's enough?"

"I'm sorry, pup. I don't know. And that indecision, I gave that to you too."

"It's not your fault."

"But I could have tried to cure myself, instead of just blindly passing it on," he said. "Other people just make up their mind and know."

"I think that I know," she said, wishing she could sound more certain, wishing for once she were more like Nelly, who always seemed sure of the answers. "If I left school, I think I could use my time far better than I do now."

"I'll tell you one thing. The times when you really do know, it's heavenly." Gilbert was looking down at the bedspread, at his hands, which cupped one another. "It does happen, even to critical souls like us," he went on. "I knew when I married your mother that it was exactly what I wanted."

"You did?" She was surprised.

"Well, I had been smitten with someone else—Margaret was her name, an absolutely ripping girl, actually—but she was not the right sort, and we both knew it. And it was she who introduced me to your mother." He tilted his head. "I don't know why your mother gave in and married me. A moment of weakness, I suppose. She desperately wanted to upset her mother, and I was the perfect fix."

"You still think it was a good decision?"

"Well, some fellows doubt their marriages every day. I never did. I loved her. Still do."

Georgie was puzzled by this. "Maybe that has less to do with her and more to do with you."

"Maybe," he said, "but maybe it has something to do with both of us. Anyway. I say you should go ahead and leave school. We'll look out for you, make sure you don't get lost without it."

"I don't think I will be," she said quietly.

———— • ————

And she wouldn't have been lost without it, she thought now, as she walked along the edge of Berkeley Square Gardens towards the dormitory, avoiding the muddy straw put down to dampen the noise of cars, her pace fast and deliberate through the dark streets. Gilbert would have helped her to adjust to life without school, and she would have had her own independence to study and translate as she wished. Still, it hadn't happened that way. Instead, in November 1909, after returning from one of her trips to Italy—from three weeks of reckless discussions and exploring ruins and painting, from laughing and dancing with Dorothy Shakespear, and watching clusters of artistic young men eyeing Dorothy adoringly—she had received a telegram to say that her father was dead.

THREE

In Georgie's first week at the hospital, the matron repeatedly instructed her to mop the floors. But Georgie discovered that if she mopped the floors right to each corner, she was too slow; if she mopped quickly, she was careless. If she spoke to the men, she was accused of being frivolous and flirtatious, but if they called out for her and she didn't answer, she was declared negligent. When she slopped water on the floor, the matron stood above the puddle and gazed at it in horror, as if Georgie had squatted down and urinated.

Still, she mopped floors, sterilised instruments, emptied bedpans. It was strange to think that it had taken a war for her to finally leave home. It was seven years since Gilbert had died in a flat in Pimlico. It had been a complete shock to Georgie—he was only forty-four, and she never found out why he had gone to that flat in Pimlico or what had happened there. But she came to realise that other people were not so surprised, that it was thought that sooner

or later Captain Hyde-Lees might drink himself to death. When
Georgie returned from Italy, Nelly sent her to finishing school, and
she lived at home until school was over and the war broke out.
Still, she wasn't sure she would ever forgive her mother for sending
Gilbert away.

As Georgie placed a clean bedpan under Colonel Fraser's bed,
she accidentally bumped the iron bed-frame, and the gentle knock
startled the colonel, who clutched his arms around his chest without opening his eyes. Part of what was so odd about the officers was
their hopelessness. Many of them did not look at her, let alone talk
to her; many of them didn't seem to care whether they lived or died.
Even Second Lieutenant Pike, who was one of the most animated,
had that odd, ghosted expression of a creature who was missing
something. Under Mrs. Thwaite's instructions, Georgie was to pay
special attention to Major Hammond, as the matron was concerned about his treatment. Although Georgie was new, she was
designated as his nurse presumably because she had cleaner, more
aristocratic vowels than Sanderson, the other girl. But Mrs. Thwaite
needn't have worried, because the major seldom opened his eyes
and didn't seem to hear a word Georgie said, and in the rare times
he was awake he kept his face firmly hidden behind his newspaper,
intermittently shaking the paper, like there was something caught
in the pages he needed to banish.

As always, during visiting hours, the ward filled with women;
men, too, but it was the women who took over the space, heaving
with sighs over their sons and brothers and husbands, reaching into
their handbags for gifts or for tissues, and filling the room with the
smell of shampoo and perfume and shortbread. A woman crouched
at Mayor Hammond's bedside, her body awkwardly turned away

from his wound as she whispered in his ear. A man, perhaps the lady's husband, stood at the bed's end, watching the two of them and kicking his heel against the toe of his other boot, gently, over and over, as if trying to knock something through the leather of his shoe.

Georgie was making one of the beds when a young lady approached her, pretty, her hair pale as cooked egg-white, wearing an expensive silk shirt and skirt, standing in a fog of perfume.

"Excuse me," the lady said. She was standing near Second Lieutenant Pike's bed, but Pike was looking out the window like he didn't know she was there.

"Yes?" Georgie straightened up. She followed the lady's gaze down to her own once-white collar, where she had smudged a fingerprint of blood. Georgie patted her collar uselessly with her fingers.

"I require some privacy," the lady announced, "to talk to the lieutenant. Would you leave us, please?"

Georgie, who couldn't see how the lady imagined any privacy possible in the busy ward, continued tucking in the corners of the sheet. "I won't be a moment."

"I'm afraid I do not have a moment," the lady said.

Second Lieutenant Pike looked over at her. "She's busy, Emma."

"She is making a bed, Thomas."

"I'll come back," Georgie said, rising from her crouched position and leaving the sheet untucked and the blanket bunched at the bottom of the bed. She was curious to know what this rather haughty lady would have to do with the plain-spoken, approachable lieutenant. Glancing back, she saw the lady lower herself into a chair like a regal personage. Like so many of the men and women on the ward, the lady had a desperation about her, but it was almost admirable how she translated that desperation into pride. She was inflicting it on the world, rather than keeping it close.

As Georgie left them to it, she could see the matron signalling to her from the doorway. She looked back at the unmade bed as she walked over to the matron, preparing for a reprimand as she rubbed her bloody collar once more. But when she reached Mrs. Thwaite, she saw that the matron was, astonishingly, smiling. Her gaze travelled up Georgie's uniform and skimmed over the bloodstain on her collar to meet her eyes.

"I'm afraid Sanderson is ill, and we're very short-staffed. I wondered if you might stay on for the night shift."

"Of course," said Georgie.

———— • ————

After the visitors had left and the night shift commenced, Georgie started to dig her nails into her palms to keep herself awake. The ward was silent and she was the only person on duty—armed with a bell, which could summon the matron, who was sleeping upstairs.

Georgie eyed the clock at the back of the room. One of the gold hands twitched. Standing for such a long time—they were forbidden to sit—meant already Georgie's back and feet ached with a cool, pulsing pain. She was exhausted. She started to pace the room. On her break she'd received a message from her mother, checking in with her and asking if they could meet soon. This was good news; that Nelly was writing to her indicated there was a chance she might consider restoring Georgie's allowance. It also meant Georgie might be able to go and stay with her at the house at Montpelier Square for a weekend. She had to admit that she already missed being able to have a proper cup of tea whenever she wanted, and having a maid to fix her breakfast and manage her laundry (and she needed someone to get rid of this bloodstain on her collar). And she missed living in a house where you didn't have to tolerate the banging and thumping and giggling and chattering of the girls in the rooms on either side. Nelly had not wanted her to take the job at the hospital, and they had quarrelled. If she really wanted to help with the war, Nelly argued, she should wait for a position at the Foreign Office instead. But although the Foreign Office would doubtless have been better suited to her, Georgie wasn't prepared to wait.

She avoided looking towards the bed of Major Hammond, who seemed to her to be near death. A part of her thought that if she didn't look too closely at death, perhaps she might escape it.

"Will you sit awhile?" It was Second Lieutenant Pike again, with his ruined feet sticking out the end of his bed. He gestured to a chair that, some hours ago, the imperious blonde lady had occupied.

"I'm not allowed."

"A pity." Unlike the other men, many of whom slept all day and all night, Pike did not seem to need to rest. She hadn't yet seen him close his eyes. She was debating about whether or not she should sit down anyway, given how tired she was, when there was a scream across the room. Then another. Strained, sharp screams. It was as though a small, howling creature were trying to burrow its way out of a body. Georgie hurried over. It was the same young officer from the first day, the blond one with the scaly face whose name Georgie had already forgotten. He began to arch his back and fall back down on the bed, arch and fall. She stood by him a moment before reaching for his wrists, but he shook her off, arms flailing in the air, scratching at nothing.

"You're all right," Georgie said, reaching for him again. He grabbed at a handful of her hair and pulled, yanking several strands out of the follicle.

"Mary!" he yelled, his breath hot. He had streams of snot and tears running down his face, and his cheeks were bright orange, from the gas. The bald patches of his scalp were wet.

"I'm not Mary," she said. "I'm the nurse."

He reached his arms up to her neck, as if he wanted to strangle her, and she stepped out of the way.

"I didn't bring your Gospel, Mary," the man said, his eyes wide. "I left it in your stupid head."

He lunged up and caught her wrist. Georgie leaned down and, with her other hand, slapped the boy's face across the cheek. The boy dropped her hand and whimpered. He thumped his own wind-pipe with his fist, making a deep thud, like wood dropping on bone.

She rushed across the room to ring the bell, and after a few minutes, footsteps could be heard coming down the stairs. Mrs. Thwaite, with a coat over her dressing gown, arrived in the room as the boy's eyes flew open again, and the matron rushed over to him immediately, speaking softly and stroking his hair, moving closer until she was holding his head in her arms like a lover: "You're safe here, you're in London, everything is all right, I've got you, you're safe, I promise." After some time, the boy fell limp, his eyes half closed, his arms resting loosely on either side of his body. Mrs. Thwaite said nothing to Georgie. She disentangled herself from the boy, looked around the ward once, left the room again, and could be heard going slowly back upstairs. Other officers were stirring; one was signalling for water. Georgie's uniform was wet with sweat. She felt sick now, as if she were waiting for someone else to wake, some other blurry horror to float into the room.

"Please, take a seat. Just sit down." From his bed, Second Lieutenant Pike spoke softly. The red-brown tufts of his hair were curved up like the horns of an owl. His eyes were unblinking and calm in the light from the weak electric lamp. It seemed to her at that moment as if he were offering her something of great worth, something she should remember. She walked to the chair beside his bed and sank down into it.

FOUR

WINTER 1914

Georgie and Dorothy had settled into a rhythm before the war, even for Georgie's final year of school, taking regular holidays to the Continent—renting a little apartment with Olivia or another chaperone, and talking and drinking and smoking and painting, and meeting with whoever was passing through. In London they went to soirées and lectures and occasionally séances, and they gave false hope to the young men who wanted to marry Dorothy. Since her father's death, Georgie had become more interested in séances, as if perhaps her father might use one to check in with her, to offer her a scrap of advice or reassurance. Although Dorothy had tried to get invitations to the occult order she'd heard about through one of her admirers, no invitation had ever arrived, and Dorothy seemed to have forgotten about it. But at one of Olivia's soirées, Georgie thought to ask W. B. Yeats.

W. B. was Nelly's age, in his late forties, and although he was a tall man, he bent over slightly to be closer to his audience. After she'd had a few glasses of wine, Georgie caught him when the woman he was speaking to excused herself to use the lavatory. As the woman left to go down the hall, Georgie stepped in front of him, and with a bravery she didn't know she had, she said,

"Dorothy and I want to join the Order."

W. B. stood up straighter and considered her. "Why?"

Georgie had rehearsed a scholarly answer, with reference to William Blake, Dante, and Swedenborg, which she thought would impress him. But standing there, she realised this answer was all wrong. She was speaking to a man, not a famous figure. He wanted something unprepared, something bare. His eyebrows were raised as he waited for her response, and the wrinkles of his forehead were like those curved lines blown into sand dunes.

"I'll do anything," she said, "to speak to the dead." She glanced up to see Nelly approaching them, about to cut in on their conversation, and to stop that happening she hastily excused herself, turning her back on her mother and slipping off into another group of strangers.

She hadn't had the chance to speak with him again. But a week later she received an envelope containing her first invitation to the Hermetic Order of the Golden Dawn. It was a pale green card with her name in the corner, announcing an appointment that evening:

144 Bassett Road, 10 PM, Stella Matutina Branch

When Georgie saw Dorothy the same evening at the regular do at Eva Fowler's, Dorothy said she hadn't received a card.

"It must be a mistake," Georgie said. It hadn't occurred to her she would have to go to a strange house, late at night, alone. "It's all right," Dorothy said. "I don't mind." She seemed distracted, continually turning around to look at the newly arriving guests, as if she were expecting someone. Georgie hoped that she didn't have another plan to set her up with one of the men she knew. Every attempt before now had been embarrassing for Georgie; either the men had clearly preferred Dorothy, or their lack of imagination had offended her. How could Dorothy imagine she would be interested in them? Did Dorothy think so little of her?

"Have you met Hilda?" Dorothy said. A woman was coming over to them, and Georgie could already tell from the way Dorothy was acting that she didn't like her. The woman was extremely tall, and had an arch expression, like a foal that has learned to gallop and is puzzled by why you are still lying in the grass.

"Hilda is a poet. From Pennsylvania," Dorothy said, still looking behind them. "Georgie Hyde-Lees, Hilda Doolittle." Georgie shook the woman's hand.

"Have you been in London long?" Georgie said politely, but any answer was prevented by a thumping across the room. All heads turned towards the sound, before everyone realised who it was and returned to their conversations. Ezra was always a demanding and slightly ridiculous presence; tonight his side whiskers bloomed from his face, his shirt had enormous pale blue buttons, and he wore, dripping from one ear, a turquoise earring. He was banging his walking stick along the parquet as he entered, announcing his arrival like he was leading a charge. Behind him, W. B. smiled at his young protégé, with a look halfway between appreciation and bemusement.

The poets joined their circle, and before anyone could say any-thing, Ezra announced the topic for discussion. "The Eagle and I are squabbling about a prize." W. B. was the more respectable of the pair; by far the senior, his poems were taught in schools; he wore an impeccable velvet jacket and stood with the confidence of a man who was planning to refuse a knighthood.

Another man had joined them and put his arm around Hilda, who kissed him fiercely in front of the group. Georgie averted her eyes and fingered the green card in her pocket.

"I don't need it," W. B. was saying.

"It's not about that," Ezra said. "It's about the magazine's rec-ognition that you are the Greatest Poet in the English Language."

"It can recognise that without awarding a prize."

"But a prize makes it clear."

"There is another man we could give it to. Who needs it more."

"You can't give it to anyone else. It's *your prize*." Ezra punctuated his final words with his stick, turning away from W. B. and towards Dorothy and Hilda. "He doesn't listen."

Dorothy laughed and Ezra smiled at her. Georgie had often wondered what it would be like to be so absolutely devoid of self-doubt as Ezra Pound seemed to be, almost as if he were gazing at the world from behind a protective film. She imagined it would be magnificent.

As Ezra switched his attention to Dorothy, W. B. said quietly to Georgie, "He's too much sometimes."

"Often, I should think," Georgie said, and she added, "Thank you. For the invitation. It came through."

He smiled. "You're very well matched to it, with your interests," he said. For now he didn't mention Dorothy, so Georgie didn't ask.

"Giddyup, Dante," Ezra called over to him. He was already on his way down the hall, Hilda and the other man behind him, and he was gesturing with his walking stick for W. B. to follow. W. B. started across the room and Georgie started after him, but Dorothy grabbed her elbow.

"Wait," she said, holding her. "Dear, I have to talk to you." She paused. "I don't want to worry you."

"What?"

"It's not official yet." Georgie watched the others leave the room, and turned back to her friend. Dorothy's pale cheeks were striped with red, as if she were ill. Worried, Georgie took her hand, and Dorothy burst into a kind of wild laughter.

"Ezra and I—we are going to marry."

"Oh?" Georgie wanted to drop Dorothy's hand, but instead she clasped it and embraced her. It shouldn't have been a surprise. But what of their plans—to join the Order, to return to Italy this summer?

"It doesn't change anything," Dorothy said.

"Of course it does," Georgie said, pulling back from the embrace. "Congratulations." As she smiled, she noticed she was already trying to extricate herself, already guarding her thoughts and feelings. She had planned to ask if Dorothy had enjoyed the parodies of Ezra in the *Egoist*, but now that Ezra was her fiancé, she could hardly bring up a text that ridiculed him. Not now, anyway. Instead, Georgie swiftly excused herself, pretending not to notice Dorothy's worried look.

She walked out of the room and towards the front door, and let herself out onto the porch of the Fowlers' house. What had she thought would happen? That Dorothy would never marry, that they would keep being independent and wandering around the Continent, painting and drinking? Looking out, she could see the darkness which marked the edge of Hyde Park. She walked around the porch until she could see inside the drawing room, which radiated a light that guaranteed that no one would be able to see her outside. She was grateful for the privacy, the invisibility. Inside, Dorothy still stood near where Georgie had left her, but there was Ezra, swooping back in to speak to her, presumably checking to see how their conversation had gone. Of course they would marry. Dorothy admired Ezra, and why wouldn't Ezra, like everyone else, be unable to resist Dorothy? Behind the glass, Dorothy was making a sweeping gesture, looking concerned, but Ezra reached and caught her hand, and brought the hand up to her cheek, and they smiled at each other.

"It won't last, you know," a voice came from behind Georgie. "These things hardly ever do."

She turned and found W. B. standing there.

"They're getting married," she said.

"Really?" He seemed surprised, and he stepped forward to peer more closely at them through the glass.

"I shouldn't have said anything. It's not official." Inside, the couple were laughing together, secure in a delight that was only theirs. "Why did you think they wouldn't?"

He was still watching them. "I don't know. I didn't think Ezra wanted to marry. Too obsessed with work. I think with the keenness of his intellect, his apprenticeship will be long. What do you make of him?"

"I think he's wonderful," she said, which was true, but she wanted to add that she didn't think his work was wonderful, or not yet anyway. She thought it wild and self-conscious, rather like the man himself. It had the man's bravado but did not show confidence, or consistency. W. B. was a far better poet. She remembered the parody of Ezra in the *Egoist* that she'd wanted to laugh about with Dorothy:

> *Come my songs,*
> *Let us praise ourselves;*
> *I doubt if the smug will do it for us,*
> *The smug who possess all the rest of the universe.*

She turned to W. B. to ask if he had read it, but his expression surprised her—a fierce expression, as if he were bracing for something—and seeing him like that, she forgot what she was about to say. She was already struggling with her own set of feelings, and here was a whole other person with his own feelings. She turned to the window to collect herself, and by the time she turned back, the poet had gone.

She went looking for him afterwards, but he must have left the party altogether. She found Nelly and told her that she was tired and she was going home early. Although she knew she should congratulate Ezra and say goodbye to Dorothy, she avoided speaking to either of them. Instead, she made her way to Bassett Road alone.

———— • ————

When the cab stopped outside the house on Bassett Road just before ten that night, Georgie almost ordered the driver to go back to Drayton Gardens. The Bassett Road house was white, suburban, unremarkable, but there was something in its plainness, its unassuming facade, that made her nervous. Who knew what might be inside? She hesitated, but having ordered the car here, she felt too embarrassed to do anything but pay the driver and get out onto the street.

As the car drove away, she walked up the steps to the house and rang the bell. She showed the servant her green card, and he took her down the hall and pointed to a heavy door.

"Please shut it after you, ma'am," he said.

She entered a completely dark room. When she closed the door, she heard the click of a lock. She could tell she was standing in a large room, although she could not see the walls. All around her she could hear people breathing. She wished her eyes would adjust. She took a few steps forward into the darkness.

Something was moving towards her. It was a figure in a long black robe, with arms out. The figure was cradling a black mass, and offered it to her. She took it. It was a long robe, with a large hood. She shook it out; it smelled of aniseed and another woman's perfume. Although the fabric was heavy, Georgie found as she pulled the robe on, she felt lighter. She stepped back and walked into someone.

"I'm sorry," she said quickly, as the body ducked away. The world seemed to be retreating from her. She wanted to reach out to feel what was in front of her, to understand where she was, but instead she stood and waited.

As her eyes began to adjust, she could see the outlines of a series of figures around the room, a crowd, all wearing hooded robes, all turned to her. Dozens of silent figures. She couldn't work out which were men and which were women. Eventually, someone came forward and took her hand, and led her slowly to the far end of the room. The figure took a match, struck it, and the flame shuddered as it was carried over to light a bright torch.

Now she could see in front of her a golden altar, laid with red cloth, and on top of that a knife, a rope, and a silver cup.

She turned to look at the other figures in the light. Each one had a hood pulled down to cover his or her face, and each robe displayed a symbol on its front: a bird with human fingers; a planet on fire; a blind man dangling from a tree.

The hooded strangers all faced her. They seemed to expect something from her. She turned back to the altar. She noticed a pair of red shoes on the floor, and she slipped off her own shoes and put the red shoes on. They were a bit too big for her and felt sticky on her stockinged feet.

The figure who had led her to the altar now spoke to her. "I am the Hiereus," he said. "Do you swear to persevere in the labours of the Divine Science?"

She smiled under her hood. Although he still had his own hood down over his eyes, she was certain from his voice that it was W. B. His robe was black with a white cross on his left breast. He was picking up the knife from the altar, and he dipped it into the silver cup, up to his fingers, and brought it over to her. He placed it in her hand—it was wet—and she could smell red wine on her fingers.

"I am the expounder of mysteries," he said, and he put his hand around her hand and guided the knife up until the wet blade was against her neck. The touch of his hand on hers was firm, each finger pressing the underside of her hand. "Repeat after me."

With the blade against her skin, she repeated:

And as I bow my neck under the dagger of the Hiereus
And as I bow my neck under the dagger of the Hiereus
so do I commit myself
so do I commit myself
through the ancient texts found by the countess
through the ancient texts found by the countess
into the hands of the Order's Divine Guardians.
into the hands of the Order's Divine Guardians.

He took the knife away and she looked up at him. She wanted to pull his hood back from his face. The people around the room were facing them, all with hoods still pulled low over their eyes, all gathered around and watching her. They were murmuring approval.

FIVE

WINTER 1916

She arrived too early for her shift at the hospital, and while she was wandering around the area, she found herself outside a small jeweller's shop. There had been air raids recently not far from here, but the possibility that a bomb could fall from the sky onto this particular cobble-strewn, sunlit street felt as likely as the sparrows opening their beaks to debate Kant's *Critique of Pure Reason*. Georgie entered the shop, the glittering of the bell above her head, to find a small array of gold and silver items under glass. She was still alone in the shop as she walked slowly around the glass cases. It was strange to be in a room that wasn't the hospital, where things might be bought and sold, and there was no muffled speech, no creaking beds or clinking glasses, no strained breathing.

She stopped above a large golden ring. It was a man's signet ring, but it appeared to be blank, with no engraving.

"See something you like?" A boy of around nineteen had appeared from out the back. It had been a while since she'd seen a young man out of uniform. He was a cautious salesman, staying back from the glass cases.

"Why is there nothing on it?"

"Sorry?" He was not close enough to see which ring she was looking at, and he allowed himself to come a little farther into the room. He peered into the case. "I see what you mean. I've no idea. I'll check the notes." He went over to a scrapbook that was hanging on a string on the wall, and flicked through the pages. "My brother says . . . it belonged to a Frenchman . . . down in the Pyrenees. No more information than that, I'm afraid. Perhaps his family disowned him, and they had the engraving removed?"

She looked closer at the ring, with its plain round face, but it looked entirely smooth. She thought of W. B., who believed you could access the Great Memory—all the memories of the dead— through symbols. Here was an opportunity to imprint the symbols herself, to stamp them into gold. She noticed the boy watching her.

"Would you like to have a closer look?" He had plucked a key from his pocket. He was wearing thin white gloves, and he unlocked the case with some difficulty, pried the ring from its glass holder, and passed it to her.

It was heavy. She turned it around in her fingers.

"It's so strange there are no markings," she said. She wondered what she might imprint on this ring, what memories of the dead she might wake.

"A blank canvas," the boy pronounced. "Quite rare, I should think."

She handed it back to the boy, and he replaced it under the glass.

"I have a weak chest," the boy said.

"Pardon?"

"I tried to sign up, but was refused."

"Oh," Georgie said. "Do you suppose the ring will be here awhile?"

"I've no idea," he said. "I shouldn't say that, though. I should insist you buy it immediately, but really, I'm no businessman. This is Archie's business. My brother. He's fighting in France, and I'm back here looking after his shop. I feel like I'm the only man in London not at war."

"Is that why you were hiding out the back?"

"Of course. People are cruel. I've had a man come in and lecture me about sacrifice. I had a woman actually spit on the carpet."

"I daresay it's preferable to going to war."

"And I daresay it's not."

"Well, at least no one will shoot at you here," Georgie said. "I suspect sacrifice is more enjoyable in the abstract."

He sniffed at her, disappointed, and she turned her attention back to the ring.

"You needn't worry," he said, "hardly anyone ever comes in here. I'm sure it's safe. If I'm not in the trenches, I can at least save your ring for you. I'll move it to one of the farthest cabinets, so no one will notice it."

"Thank you," she said.

When she returned to the hospital, the tasks were just as monotonous or disgusting as they had been the day before, the matron was still cold and disapproving, and Major Hammond ignored her as usual. Still, she found that she could perform her role calmly, without overthinking. Although she wouldn't say she liked the job, it was a relief to know exactly what she should be doing, and she had the feeling that her life was following a logic. When the matron asked if she would take another night shift that evening, she found herself responding as if she were being offered a great prize.

When the night shift came, although she knew she wasn't allowed, she permitted herself her one indulgence: to sit down beside Second Lieutenant Pike and look out at the white-sheeted beds. Pike was silent beside her at first. There was something about sitting there that felt safe; she felt she might sit there for hours, listening to the slight snore of a sleeping captain, the soft rumple of woollen blankets, and the muted hooves on the straw-strewn roads outside.

SIX

PIKE

Here again. She was like a fine-boned bird, perched here. He couldn't help but smile, couldn't help but think that this alignment of circumstances was some kind of gift. He had earned some kind of gift, hadn't he? Then again, she wasn't smiling. She seemed to be looking past him, thinking about something else entirely.

Lately all of it was unreal to him, as if part of him had died in the car on the way here, with the taste of soil, steady clanking, groans; butter where his feet should be. Part of him had died, smudged on that leather seat, with mud between his fingers, under his nails, mud deep in his cuts, in his ears, and each time he wiped the mud off his face, he wiped more over himself, into himself, dear mud, dear muddy bodies all in a shambles, all in a row. They'd washed him, but only on the outside; inside his skin was lined with mud, it had crept down into his veins, it crouched there now, in puddles mixed with blood.

"You have a sweetheart, don't you?" he said to the nurse sitting beside him. He wanted to get this clear. And now she did smile. Her whole face held the light differently; it would be fair to say she beamed.

"Perhaps."

"Who is he?" Pike concentrated on keeping his voice level.

She had tipped her head towards the window. "A poet," she said.

He remembered having this kind of belief in someone. He'd had it in Emma. How could he tell this nurse this, how could he warn her? He'd written to Emma from the infirmary in Gallipoli, declared she shouldn't wait for him. He was going to lose his feet, and she should be free. It was spring; he imagined there would be dances for her to go to. That was the extent of his letter. It had felt good to write it—he was a man of virtue. He couldn't bear for Emma Wetherford to become the wife of a half man, one who couldn't walk, couldn't take himself to the lavatory. She was pretty, if a little stiff, but boys like that kind of reserve, they like to think they can crack it. They like to think they can break it open. (They can't, but they don't know that yet.) And of course, she wrote back to say she would wait for him, that she loved only him—oh, Emma! It gave him the chance for another noble rebuff: *I do not want to be unfair to you*, he had written as he lay in the infirmary, smelling of piss, his feet rotting under him, and now it seemed to him that as he wrote this he might have sucked the end of the pencil, tasted lead.

Because not a month later—hardly three weeks!—he received another letter saying she was dreadfully sorry but she was engaged to marry another fellow. One of the chaps with the sense to stay home, and one with a name her daddy approved of. She wanted

Pike to be the first to know, and if he didn't want her to marry—if he wanted to go back to their being engaged—he should let her know immediately, and she would marry him instead. As if he could write back, with no money, no name, feet rotting away to nothing, and say, *Marry me!*

Her letter had tried to seem solemn but somehow managed to announce the full name and rank of her husband-to-be, like she was brimming over with pride at being his fiancée, an admired thing, like a fine thoroughbred or a twirling windmill. Well, to hell with her. To hell with her, and particularly since she had started showing up to the ward, all gussied up as if on parade, forcing him to remember her, to remember everything. They'd had pink champagne for their engagement on the lawn. Pink champagne! Only Emma's brother Eddie had stepped forward to shake Pike's hand; her father simply stared at him like he was a child murderer. Fancy a poor student of medicine snapping up his beautiful, clever daughter—when all the time she had snapped him up, really, just as afterwards she'd opened her lovely jaws again and let him drop, so now she could marry a far more worthy gentleman. A huge relief for the family; apart from Eddie, the whole family had sticks so far up their asses probably none of them had ever glimpsed their toes. She had come into the ward the other day, bossing around his lovely nurse and then sitting upright in her impeccable clothes with her impeccable posture. The worst bit was that he found he couldn't talk to her, could communicate only in brief snatches, couldn't tell her what he thought of her. She loomed over him, and he couldn't tell her to leave him be. She never stayed long, retreating like a sleek spider which creeps out from the floor and the wall, only to crawl back into its crevice. There would be no doubt in anyone's mind she had made the right decision. When the father-in-law shuffled off from this earth, she would be a countess.

A poet. The nurse was still staring at him with her eyes gleaming with hope so strong you could almost smell it. It was the first thing he didn't like about her. Not that she had a sweetheart—of course she did, a girl like her—but that the fellow in question was a poet. You couldn't trust a poet; either he was a fraud, a bad versifier, tapping his scuffed little loafers together while he proudly beat out bad rhymes; or, perhaps worse, he was a real poet, in which case he was self-important, a gentleman surely (no one could make money out of poems), with an enormous oak desk and a pen clasped between his fingers with the worthy expression of someone holding a sword. All that was certain was that a poet was never a serious person.

Then again, was he himself a serious person? A student. A student of medicine with ruined feet who wasn't sure he could bear to continue his studies. Who couldn't properly talk to Emma Wetherford (who wasn't a Wetherford anymore, of course, although he'd mercifully forgotten what she was now) after she'd spurned him. When he'd arrived at the hospital, he'd found another space for himself—a pressurised, underwater space, where he didn't need to think, where all his decisions could be suspended. It was like going under with his eyes open in the lake he used to swim in each summer, that green low world, with its stringed lake-weed that would shift in slow motion before him. He might quite comfortably die there. It was only when he came up, kicking, that he found the surface floating with women, like bushy-feathered swans.

One afternoon he'd come up to discover a particular creature waiting for him, and for the first time he found he didn't want to go back down. It didn't have a beak but a soft human nose. A woman, then, stubborn, with dark hair and a severe, slightly chubby face. She wasn't really swanlike, or pretty, or especially feminine. She was young but had the seriousness of someone much older, and her face wasn't impassive but crinkled and irritated, her complexion rather pinker than was attractive, and she had dark half circles slung under her eyes. Still, she was awake, even if she didn't seem overly delighted to be there. She had a name: Hyde-Lees. Her eyes were always moving, as if she were outraged with the world for not giving her more. This intense gaze was reason enough for him to kick and kick, to stay above the green surface for as long as he could, just to watch, until eventually he realised he had forgotten how to get back to the green space at all. Now this was all the world he had.

"And what is his name, this poet?"

Hyde-Lees looked at him before she uttered the familiar name of a man twice her age, an ungainly, pretentious Protestant Anglo-Irishman who, it could be conceded, was a reasonable poet (if you went in for faeries and dream-dimmed eyes), but could under no circumstances be called a gentleman, or remotely right for this charming girl of no more than twenty-five. For a moment, he was disgusted. Why? Why was she so weak to fall for such a man?

But looking at her face, half in shadow, he recalibrated. If she were weak enough to fall for the poet, did this not mean she might be weak enough to fall for him? And wasn't the poet a pathetic enough object that the girl's affection for him could be broken down, diverted? He would get closer to her, he promised himself. He would start immediately.

SEVEN

SUMMER 1914

It had been the last of the Shakespears' soirées before the war broke out. The usual crowd was there, and Dorothy and Ezra, newly married, would not stop gazing at one another. There was something vague about them; Dorothy could only half kiss Georgie hello, and Ezra smiled and ruffled her hair as though she were twelve years old instead of twenty-one. Georgie asked them about W. B., and Ezra managed to say that he had been feeling unwell and had left early.

To fend off boredom, Georgie drank too much wine and eventually found herself in that easy, dizzy state where her words were coming to her fluidly, and everything was imbued with a heightened sense, as if each word or movement contained great promise. She noticed, around Dorothy's neck, a silver chain with a hanging butterfly, which quivered at her throat when she laughed. Georgie's knees felt loose, as if the bones had gone soft, and no one seemed to notice when she wandered away from the group and stepped into the cool, dark hallway. There was a light on in the library, and she walked in.

"Oh, hello," a voice said. W. B. was under a lamp, sitting on a narrow wooden bench with a book on his lap, and when he saw her come in, he pressed a finger on a particular passage. He was about to rejoin the party, he said, but he was checking something for a moment. Even though his accent was almost English, he had that lovely Irish turn to his consonants—she'd thought it was all in his vowels, but really it was his consonants. She came in and leaned over his shoulder to see what he was reading.

He looked up. "Didn't Harkin say something about Taylor?" Dr. Harkin was the leader of the Order.

"Not that Taylor," she said. "The translator of Plotinus. Thomas Taylor."

"Oh," he said, resting the book back down on his lap. "You're right, of course. You've read him already, I suppose."

"Of course," she said. They smiled. Her thoroughness was a kind of joke between them. She sat down beside him; the wooden bench was rather high, and she swung her legs back and forth, thanking the wine for the ease she felt. She liked sitting close to him, being alone in the room with him.

"Are you quite well?" she thought to say. "Ezra said you were ill."

He hesitated, and it was only when she saw his lips twitch and noticed the handkerchief between his fingers that she realised he wasn't ill at all—he was upset. He must have come in here to get away from everyone. The book had been a ruse; he had shut himself in here for some privacy, and she had come in oblivious, with her wine-soaked boldness, and not only interrupted him but corrected him, and gone ahead and sat right down beside him. Embarrassed, she began to get up.

"Oh—I'm sorry—"

"No," he said. "Stay if you like. I've been—you're far too young to understand this, but I've been fussing about being too old. Regrets. You're too young for regrets." He was pushing the handkerchief back in his pocket.

"Like what?"

"I should have married."

She sat back down and slowly returned to swinging her legs, as if to insist on the lightness of the conversation. "Don't be silly. You're not too old for that." He was twice her age, but he was still attractive enough. He had been involved with Olivia at some point, and she knew there had been others too.

"Do you mean that?" He was looking at her.

"Of course." She looked back at him and stopped swinging her legs. What was he asking, exactly? She looked away.

He had turned his attention to the desk, and as she watched him search for something in a drawer, flicking through the contents with his long fingers, she considered those fingers, that familiar mass of dark, greying hair. All the younger men she knew were unoriginal, fickle, and—despite Dorothy's newly married status— still too busy pining after Dorothy. Willy Yeats turned his attention back to her and produced a rectangular box. He flipped a clasp, she heard a click, and the box sprang open. Inside was a pack of cards, the backs dark blue drizzled with silver. He tipped the pack into his hands and tucked the box back into the drawer. He shuffled the cards and splayed them out in his hands, face down, offering them to her.

"Pick one," he said.

She reached forward and brushed her fingers over the cards. She paused her index finger on one, then another, then finally pulled a third one away from the pack. She turned it over so they could both see it. It showed a handsome young blond man, strolling jauntily towards the edge of a cliff. The black text said *THE FOOL*.

"The beginning of a journey," he said, and he leaned back and smiled. "I had wondered, hadn't you? What do you think?"

She stared back at him. They seemed to be sitting very close together, and she could feel sweat tingling at the base of her spine. He reached his hand out to her.

She looked at it.

William Butler Yeats, the poet, the occultist, the scholar, the Irishman, this man, sitting next to her, asking her—she couldn't quite believe it. After a moment—after all, why not?—she took his hand.

There was a knock on the door and Georgie dropped his hand just as Olivia came in to call them back into the party. The whole room seemed to vibrate with a violent pulse she knew must be her own.

As Olivia explained who was leaving and who was yet to arrive, Georgie glanced down at the card on the table. The cliff's edge at the man's feet was sheer.

She looked up and managed to tell Willy and Olivia that actually she had to go, that Nelly would be wondering where she was. But before she left, Willy followed her out to the coatrack and helped her with her coat, and he kissed her cheek close to her mouth. Georgie's lips prickled and went numb, as if they were no longer hers.

———— • ————

That feeling of a not-quite-uttered agreement had hung between them ever since, as if someone had cleared all the dust from the air and they were seeing each other for the first time. Each time they met, he kissed her cheek near her mouth, and sometimes they alluded to their *journey*. On the outside, not much had changed; they had not been properly intimate, or spoken of an engagement. They still attended the monthly meetings of the Order together, and shared discussions about the thin layer between this world and the next. But on the inside, everything felt different. The future was there to be leapt into, whenever they chose. It was unspoken, but it was clear.

EIGHT

WINTER 1916

After another night shift, Georgie forced herself to get up in the
early afternoon and go to the reading room at the British Museum.
Because of her work at the hospital, she had fallen behind on her
studies for the Order.

She'd had a note from Willy that morning. He had already gone
down to Sussex, to the small cottage he rented for the winter with
the Pounds, and he would regretfully miss the next Order meeting.
He had signed the note, *Yours faithfully, W. B. Yeats*, and the formal-
ity of this seemed strange to her. At least, she supposed, he had let
her know. Perhaps in his next note, he would invite her down to
Stone Cottage to visit.

As she walked from the dormitory, she thought of being outside the city, out where the world thinned out, dirt disturbed itself,
light flashed out the corner of your eye. It was outside the city she

seemed closest to the anima mundi, that great mass of all human memory, which was the object of their research. She had glimpsed it only once, when she had been on a ferry in the Bay of Naples, not long after her father had died—she had been exhausted then too, sleepless, and desperate to get away from Nelly and the cousins. She had gone up to the top deck to watch the sea restlessly push past, and the foam gather along the boat's edge like rough lace, while black smoke gushed from the steamer—and standing alone on the deck there, looking out at the lazy black flank of Vesuvius, she had felt something grip inside her skull. Something had forced itself into her brain, a map of another human's thinking, trying to crack her own open. It was a shock—to have someone else's voice driving her own out; to have another's eyes looking down at her new navy leather shoes. *Cielo*, the mind had said, traveling over her suddenly tasteless clothing—*e le scarpe, che malgusto!* Her eyes travelled over her own body, her ankles, her legs, her torso, her breasts, her hands, half predatory, half disgusted. The mind seemed unaware of an audience—her—and had simply taken her over, made her silent.

The eyes looked out of her own body, out to the mountains closest to the boat, and identified a particular cleft between them, a dark ravine, a woman's shape. A name had repeated in her head—*Dorlowicz, Dorlowicz*—she had seen the word, scrawled in red ink—and in the moment the feeling left her, Georgie leaned against the railing, grasping to get the voice back. For a terrifying minute the map of her brain seemed wiped pale, as if it had taken her own personality with it. She'd looked out over the railings of the ferry, and there had seemed to be a relationship between the creamed white foam in the boat's wake and the point where the smoke was gulped by the calm sky's blue. There was a relationship, she thought, between her own face and the face of the Madonna in the tiny church she had seen earlier that day, golden-cloaked and staring out, who lacked the usual Madonna's sleepiness. This one had stared straight, unafraid, her mouth half turned up, as if she were a little cruel. A moment later, as she pressed up against the ferry's railing, she had seen one of her cousins waving to her, and all her own feeling had flooded back. It had not happened to her again.

Ever since she had looked for this word *Dorlowicz*, but so far, she had not found it. But she was sure it must be connected to their teachings at the Order, and that she and Willy might find it together. She could mop a thousand floors, listen to a thousand jeering officers, if only she could get a glimpse of what it meant.

And yet, now she had arrived at the library and sat at a narrow desk with her books in front of her and her notebook open to a blank page, all she could do was stare. It was as though heaviness were stacked on top of her. Her brain was full of the hospital. The news from the front was the same; at Verdun the Allies were launching yet another counterattack. It was generally understood that what was reported was only the good news, and that this was always exaggerated. Most of the officers had stopped reading the news and asked the nurses not to bother with the wireless. A nurse by the name of Sanderson, whose fiancé and brother were both fighting, had developed a red, crisp rash between the bridge of her nose and the corners of her eyes.

Georgie found Harkin's notes from the Order's last lecture and scanned the loose pages. Ever since Willy had sponsored Georgie to join the Order, she'd risen up the ranks faster than any neophyte in its history. She had memorised the elements, the patterning of the stars; she had drawn her own major arcana cards. She cast the most accurate astrological horaries. She also attended any meeting that Willy missed and took notes for him. They had intended to go to séances together, but so far the hospital had kept her too busy and Willy had been often away from London. She was also secretly relieved, because the Order did not allow its members to attend séances, and she was worried that Harkin could find out. This never worried Willy, who did as he pleased.

At the bottom of the page of notes, Harkin had drawn a coloured picture, the thin black outline roughly sketched. It showed a person's arm, bent at the elbow, forearm raised and palm facing outwards. The hand had two fingers and thumb raised, with the other two fingers curled down. The gesture of benediction. A blessing. The arm was wrapped in a white sleeve, with the hint of a red cloak at the shoulder. She had no idea what Harkin had meant by drawing it here. Perhaps it connected to George Mead's theory of the migration of souls. But when she thought of Mead, she thought also of Pico and Swedenborg and Plotinus—and for the moment all these texts seemed to combine, all interlinking and knotting together and referencing one another, and she could not connect them to the world. She saw each idea as a string or a rope, so in her mind the library became a series of tangles, all doubling back on one another and tied together to form a giant knot. In the past it had seemed she could see each silky strand so clearly she could separate them cleanly with her hands, she could see a point where she would weave herself a long, slender rope, with which she could do what she liked. But today she felt as if the job she had set herself was not to untangle this knot but to eat it, in a huge hairball that would choke her.

She heard a light tap on her desk and looked up. Standing there was Dorothy, pretending to survey the books in front of Georgie.

For a second Georgie thought she was hallucinating. She often saw other members of the Order here, or writers like Ezra or Willy or lately Hilda Doolittle, but it was unusual for Dorothy to come. She had never joined the Order, never again showed any interest in the idea, and these days she mostly spent her time painting and helping Ezra. Shouldn't she be down in Sussex with him and Willy now?

"Study break?" Dorothy whispered and held up a large silver flask, which certainly didn't contain tea. Georgie almost laughed. It was barely two o'clock in the afternoon. She gathered her books together and followed Dorothy to the museum cafeteria, and after the waiter had served them tea, Dorothy, without any pretense of hiding what she was doing, poured a generous slug of brandy into each delicate teacup. Georgie, who had lately found herself very critical of Dorothy, felt a surge of great warmth towards her kind, clever friend. She had always loved her, it seemed now. Both Ezra and Dorothy were staying with Willy at Stone Cottage, the poets working on their poems, Dorothy working on her paintings. As she smiled, Dorothy's eyes dragged Georgie's in. Dorothy was beautiful; her cheeks pale and glowing, her profile like it belonged on a coin. Georgie reflected that she desperately needed more sleep.

They drank to each other's health.

"You look awful," Dorothy said, and Georgie's feelings cooled somewhat. She took another sip.

"What are you doing here?"

Dorothy's small teeth showed for a moment. "We were worried about you."

It was clear to Georgie that *we* did not refer to Ezra and Willy. It meant Nelly had sent her. At the thought of her mother, Georgie stiffened. So Dorothy had not come to see her voluntarily after all. She wrinkled her nose and took another gulp of tea.

"How is the hospital?"

"It's great."

"Really?"

"Yes. It's good to be helping. The men are interesting. The matron has good control of the place."

"I can say whatever you like to Nelly. You can tell me how it really is."

"I just did." She felt weak enough without telling anyone about it. Dorothy reached over and refilled Georgie's teacup with brandy. The drink had already started to do its work; Georgie's head had become fuzzier and easier. Dorothy was looking around languidly at the waiting staff, who had definitely seen her with her flask but would not come over to bother them. Like any extremely attractive woman, Dorothy was accustomed to getting what she wanted. Georgie was never sure if it was because of Dorothy's looks or because of her unshakable confidence, but in any case, she had never seen it fail.

"You are getting your work done, then?"

"Of course I am." Georgie realised she now sounded standoffish, and softened her voice. "Has Willy said something?"

"Willy who?"

"Willy Yeats, of course."

Dorothy frowned. "Why?"

"It is possible we might have some kind of future together."

"You and Willy?" Dorothy gave a half laugh, half cough. "Don't be daft."

"I'm serious."

"You can't be!" Dorothy was laughing now, and Georgie took another sip and wished her head were clearer.

"Why not?" When Ezra had come over from America, knowing nobody and with no money, he had spent months elbowing his way into soirées and readings until he'd won himself a winter alone with the great poet, out on the waste moor. Now Ezra had a beautiful wife to take there with him for the poets' winter retreats. Not for the first time, Georgie reflected on how Ezra was exceptionally good at getting what he wanted.

Dorothy's laughter had evaporated when she realised that Georgie wasn't joking. She held up one slender, pale hand and started to count items off on her fingers. "Because. He's a hundred years old. He had an affair with my mother. And many more since. He's completely, utterly cuckoo"—she paused, her little finger hovering in the air— "and, of course, Maud Gonne. He's still in love with Maud Gonne."

"He is not." She was irritated. Willy was old, yes, but that wasn't his fault; he'd had an affair with Olivia, but Olivia was wise, an excellent novelist, witty, and beautiful—how could that count against him? And the accusation that Willy was still in love with Maud Gonne! Of course he wasn't. Yes, he had been in love with her for decades, everyone knew that, just as everyone knew the poems praising her beauty like a tightened bow. But that he wasn't in love with her now was just as obvious. His poems said as much, and besides, he had told Georgie so himself at one of their late-night Order meetings. She was naive, Dorothy, refusing to embrace the supernatural, determinedly, unimaginatively placing herself only in the world she could see.

"Georgie, he is; surely you see that. I've spent weeks with him and Ezra and he is definitely still mooning after Maud. What could you possibly like so much about him?"

She considered. "He understands the contradictions. He doesn't give in to the abstract. He doesn't stop; he's always asking. Why are you smiling?"

"You sound like you're describing yourself. You don't need him, you know."

"I never said I did. I didn't say I needed anyone."

Dorothy tilted her head. "Are you sure you're all right?"

"I'm tired." The brandy was bothering her, her woozy brain lunging at nothing. She was supposed to be working, for heaven's sake; why had she let Dorothy interrupt her? She stood up from the table, putting out a hand to balance herself.

Dorothy looked up at her. "So I can tell Nelly—you're tired? But all right?"

"You can tell her whatever you please." She was stung that Dorothy would come only on Nelly's instructions, stung that she would reject so heartily Georgie's notion of Willy as a suitor, would make mindless claims about Maud Gonne. She wished she were the one who could spend the winter at Stone Cottage with Willy and Ezra. Dorothy was tucking a loose strand of dark hair behind her ear. She seemed as bad as the worst members of the Order, who repeated the same sentences without any kind of reflection or revision. They were all like gramophones, playing the exact rendition of the same song when life required variation, adaptation. Willy never spoke this way—he was always improvising, testing his theories; even in a formal setting, he was still straining for new, unlikely connections. His thoughts played out as if he had discovered a foreign instrument, and rather than touching one key timidly to see how it sounded, he pounded the keys, trying every note, unafraid of the resulting music. She couldn't begin to explain this to Dorothy, who would never understand.

"Perhaps you could come down and visit us?" Dorothy had stood up, fussing now that she realised she had said something wrong, upset her.

Georgie nodded. "I'd like that." She kissed her friend and felt something cold pressed against her hand; Dorothy was handing her the flask with the rest of the brandy. Georgie took it and thanked her. Out on the street the late afternoon was glorious, last light grasping the buildings, forcing the windows into gold. Once she got back to the dormitory, Georgie opened the window a finger's width and lay down on the narrow bed to sleep.

NINE

Georgie had been summoned to the Order for a meeting with Dr. Harkin that evening. She had never had an audience alone with the Order leader before, and she couldn't imagine what he might want. Because she had a spare two hours, on a whim she decided she'd walk to the Order. Perhaps, after all, the walk would do her good. She went walking often enough in the country; why not in London? Turning away from the gardens, she cut through the old cream-walled alley and out onto Mount Street, with the buildings balanced around her.

She walked quickly, cursing at the muddy straw that had blown up from the road, leaving curls of wet dirt up her skirt. It was just after six, but it felt much later with the streetlights out. Dark London was an entirely different city. Through the low cloud Georgie could hardly see the jagged line where the blackness of the buildings met the dark blue of the sky. She often wondered what a shock it would be, when the war was over and they turned the lights back on, whether the streets would be blinding.

Closer to the park, a man tipped his hat to her. In his left hand he held a child's knitted hat, but there was no sign of a child. Georgie walked faster. The countries of Europe seemed themselves like children, stuck in a tug of war, and all falling over together because they held the same rope. It felt so much better to be moving, to walk everyone's words out of her. She moved faster under dimmed and dead streetlights, past the buildings of orange brick, peach brick, scarlet brick, all with their narrow balconies. She passed a drooping Union Jack, its folds tremoring in the slight winter breeze. A pair of men walked past her, each with a furled umbrella tapping at his ankle, each glancing at her as he moved on. She crossed into Hyde Park. These men, looking at her, would not see any kind of hero, nothing remarkable in her. Dorothy more closely resembled a hero; although, then again, it was men who were heroes, really: wanderers, magicians, politicians, generals. What quest did Anna Karenina or Emma Bovary ever have? What grand plan did the world have in store for them? Was that why she was drawn to Willy, because he was heroic, in his fame, in his public standing as a poet, in his Irish rejection of an English knighthood? It wasn't that exactly—it was more that she admired his work—and she liked how fallible he still was.

A month after she had sent a draft of some of her Pico translation, he had sent her a note to say that he thought their souls were bound together. He sent her letters about séances he'd been to, and she looked up facts for him in the library. She was accustomed to being well liked but not needed, and there was a part of Willy that seemed to need her; he admired her learning, her diligence, the meticulousness that contrasted with his own more haphazard approach to study. Wasn't this what mattered? What did Ezra see in Dorothy? The magnetism of a beauty, a clear, discernible charm and a mind to go with it; but how much did he truly admire her beyond her low voice, the smoothness of her cheeks, the flash of her teeth when she smiled that lazy, clean smile?

She occasionally worried that Willy might not come through, but she didn't worry that she wouldn't. It was as her father had suggested; it was a luxury to have found something she didn't second-guess. She knew marriage was difficult, knew that marrying someone twice your age would be even more so. But what a luxury to have found herself asking *why* she loved him, not *whether* she did. That was a gift.

Along the park's dark lip, plane trees tangled into one another. Time had erupted an unexpected pocket, where she might walk and walk as the world fell still around her. The thin branches might be the contorted limbs of Swedenborg's angels. She turned away from the trees and headed up through the web of streets to North Kensington.

——— • ———

A servant ushered her through to the cloakroom, where she hurriedly put on her robe and went through to the meeting room, but she found no one there. She kept on walking, through the meeting room and out a tall oak door and back into the cool air. She entered a small, untidy garden. The grass grew up past her ankles.

Dr. Harkin was standing beside a small tree out in the garden. The tree was the same height as he was, and for a moment in the dimness they seemed like similar creatures. She was surprised to realise he was wearing his civilian clothes, a navy suit with a wide lapel, and he had a lit cigarette which he held loosely. She felt self-conscious that she was wearing her robe.

"Nemo." This was her Order name—Nemo Sciat, meaning "let nobody know."

"Hello, Doctor." Having his eyes on her made her nervous. He offered her a cigarette, but she shook her head. "I'm sorry I've missed so many meetings lately."

"I know you have other commitments."

There was a pause while they both stood there, and he took an occasional draw from his cigarette. She knew that he could take a long time between sentences. The Order was his life's work. There was a sense in which it had become her work too; while Willy only dipped in and out of the core texts of the Order and read only in English, Georgie read every text from cover to cover more than once, and she read in Italian, French, German, and Latin, and was teaching herself Sanskrit. This year she would sit an examination that would allow her to rise to the rank of 6=5, the same rank as Willy.

With his free hand Dr. Harkin reached up to smooth his moustache with a finger and thumb. He had all the Order organised in his mind, each level, each element you'd passed and all those yet to pass; he knew the system and its long history, and where each of the present members belonged in the hierarchy; presumably it all took time to sort through. But tonight she was anxious to know what he wanted.

"Is everything all right?"

He nodded. "And you? You are—well?"

"Quite well." She waited, directing her gaze at the few strands of hair that lined his throat.

"I have heard—" he started, paused, solemnly eyed his cigarette. He didn't seem to breathe between puffs, but when he inhaled he did so in loud breaths. She stood very still, in the hope he'd get the words out. "I've heard that you have been going to séances. With a Miss Radcliffe."

"I don't know anyone of that name." This was technically true. Willy had seen the Radcliffe girl and had asked Georgie some questions about the scripts from her séances. But when Willy urged Georgie to make an appointment to see her, the lady's calendar had been so full that she couldn't get a slot for months. She had made an appointment, but it was not until April, meaning she didn't know Miss Radcliffe, per se.

"I have heard—that you and Demon est Deus Inversus—"

"People say all sorts of things about Mr. Yeats. Almost none of it true." She looked at Dr. Harkin as he lowered his cigarette, a gleam of silver at his wrist. What did he care about Nora Radcliffe? Some girl claiming to channel ghosts—how could this possibly affect an organisation as powerful as the Order?

Dr. Harkin's mouth twitched. He straightened up. "I know— you wouldn't partake in vulgar parlour games," he said. "I'm talking about genuine attempts to rouse spirits. It's dangerous for someone at your level to be exposed. You know there's a risk of losing control of your thoughts. We will expel those who try, and we would really prefer not to lose our highly valued members."

"Of course," Georgie said, "we know." She liked to use *we* to refer to her and Willy. "I'm looking forward to my examination."

"Don't be so sure you will pass." He was frowning at her. She didn't understand what he was saying. Reading all the books in the world could not prepare you for the Order's practical

examination—and it was true that Georgie's talents were more
bookish than practical—but surely, as the most accomplished student, she would pass? It was true your success relied on your nerve,
but she had always managed before. He threw his cigarette and it
vanished in the long grass.

"Please don't risk all your hard work," he said, "for a séance with
a pretender." The doctor had shifted his hand to his neck, plucking
at the loose skin with two fingers as if he were pulling lint from a
blanket, or pulling words out of his throat. "We have other plans
for you."

Georgie nodded, wondering what he meant. "Thank you,
Doctor."

"I spoke to your friend Mr. Yeats too, but I'm not confident
he obeys any orders but his own." He gave a dismissive nod.
"Goodnight, then."

He had already started to head inside. She followed him, but
instead of turning into the hallway, she went to the empty cloakroom, hung up her robe, and pulled on her coat.

She went down the steps of the house and into the dark street,
where the other houses looked closed off, like faces turned away
from her. Willy had said that Nora Radcliffe was like no other
medium he had ever gone to. Should she keep her appointment to
see whether he was right? She walked back towards the dormitory
slowly, in no hurry to arrive. It was only a handful of hours until
her next shift at the hospital. The sky had turned a watery brown
colour, like a shallow river, and all along the street, she looked into
each darkened blue light, wondering if she could be seen by any
Germans who lurked above the clouds, gazing down from the air.

TEN

Right before her shift, Georgie went to use the telephone in the hospital corridor. She did not like to use the telephone, did not like to converse with those hollow voices down the end of the line, particularly when she was speaking to a stranger. There was something about talking to someone whose eyes you couldn't see that felt terrible, like you had been blindfolded. This along with the prospect of the night shift made her feel a furry film down her tongue, reaching into the back of her throat.

She breathed slowly as she dialed.

"Radcliffes' residence." A man's voice.

"Yes, hello. I have an appointment—"

"Appointments are dealt with through Mrs. Euphemia Radcliffe, the lady's mother. Would you like me to find her for you?"

"Please. Yes."

She held the receiver and waited for what seemed like a very long time.

The man's voice again: "May I ask who is speaking?"

She hesitated. You always gave pseudonyms for séances. "It is—that is"—she glanced behind her to make sure no one was listening—"it's Miss Selden."

A rustling in the receiver—some muttered words in the background—and a woman's voice, impatient. "Well?"

"Is this Mrs. Radcliffe?"

There was no reply.

"I am wondering if I might cancel my appointment."

"Who is this?" the voice said suspiciously. "Really, who is it?"

"Miss Selden," she said, louder.

"Don't shout, girl."

"I have an appointment," Georgie said more softly, "next week, but I am working at one of the hospitals, taking care of the officers"—she swallowed—"and I must cancel. I am very sorry for the inconvenience."

"How extraordinary."

"Pardon?"

"I don't even know who this woman is," the woman said, evidently addressing someone else in the room with her, "and she's asking to cancel her appointment. Quite extraordinary."

"Extraordinary," said another soft female voice in the background.

"I don't think you understand, Miss—Sheldon, was it?—what kind of talent you are dealing with. We have filled our calendar until September, you know. I say, there is no hope of postponement, unless you want to wait for seven months. Do you? I suppose the dead will wait. But more than one person has said an appointment with my daughter has entirely changed their life. I assure you there will be a number of people very willing to take your place. What was the date of your appointment, Mrs. Shelldown?"

Georgie stared through the open door into the ward, where she could see one of the nurses running over to a blond officer, who was thrashing once more in his bed.

"Are you still there?" the woman called. "Hello?"

"Never mind," Georgie said. "I'll come after all."

"Suit yourself." The woman banged the phone down. Georgie held the receiver for a moment to her chest before gently replacing it on its cradle.

———— • ————

She checked the roster, to discover that she had a shift at the same time of her appointment. There was nothing for it. As soon as there was a moment of quiet on the ward, she approached the matron.

"Excuse me; I'm sorry. I need to ask you something."

"Yes?"

"I need to take off my shift on the twenty-fourth of April."

"And why is that?"

Georgie frowned. "I have a personal appointment."

"Personal?"

"That's all I am able to tell you." She was annoyed with the matron. Yes, the matron could dismiss her from the hospital; yes, this would make it impossible for Georgie to find a position elsewhere—but she had just agreed to stay on yet another night shift; did she not deserve some kind of credit? Why was this woman so rude to her, so often? Why did she have such ridiculous expectations? Why did she act as if missing a fleck of dirt on the floor was akin to killing a man?

Mrs. Thwaite was staring at Georgie as though she had cursed at her.

Georgie looked away. "I am afraid," she said, more confidently than she felt, "that this is non-negotiable."

"I will note it in the book," the matron said. She walked away without saying anything more.

ELEVEN

Something was hovering over her in her sleep. It had its hands out, and it seemed to be taking the light in its hands and crumpling it, so that there were shadows everywhere.

"Miss Hyde-Lees." The voice was carrying an envelope. A crumpled yellow, on one of those days where every leaf seemed to have conspired to fall and form a carpet of crunchy leaves underfoot. The envelope might break free and develop wings. Or it might be dropped.

She was in her bed in the dormitory, but she knew somewhere there was a telegram. For a moment she was sure her father must have died again. She shifted the sheet so it covered her face. She had been awake the first time. She'd put a glass of water down on the table, and it had hit with a decisive knock. Perhaps to die for a second time was like a double negative; it would mean that he was still across town, laughing at her crunched brow or pulling Brahms by the tail or tearing strips from the newspaper and making paper planes from the war news. Childish, Nelly called him, and she was right, but while this made him a terrible husband, it made him a charming father. Perhaps that was him here right now, ready to laugh about it. *Really, pup? Delivering a telegram? Your old father?*

She opened her eyes and saw a girl standing in the doorway. She jumped up from her bed, grasping at her nightgown. The girl kept her eyes on the floor.

"Miss Hyde-Lees," she said again.

"Who let you in?" Georgie said, and the girl shrugged and did not move. Georgie glanced at the watch on the night table; it was already nine thirty! She had planned to be at the reading room hours ago.

The girl was holding out an envelope.

"Who is it from?"

"I don't know, ma'am."

"Bring it here," she said. Perhaps it was from Willy. Perhaps he had come back early and wanted to see her. The girl rushed in to slip the envelope into her hands and rushed back to the door. Georgie fumbled for a coin to give her, but the girl had already gone, and the door banged so hard it bounced open. Georgie walked over and closed the door properly. She returned to sit on the bed and broke the envelope's seal.

The message was unsigned. It read:

STAY AWAY. IT DOES NOT END WELL.

Georgie checked the envelope again. It was addressed to *Miss G. Hyde-Lees.* What did it refer to? And who could have written it?

Surely Dr. Harkin wouldn't write such a thing? After a moment of tracing the type with her finger, she stuffed the envelope into the pocket of the dress hanging on the back of the door, and lay back on the bed.

TWELVE

She had meant to return to the reading room, but thick, syrupy sleep took over, and when she woke up she realised she was late to meet Nelly, who had finally arranged an appointment with her. Georgie rushed to meet her, and, with barely time to kiss her mother's cheek, she was whisked down the street and into the opening scenes of a chamber opera of *La Traviata*.

She did not like opera, although now it was wartime the scale had become smaller and the approach more eccentric. Still, from the opening bars, she returned to thinking of the strange message, which she had in her pocket, the folds of which she could feel through the lining of her dress. While watching the reduced orchestra with its sharp elbows and glinting instruments, she thought: *It does not end well.* She watched the soprano playing Violetta spin around the party scene, her head tipped back as the aria's notes erupted from her mouth. *Stay away.* The message was cryptic, and the writer seemed to want it to be cryptic, but it was difficult to consider a warning when you didn't know what you were being warned against. From her regular horaries, she had also had a warning; because Neptune was currently in the ascendant, it suggested a major deception between her and Willy. She supposed the message could refer to this deception, but how? And who would have sent the note?

Nelly was watching the singers with a fierce attention, seeming almost angry in her hunger for detail. She had appeared to forgive her daughter's lateness; she might be open to her coming to stay, and perhaps she would agree to restore Georgie's allowance. Nelly used to go to the opera alone and leave young Georgie with her father. This had lasted until one night when Nelly had come home to find eight-year-old Georgie cheerfully sipping a glass of watered-down whisky under her father's generous supervision. Nelly no longer let him stay home alone with her after that. It was sometime later, on a morning when Nelly was also at home, that Gilbert, already drunk, playfully chased his daughter down the hallway but slipped and fell on top of her, and, with the weight of all six foot three of his bulk, snapped her collarbone. They were lucky it hadn't been worse. Georgie had had to go to the hospital, and by the time she came back home again, Gilbert was no longer there. That was the first time Nelly had sent him away, to the inebriates' home—everything hush-hush, because divorce was not an option.

After Gilbert had died, Nelly became even more aggressively social, attending salons and exhibitions and charity lunches, and in 1911, just over a year after she was widowed, she had remarried, this time Dorothy's uncle Henry. Mrs. Nelly Tucker, as she was now called, had wrapped herself tightly in this new life she had made for herself. Georgie marvelled at how easily she seemed to have replaced Gilbert.

Still, Georgie had already decided that it would be best for her to go to stay with her mother for the weekend. She would benefit from two days of proper sleep, and time with her books. The hospital was interfering with her work, and she needed to set herself on a clearer path—and it made sense to do this while Willy was still away. She would recast her horaries, study for her Order examination, and prepare for her meeting with Miss Radcliffe. All she had to do was convince Nelly to let her stay.

On the stage, the soprano playing Violetta clasped the tenor playing Alfredo to her not ungenerous bosom, and Georgie glanced off into the enormous folds of the curtain. She found the show offensive in its lack of ambition, the music cloying, the melodrama senseless. Yes, the singing was beautiful, but why the staging, why these humans improbably flinging themselves at one another? She let her mind loose and it drifted to Willy, to his note to her, to how soon he might return to London, to what he would say to her. On the stage, Violetta had begun the seemingly endless process of refusing to die. How were you supposed to mourn someone so insufferable? When she finally fell to the floor, and the orchestra stood for the curtain call, Georgie applauded with relief.

After the show, Nelly handed her an envelope—"From us, to help you along, darling"—and they went to dinner, where the waiter recorded their order so slowly it was as though he too were penning a masterpiece. Nelly had been talking about the soprano's performance—she had a weak low register, according to Nelly, depriving Violetta of her usual pathos—but she seemed to realise that her daughter was not really listening, and sharply switched topics.

"And how is the hospital?"

Georgie looked up. "Fine."

"And the men?"

"They're lively." She didn't bother to add that she had managed to work her way up from bedpans and was now entrusted—

entrusted!—with the tremendous responsibility of cleaning the officers' wounds, despite the fact that Mrs. Thwaite appeared convinced that at any moment she was bound to accidentally slip and stab the patient through the throat with a needle, or spill a basin of hydrochloric acid over his face, or faint and fall on a patient, thus asphyxiating him.

"You don't wish to come home? You could come with me tonight if you wanted."

Georgie was surprised at the bluntness of the question. She was careful.

"I suppose I didn't realise quite what the hospital work entailed. I had wanted to work on my translation, but I find I don't have any spare time."

"Dorothy said you were struggling."

"Oh?"

Nelly gazed across at another table, where the diners—a well-dressed, middle-aged couple—had their backs to them. "You know, when I married your father, I thought it was absolutely the right thing to do. And of course, it was a terrible decision."

"I'm not sure I follow." She wasn't sure she wanted to. She knew that her mother had never especially wanted to have children, and that it was not long after Nelly had met the charming and clever Gilbert that she realised that Gilbert's devotion to his wife was outweighed by his devotion to whisky. Nelly had often said she had raised her two children on her own.

Georgie reached down and rustled the contents of her purse, as if to check for the key to the dormitory. Sometimes when her mother spoke, she tried to do something else, in order not to be swallowed up by her words, in order to keep her thoughts her own.

"Dorothy told me you had a thing for Willy Yeats."

Georgie felt a flush of surprise, followed by embarrassment. She pulled her hand out of her purse. Dorothy had just gone ahead and told her? She tried to keep her voice soft.

"Mother, I'm rather good at taking care of myself. Of myself and two dozen English officers, I might add. I don't need your advice."

"I wouldn't go near him, is all I'm saying. And if you need to come home, you can."

"All right."

"He's twice your age, darling. He's older than me. It's not appropriate. As I said, I made my own mistakes. I wouldn't want you to repeat them. I also have it on good authority that he is about to marry."

"You don't know anything about him." Why was it her mother only ever wanted her close in order to control her? And why was it Nelly couldn't imagine that Willy Yeats would want to marry her? Was she so undesirable? Was it so impossible?

"I'm just repeating what I heard."

"Don't you think you might have asked me what *I* thought?"

"He is a famous man, a ladies' man—he strings along so many girls at once—catches them up in all his glamour, you know. You wouldn't want to marry him even if it were an option."

Georgie stood up, furiously. "It is an option."

"Darling," Nelly said calmly. "We all get caught up in things we can't have. But this isn't something you ought to even want. Be sensible for once."

Georgie's whole body was burning up. *For once.* The waiter was returning with bread for the table, but Georgie grabbed her purse.

"I am perfectly sensible," she said loudly to the young waiter, and walked right out of the restaurant.

———— • ————

Out on the street, she was so angry she walked right into the path of a cab, which screeched to a stop and blasted its horn. Georgie strode across the road in front of it, feeling invincible. How dare Dorothy tell Nelly that she was interested in Willy, and how dare Nelly suggest that this was a futile pursuit! How was it everyone thought they could live her life better than she could? How would they feel when she and Willy got married, what would they say, how quiet and meek would they be then? She would cut off all contact with Dorothy, she thought. She would disallow Nelly from seeing her own grandchildren.

Turning right onto Piccadilly, she looked above the buildings to the white sky, imagining the entire whiteness filled with zeppelins spitting angry bombs all over the city. In her mind, the bombs exploded like brick-coloured magnolias. And still, she thought, pieces of the city would remain; even if they bombed every single building, no one could eradicate every brick, every bit of road. In a sense, the city was permanent.

When she got back to the dormitory, her notebook was missing. With her remaining anger, she had the idea someone might have taken it, broken in and stolen it from her. Someone might be trying to take all her research, to steal it away. She was so agitated, she tried to go to bed but kept getting up to open the window, and close it again, and check if she might have left the notebook in her other cloak, or put it in one of the drawers, or somehow lost it behind her books. But in the tiny room, it was nowhere to be found.

THIRTEEN

PIKE

She had left it on the windowsill, and on a whim he'd slipped it under his covers, purely, he told himself, to get a better idea of who she was. He skimmed through the pages, but after not too long, he felt a gripping in his gut. He realised, flipping through, that he was looking for his own name. He was looking for a glimpse of himself through her, evidence that she thought of him, that he was not entirely forgettable. But as he turned the pages, through this strange mingling of subject matter and different languages—English, Italian, Latin, and a language he didn't recognise—he noticed so many references to the same W—*D says W still in the country*, for instance, and *Visit NR before W's return.* There were other notes—about the journey of the soul after death; a scrawled recipe for beef tea; and he recognised a list of the circles of hell: limbo, lust, gluttony, greed . . . Why did she never write about the hospital? Was it so bad? Perhaps she wrote about it somewhere else, or her thoughts were taken up with it much more than this document suggested. Perhaps she had noticed he was handsome and kind but did not write it down. Or otherwise, she was selfish, and she didn't think of them at all. They had given their lives, hadn't they? And he had given all his time to think of her, while she couldn't even wrench out a couple of words for him.

Folded into a small square was also a letter from the poet—the illustrious W—a distant, unloving letter, saying he wouldn't make it to some meeting or other, written in a rush, with a glut of spelling errors, by someone who apparently cared not a jot for the addressee. *Yours faithfully, W. B. Yeats. This* was what she called a sweetheart? Once more Pike had the reservation that this girl was not who he thought she was; perhaps she was more of a fool than he'd imagined. He continued to read through her notes. There was a table of phases of the moon, and of how memory was transferred from one soul to another, and a list of the meanings of the tarot: *the Tower: profound and sudden change; the Hanged Man: release from control; the Fool: a leap of faith; the Magician: awareness and attention.* There was a page with the large heading *Deception (Neptune)*, and there was nothing written underneath.

He tossed the book down on the covers, and when he looked up, she was standing at his bedside, staring at the notebook.

"Where did you get that?"

"You left it behind."

"And you took it?"

"I was only looking after it."

"You were reading it!"

"I wanted to know more about you. You left it behind," he said again. He was still disappointed in her for not including him, not thinking of him, for believing in foolish things like tarot and astrology. For not being the person he'd imagined.

"It's *mine*."

"I'm sorry." He paused. "I suppose I wanted to find myself in it."

"Are you such a child?" She snatched it up from the bed, and she was already looking through the book herself, as if to reassert her ownership, or to see what he might have seen. In her rush, several loose pages fell onto the floor, and she knelt down to pick them up. He reached his arm down to help her but she cut him off with a gesture.

"It's private."

"I'm sorry," he repeated. She concentrated on gathering up the pages.

He tried to soften his tone. "Are you—religious then?"

"No."

"The war'll squeeze it out of anyone, I suppose." He was trying to coax her into forgiving him, into looking at him. "At least you seem to believe in something."

"And you don't, I suppose?" She had a sulky tip to her head, pretending not to listen to him, trying to punish him.

"The only superstition I believe in is third light."

While she said nothing, she glanced at him, as if waiting for him to explain.

"That it's bad luck to light a third cigarette from a single match. It makes sense, that."

She didn't reply, so he went on: "Because the time it takes to light three cigarettes is the same time it takes the Hun to spot you and take a shot at you. I've seen it myself. You can pay a lot for generosity." He hesitated. "You write in other languages. Why?"

"To test myself."

"Is that the only reason?"

She considered. "No. I want to make sure they're my notes. That no one's looking over my shoulder." Her voice had thawed slightly. "It helps me to feel invisible."

He didn't want the conversation to end; he wanted to keep her near him. If she walked away now and ignored him for the rest of the day, the week, it would be unbearable. "Listen, I shouldn't have read it." He spoke fast, without thinking. "I think—it's a tragedy to have a clever young lady like yourself wound up in such an infantile creature."

"Pardon?"

"Your poet, I mean."

She shook her head at him again. "Isn't he a little old to be infantile?"

"That's exactly what I mean. He is. I wanted to offer you some advice."

She laughed. As if all the tension had reached such a point she had to laugh. He hoped it was a good sign. He kept talking.

"That kind of man—an ambitious man—likes to have to fight for something. It's better not to make it too easy for him. He should have a competitor."

"Well, he doesn't." She laughed again, in one sharp breath. A couple of the men in nearby beds were looking over at them.

Pike pretended not to notice. "What about me?" he said quietly.

"Excuse me?"

"It wouldn't have to be—a real competition. You could just say you'd met an officer in the hospital."

She laughed, a little gentler now. "You're lucky that your impudence is amusing, Lieutenant."

"Lucky? I don't believe in luck. Do you?"

She paused, and smiled. "Perhaps I'm waiting to see."

FOURTEEN

She had received an invitation from Dorothy and Willy to go down to Stone Cottage, and she left for the station as soon as her morning shift was over. Her earlier anger at Dorothy had dissipated; she knew that Nelly had a gift for gleaning information that you hadn't intended to part with. She also understood that Dorothy intended to show her that Willy was an inappropriate suitor, but Georgie was just as determined to prove her wrong.

It was cold, and she wished she had brought her gloves. She wouldn't have much time at the cottage, as she had to return to the hospital for the night shift, but still, it would be worth it to see Willy and Dorothy and Ezra.

On the train she tried to concentrate on the blurring hills, the small towns with a church at each town centre. Her fingers were still cold so she put them in her pockets, but she was restless, and

she pulled them out again. She took out her newly reclaimed notebook and found a page with a note from *Henry IV*:

GLENDOWER.
I can call spirits from the vasty deep.
HOTSPUR.
Why, so can I, or so can any man;
But will they come when you do call for them?

It was early afternoon when the train pulled in, and Dorothy was
at the Forest Row station to meet her. Seeing her waiting at the
station reminded Georgie of when they had gone on painting
trips in Europe, galloping about colluding and drawing; march-
ing up hills arguing about books; and wandering among ruins
to escape their chaperones. She supposed they wouldn't do such
things again.

They kissed, and Dorothy took her arm, directing her to walk
back towards the cottage.

"You look much better," Dorothy said.

"How is it here?"

"Oh, fine. I'm working on a painting," she said. "Otherwise,
Ezra tries to shock Willy by reading obscure poets and Willy tries
to shock Ezra by reading Wordsworth. And both fall into such
great smugness, they forget to listen to the other."

Georgie was glad to have her friend's arm entwined in hers.
"Do they listen to you?"

"Oh, sometimes. I mean, they do listen, but never quite so atten-
tively as when they are listening to themselves. There's this expression of absolute wonder on their faces, when they are stumbling

into what they think is a deeply profound thought. Like they think their words are divine."

"I can't imagine Ezra as anyone's secretary."

"You can see for yourself. He does dictate letters, and reads to Willy. But he often tries to control things. Ezra is sort of—thirsty to make his mark on the world."

They had arrived outside the cottage. Georgie had seen the house before from the path; it was only two hundred yards down the road from the Prelude, where Nelly and Henry and Georgie had spent some of their summers. The Prelude, a far larger, brick house, backed onto Ashdown Forest and its miles of faery woods. Stone Cottage, however, was a more modest dwelling, and it sat on the waste moor.

As Dorothy let her into the house, she called up, "She's here," and they both listened to the banging about in the rooms upstairs. Down the stairs came Willy himself.

"Wonderful," he said, leaning in to kiss her cheek. "Welcome, my dear."

"Welcome to the secret society," a voice called from above. Ezra bounded down the stairs, kissed Georgie's forehead, pulled a lock of Dorothy's hair, and said, "I will be there in a moment—I have to finish something," and abruptly turned around and ran back up the stairs.

"I have a very eager secretary," Willy said as they walked on into the living room, "although his extracurricular activities can be a little alarming. Have you ever heard of a poet called Lascelles Abercrombie?"

Georgie shook her head, wondering if she should have, and trying not to smile too much at being near him. Dorothy gestured for her to sit by the fire, and she took the seat beside her friend. Willy sat on the other side of the fire, in a large blue armchair. "A fortnight ago Ezra invited him to France to fight a duel, because his poetry is such an affront to the reader."

"Well, it *is*." Ezra had already arrived in the doorway, somehow having finished whatever it was and returned in barely a minute.

"What happened?" Georgie said.

Ezra shrugged. "Apparently I depressed him. Which depresses me."

"Better than you being bested in your own duel," said Dorothy, as Ezra wandered over to his wife and perched on the arm of her chair. Dorothy and Ezra looked at each other with a kind of studious awe, some space between unknown affection and known tolerance. Georgie glanced at Willy, who was also watching the couple.

"I have to watch his dictation," Willy said, turning to look at Georgie, "lest he invite anyone to duel with me. The prerogative of youth."

"You're not so old," Georgie said.

"I can hardly read in bad light. Ezra is my eyes."

Georgie couldn't help but think what a better secretary she might make. She was not as wild as Ezra, not as furious. She would stay on task. Over the course of the next hour she envied the closeness of the three of them, how when Ezra got up, he casually stroked Dorothy's cheek on his way past, and Willy pulled in his chair to make space, while the fire shot out sparks. They were comfortable with one another, and Georgie did not feel altogether comfortable.

———— • ————

Dorothy took her out walking on the waste moor before they lost the light. They put on their coats and scarves and boots and plodded out into the fields. The air was freezing. Georgie wished she could stay in one of the cottage's upstairs rooms and not go back to London at all. How far away the hospital seemed right now.

"What do you think it would be like," Dorothy said as they walked, "to be extraordinarily beautiful?"

Georgie frowned. "What? You're quite beautiful enough."

"That's not what I mean, though. I mean, what do you think it would be like to have a kind of otherworldly beauty? As a man or a woman."

"I think it would be tedious."

"Why?"

"What use is beauty? What does it do?"

"It draws admiration."

"But is the beauty active, or are the admirers active? And what use is admiration for something that you can't take any credit for, something that doesn't *do* anything?"

"Well, it's of some use," Dorothy said. "The admiration is real."

"But what does it lead to? Where does it go?"

"Where does anything go? I was only wondering what it would be like, to be wildly attractive. I didn't mean to upset you."

"I think everyone feels that there is something wrong with them, no matter how attractive they are. Why must women be attractive and admired, while men can be invisible but still heard?" She realised she was almost shouting, and Dorothy was staring at her.

"All right, dear. I only asked."

Georgie tried to change the subject. "Do you like being married?"

Dorothy nodded. "It's not what I thought," she said. "But I do like it."

Neither of them had mentioned their earlier conversation about Willy, or the fact that Dorothy had prattled to Nelly, but after a while Dorothy said, "Willy told me that a woman who marries an artist is either a goose, or mad, or a hero. Have you heard this already?"

Georgie shook her head.

"A goose tries to force the artist to earn money; a madwoman drives him mad. But a hero suffers with him, and they come out all right." Dorothy loosened her scarf around her neck with her long fingers. "I'm not sure if I'm mad or a hero. I expect I am a mix."

"I think we're both heroes," Georgie said, "married or not."

———— • ————

When they got back to the cottage, Willy was standing in the hall-way. "I have to catch the post office before it closes, but will you still be here when I get back?"

Georgie shook her head and tried to hide her disappointment. "I have to get my train."

"Are you sure?"

"I'm needed at the hospital." She had written to tell him about Neptune's warning from her last horary, of the impending decep-tion between them, but they had not had a chance to talk about it.

"That wretched hospital," Willy said. "Did you make it out to see the Radcliffe girl yet?"

"Not yet."

"I wish I could join you."

Dorothy was watching the two of them, clearly registering their affection for one another, and sensing the need for an intervention. She was checking her wristwatch. Georgie wished she could throw in her hospital job this minute. She wished she could telegram Mrs. Thwaite and move into one of the spare bedrooms to continue with her Order study and her horaries, while the poets wrote their poems and Dorothy painted, and in the evenings they could sit around the fire and talk.

"You still have time," Dorothy was saying to Willy. "Perhaps you could let Georgie read your new poem before you go."

"The young ones have no patience for my poems about the old days," Willy said.

Dorothy smiled. "Georgie might, though. You could read her the one you read us last night."

He didn't seem to register anything unusual in Dorothy's request. "I tried to read it," he said and, turning to Georgie, led her back into the living room, "but they silence me now, when they feel I am too passé. They think I am in my dotage. Ezra actually 'corrected' some of my poems recently, without asking. The mentor has become the mentored."

He went across the room and plucked a page from among the array of papers splayed about. He offered it to Georgie, and Dorothy said, "Won't you read it aloud?"

But he shook his head. Georgie took the page from him and read the first few lines:

She is foremost of those that I would hear praised.
I have gone about the house, gone up and down
As a man does who has published a new book,
Or a young girl dressed out in her new gown,

At this moment Ezra walked in and saw Georgie reading the poem. He smiled and wagged his finger at Dorothy. Georgie returned to reading. The poem was about a man trying to turn the conversation to the topic of his beloved—who was clearly Maud Gonne—and how he was thwarted by all the people around him, who seemed to want to talk of others. It ended with a declaration:

> *I will talk no more of books or the long war*
> *But walk by the dry thorn until I have found*
> *Some beggar sheltering from the wind, and there*
> *Manage the talk until her name come round.*
> *If there be rags enough he will know her name*
> *And be well pleased remembering it, for in the old days,*
> *Though she had young men's praise and old men's blame,*
> *Among the poor both old and young gave her praise.*

The writing was in tight cursive, with occasional crossed-out words and their replacements provided above. *In the old days!* Was he truly stuck in those days? How could he cling to this woman he had once loved, who had never loved him, as if she hadn't led him on, decade after decade? Why did he talk to Georgie the way he did, if he was so caught up in this? She put the poem down on the table, and for a moment she didn't look at Willy or Dorothy, although she could sense Dorothy glowing beside the fire. Did he not sense a contradiction between this poem and the way that he thought about her?

"It's beautiful," she said to Willy, who stood waiting for her response. He was still holding his letter. He kissed her cheek, lingered, and pressed her hand. She couldn't tell what he was thinking.

"I'll see you back in London," he said.

As Willy left, Ezra bowed theatrically to his mentor. Georgie glanced down the hallway as Willy walked out, as the door closed gently behind him. Would he really keep at the same subject matter until he died? Was he truly that far away from her; did he see such a gap between old and young? Why had he looked at her the way he had? Why would he allude to a possible relationship between them? Dorothy had gone over to her canvas in the corner.

Ezra's expression towards Georgie was level. "What do you make of it?"

She was startled at first, before she realised that he meant the poem.

"I admire it, of course. But I'm less convinced by this old-man's-ad-nauseam-nostalgia-for-his-lost-love."

Ezra was nodding sharply. "He can't move past it. He's truly stuck in old themes, old style; there's no development. All Maudlin rants. It's a sad thing." He looked fierce. Dorothy had picked up a paintbrush and started to thicken one of the black lines on the white canvas.

"There is something new though, sparer, in some of the work," Georgie said. "I think he will change."

"He won't listen to me. Just keeps writing away to no one. I will be the only one to ever love her, down Ballykillywally way, haw haw."

"He needs to decide to change himself."

"I can hardly believe that Joyce is Irish. He doesn't wallow like our Willy."

Dorothy sighed and put down the paintbrush and walked back over to the blue armchair, where she crossed her legs underneath her.

Ezra glanced at her, and back at Georgie. "I heard you were thinking of Willy as a mate. I think it's a terrific idea."

Dorothy made a noise in her throat. "You do not, Ezra."

"I absolutely do. She would be good for him. He needs someone to shake him up. Gonne begone! Georgie understands his poetic weaknesses. He needs someone as clever as her to get him back into line."

"I'm sure he does," Dorothy said, "but what does she need?"

——— • ———

Dorothy walked her back to the station as the light was starting to leach out of the sky. She was gentle as she kissed Georgie on both cheeks.

"You thought Willy would come out of that badly," Georgie couldn't resist saying, "but he didn't really."

"You don't think so? Dear, you don't know him."

"And you do?"

"More than you do, yes. He's stuck in the past. He's not worth wasting your time over. I do hope you see that."

Back on the train, as she watched the trees flash past, blurred as the slip from second to second, she thought of Dorothy's paintings lying around, and she realised that she had not examined them or asked about them, that the men had not mentioned them either. They had talked only of poetry. The retreat was not about Dorothy's paintings, and still, Georgie felt guilty she had not asked her friend about her own work. As the trees faded into the darkness of the landscape, she resolved to take more notice the next time.

FIFTEEN

SPRING 1916

Every afternoon since she'd received the money from Nelly, and even though she knew she did not quite have the sum required, she had returned to the jewellers, but every time she had found the same Closed sign taped to the door. It looked as though the sign had been scrawled hastily; she wondered if the brother had died at the front and the business was going to be sold. What was the fate of the proud, self-conscious boy behind the counter, and what she had come to think of as Willy's ring?

Finally, she noticed the Open sign was out once more, and when she entered to the sprinkle of bells, she found the boy standing behind the counter, this time greeting her with a broad smile.

"I knew I would see you again," he said cheerfully. She realised he was in uniform.

"You see they got desperate," he said. "They're even letting me go." He was already unlocking the case on the far left of the shop, and he pulled out the signet ring. "It's been waiting for you. I hid it away." He held it out to her.

"I'm afraid I'm still a little short," she said.

"Oh, I don't care," the boy said.

She handed over all the money she had, and he gave her the ring. "I hope it brings you joy."

SIXTEEN

Visiting hours were quiet. Georgie was checking the major's wound when he not only lowered his newspaper for the first time but actually folded it and placed it in his lap. And then she heard him speak for the first time.

"Miss Wetherford. Emma Wetherford? Is that really you?" He was calling over to the silvery blonde woman who came to visit Second Lieutenant Pike.

The silver-blonde head turned. "Major Hammond!" She walked over to him. "Fancy that! And it's Mrs. Haworth-Ray to you, sir." She flaunted her ring and scrunched her lips together.

He laughed. "Good Lord, look at you! Charles finally talked you round then. Lucky devil. But—what in God's name are you doing in this hellhole? Your mother would be mortified."

"You won't tell her," she said, her hand retracted and her voice stiffening. "I am visiting a friend." She nodded towards Pike. As they glanced in her direction, Georgie pretended not to be listening to their conversation.

"The second lieutenant is your friend? How amusing."

"We met at Cambridge when I was visiting Eddie," she said, "and I do try to follow up with my friends."

"Heavens. Well. Don't forget to follow up with me then, little Emma. And say hello to your mother for me, will you? I am off to convalescence for the moment; the Hun got me in the side, you see, a real nuisance. But I'll be up again in no time. Such a pleasure to see you. You'll give an old man a kiss, won't you."

Georgie was amazed that this man could put on this display, when only half an hour beforehand he couldn't bring himself to wipe an inch and a half of snot from his nose. Now the major's face was clean and animated, and Emma Haworth-Ray leaned forward to kiss his cheek. Georgie glanced over at Pike, who caught her glance and winked at her.

SEVENTEEN

"It would have killed me," the woman was saying, "not to acquire it, to come across it in someone else's drawing room."

Georgie peered in the doorway of the Radcliffes' house. A woman was standing in the wide hallway, stroking the arm of a cheap mahogany chair that was aspiring to be a Chippendale; but the arms of the chair, supposed to be sleek, were blunt, and instead of resembling swans' necks, they looked like the paws of an awkward mammal. The woman was addressing someone out of sight, but after a moment she turned around and noticed Georgie.

"Who on earth are you? Where is Rogers?"

"Excuse me," Georgie said. "I'm here to see Miss Radcliffe. I am Miss Selden."

There was a maid standing nearby, the recipient of the woman's conversation. She bobbed her head at the woman and dropped a sloppy curtsy. "I'll get Miss Nora, ma'am."

"I remember you," the woman said to Georgie, moving away from the chair and squinting slightly, her eyes not reflecting the light. "You're the one who made that telephone call. You might practise your telephone manner, you know. It was quite off-putting."

Georgie didn't know how to reply. Mrs. Effie Radcliffe was a thin, sharp-nosed woman, and her eyes were very big indeed, and so wide-set she gave the impression she could not see right in front of her, but rather could look either side of her, like a fish.

"You had better come in." Her voice was scratchy with disdain.

Georgie followed her down the hall, catching glimpses of the adjoining rooms. The house was filled with furniture of the kind that was made to look expensive but was worth very little. Then again, as her father used to say, a thing was only worth what someone would pay for it, and Georgie imagined that Effie Radcliffe might have paid a lot for these items. But the curlicued mahogany coatrack did not match the pale sideboard, which did not match the one interesting item, which was a print of Blake's *Newton*, his beautiful muscular body crouched over a long white scroll, his cheekbone sliced across his face, his fingers measuring distance on the scroll with a compass.

"In here," Effie Radcliffe said, motioning her to go first.

Miss Nora Radcliffe was sitting in a small library, and she jumped when the door opened. She was not like some of the other mediums; there were no long trailing scarves or ringed fingers or wild frizzed hair. Instead, she was a skinny, anemic-looking creature, with plaits on either side of her face. She resembled a girl, but the curled lines around the sides of her eyes and the little slant between her eyebrows showed that she was older than that, maybe more than thirty.

The room they were standing in was lined with wooden shelves of books, although there were also gaps where books were missing. Effie Radcliffe indicated for Georgie to sit on the left side of her daughter.

"Nora is very gifted in the study of astrology," Effie Radcliffe said, seating herself on her daughter's right. "She always has been, as well as being a talented medium. She has an exceptional gift."

Georgie sat down obediently, imagining Willy sitting between these two women. "I cast horaries myself," she said.

"But few people have the intuitive touch that Nora has. It is quite a complex practice, you know."

Georgie glanced over at Miss Radcliffe. She was shifting in her chair. She passed a sheet to Georgie, wordlessly. It had spaces for her details: date of birth, time of birth, place of birth. Georgie noted down:

16 October 1892, 8:42 AM, the Grove, Branksome Wood, Fleet.

Once she had returned the paper to Nora Radcliffe, the girl looked back at her, blinking.

"I am not sure I should say this," she said in a quiet voice, "but perhaps you are also aware—that there is someone who has come here before, with your astrological data. Who is also interested in what the stars have in store for you."

There was a knock at the door, and the butler opened it. "I'm ever so sorry to interrupt, but there is a telephone call for you, my lady."

"For me, Rogers?" Effie Radcliffe stood up. "You must excuse me." She peered from her daughter to Georgie and bustled herself out of the room.

Nora Radcliffe waited for her mother to leave.

"You were talking about Mr. Yeats," Georgie said.

"The person doesn't use that name. But you are—connected to—the person in some way."

"Yes. And I'm interested in your script, from what I've heard about it. Do you think we might try now?"

"Now?" Nora Radcliffe said, as if she would prefer to simply discuss astrological issues, as if a séance were not the entire reason for Georgie's visit. She glanced up at the ceiling. "I suppose we can try." She concentrated for a moment on the large notebook in front of her, like she was counting inside her head, before she closed her eyes.

The room was silent. The girl's eyebrow twitched, but her hands stayed still. Georgie looked away, trying not to disturb her. She could hear faintly the sound of the girl's mother, her voice carrying down the hallway from the telephone. Above the table, a small window looked out on a triangle of soil which might have once been a lawn, with a thin slice of afternoon sun. She thought of the hospital, of the light through the high windows falling on the beds. She thought of Second Lieutenant Pike holding her notebook, turning the pages as though they belonged to him.

There was a sharp intake of breath, and she turned to see the girl's body quivering.

Nora Radcliffe pressed the pen to the empty page but could not seem to move the pen on the paper. Her eyes stayed shut. Her hand paused and shook. Her body crouched over the page, now more like a hunchbacked creature than a woman. She changed the grip on the pen, holding it between her thumb and her fist.

Now the pen drew a shaky curve. It was not a letter, just a half circle on the page. Her hand lifted and made another half circle.

"Is someone there?" Georgie said.

The pen hovered above the page, as if it were deciding whether to reply. Finally, in mirror text, it made a shape, a thin *S*, and to the right of it, an *A*, and an *M*, until it spelled out

THOMAS

The girl's eyes remained closed. The pen was still clutched at the same painful angle. Georgie lifted her own hands from her lap and clasped them together before asking the question.

"Why are you here?"

The air felt as if it had thickened, and Georgie struggled to breathe. She watched the girl write for a solid minute, the words appearing slowly:

THE ONE YOU THINK OF KNOWS
NOT HIS OWN MIND
ONLY I CAN MAKE PROPHECIES
FOLLOW ME OR YOU WILL BE LIKE THE
CHILDSPARROW
WHO FALLS BEAKFIRST
FROM ANOTHER'S TREE

Georgie frowned.

"What do I have to do?"

FIND THE OLD STORY
BEFORE IT FINDS YOU
DO NOT LET IT REPEAT

"Where? Where do I find it?"

The pen hovered above the page a moment more, but at the moment it pressed once more against the page the door opened, and Georgie saw, for a second, the looming face of Effie Radcliffe in the doorway. The pen dropped to the floor. When she looked back up, the woman had slipped away.

But Nora Radcliffe had opened her eyes. She took a long breath in before recovering her voice.

"I'm so sorry." Her head drooped between her shoulders. Georgie noticed the door to the hallway remained open.

.After a moment the girl raised her head and saw the writing in front of her. Her head snapped to attention.

"Something—something happened?" She looked from the text to Georgie and back at the text. She seemed genuinely surprised, although Georgie wasn't sure whether to believe her.

They both stared at the notebook for a minute. Laid out on the pristine page, the words did seem to have been summoned from somewhere else; it was difficult to imagine they were the product of this young woman's mind. Nora Radcliffe was staring down at the strange words, breathing out with her lips pursed as if she were whistling.

"Are you quite well, Miss Radcliffe?"

Miss Radcliffe's eyes flicked up to the ceiling, and she pressed her lips together and squinted.

"It's only—" She paused again, and coughed, and as she stared at the doorway where her mother had been standing, words came pouring out of her. "I am not a fraud," she said in a low voice. "The voices do come to me. But they wear me out. And they do not always come."

"I see."

"I am worried that if I try again now, I might—get stuck—or worse. I admit I am scared to try."

"I don't want to make you ill," Georgie said.

Miss Radcliffe was reaching into her pocket and produced some coins, which she offered to Georgie.

"You must pay Mother when you leave."

Georgie shook her head. "I can pay." That was already more than good enough, she wanted to say. Miss Radcliffe was looking blankly at the empty doorway, as if she weren't listening.

"May I take this with me?" Georgie said, indicating the page.

Nora Radcliffe nodded and tore it out of the notebook to hand it to her. Georgie took it and folded it carefully. When Georgie offered her hand to shake, the young woman grabbed it. Her grip was tight, her hand sweaty and cold. "I hope you will come back." Her eyes were lined with a greyish rheum.

After Georgie stepped out into the hall, she stopped a moment. Was it worth sacrificing her place in the Order for this? All those years of work for a few minutes of communication too vague to give her anything to properly chase up? Of course not. But there was something, she thought, looking down at the folded paper in her hand. Willy had been right. There seemed to be something in it.

"How did you find it, then?" Effie Radcliffe had returned, holding a thick appointment book with a gold spine. She opened her book and flicked through the pages.

"Very interesting."

Georgie had found her purse, and collected some coins to pay Mrs. Radcliffe. She even tipped her, feeling sorry for the girl. The woman accepted the money without comment. "You would like another appointment."

Georgie glanced over the woman's shoulder at the book, which was showing July and August. There were many more empty appointment slots than the woman had led her to believe on the telephone.

"Perhaps you might come again soon?" Effie Radcliffe said.

"Please," Georgie said.

EIGHTEEN

Later, in the dormitory, she felt restless. From the handful of mediums she'd gone to before she joined the Order, she knew they were exhausting; even with bad ones, the hope you would discover something led to a nervous agitation that, when it was over, left you weak and useless. And Nora Radcliffe had not been at all bad. Or had she? Sometimes it took a few hours for you to realise that it had all been a ruse, that you had been manipulated.

Dorothy had written to say that they should meet now that she was back in London. But there was no new note from Willy, although he, too, must be back in London. Now when Georgie reread his last message, it seemed cold, distant. She was beginning to doubt him. Perhaps she was naive to have believed they could ever marry. That new poem was evidence enough. *She is foremost of those that I would hear praised.* Had Dorothy and Nelly been right all along? Could the real reason for his failure to write to her be Maud Gonne, his old love of so many decades, still pulling him back to her? Or someone else, maybe; there were plenty of other women with creamier skin than her own. She found herself doubting the Radcliffe girl too. There was the overeagerness of the mother, presiding over it all, and the little quiver in the girl's forehead, as if she were anxious that the game would be found out. The spirit—*spirit*—had given nothing away. What if Harkin found out she had gone? She would lose her place in the Order, and it all would have been for nothing. Did Willy's determination to believe the Radcliffe girl come from some weakness in him? In any case, she knew she would keep her next appointment—and in doing so, maybe she was just as weak as Willy.

She had recovered the flask of brandy Dorothy had given her, unscrewed the lid, and sipped. That was better. It was windy outside, and the old building seemed to settle and resettle in the wind.

She took another sip. At least no one would come in and bother her. Really, it didn't matter that what he'd written was distant. It didn't matter that he might not be thinking of her. That she had a drink mattered. That she had the time to drink it. That her father, whom she would never see again, nonetheless still had a remnant of thought remaining in the air, a spindle of memory, a spatter of words, right around this drink, like a fruit fly gliding on the surface. He was not simply the dust. That mattered.

She had never seen her father's body. His body had been sent to the mortuary, and at the funeral, the coffin was closed. Not seeing him dead meant she could believe, for a time, that the footsteps approaching from down the hall were his, that the door handle turning was from his hand. They never were, of course, but for a time she'd allowed herself to hope.

The soul's existence after death mattered; but whether or not Willy Yeats wanted to marry her? That made no difference to the small numbers of the living or the innumerable numbers of the dead. He couldn't take a thing from her. Nor could this major deception looming between them, which was still promised by the ascent of Neptune in their horoscopes. She could hear voices down the hallway, and she smiled to herself. What was the use in deception if someone wasn't even here? Probably the deception was that he had once mentioned marriage, and it would come to nothing. She would get over that, she supposed. She tapped out a tune she'd heard on the gramophone onto the flask with her fingers, and drank again. She would try to forget him. He had been proposing to Maud Gonne for thirty years, been rejected for thirty years; perhaps it was too late for him to truly find a way out of that pattern.

She put down the flask, closed her eyes, and ran her finger along her books, pulling one at random from her little shelf. It was Morison and Lamont, the Oxford academics who, when visiting the Petit Trianon at the Palace of Versailles in 1901, had been transported back to the eighteenth century. Georgie had turned to the page where one of them had seen Marie Antoinette, sketching in the grass. But as she read, the rumble down the hallway became louder, and now the women's voices were accompanied by the bleary crunching of the wireless. Georgie put the book down and opened the door, and in her nightgown and socks, she followed the noise down the hall. The room at the end of the hall was filled with nurses and VADs, all crowded together and listening in their dressing gowns. *They have occupied the buildings*, the voice on the wireless was saying. *Civilians are being shot on the street.*

Georgie moved up to one of the nurses and asked what was happening, and the woman glanced back at her.

"Uprising in Dublin. They're shooting." Georgie listened for a while to the news, watching the startled faces of the half-dressed nurses, blonde and dark, pale and pink faces, all stricken. The British Army were trying to round up the perpetrators; the dead were lying out on the city streets. The rebels were declaring Ireland a republic *in the name of God and the dead generations*. Georgie realised she was holding her breath. What if he had gone to Ireland? What if he were hurt? She slipped back down the hallway to her room, her socks making no sound on the wooden floor. She thought of women and men shot, lying face up on the cobbles, and this thought blurred with the idea that perhaps it was not a creamy-skinned woman that had distracted Willy after all. She thought of Willy's body lying cold on the road, his lovely dark eyes staring up. Of course he hadn't written. She only hoped he was all right. At that moment she forgave him, impulsively, for everything.

NINETEEN

PIKE

He had become dependent on this swan duckling, this nurse creature. Her low voice, how she carved her steps out across the tiles, that persistent shadow of a bloodstain on her once-white collar. He hadn't made much progress, however, with courting her. With the exception of a few snatched conversations, a few smiles, she mostly treated him as she did everyone else at the hospital.

And then Emma had come again today, to wave at him like a princess and talk at him about their old acquaintants as if nothing had changed between them. He still felt stilted around her, still couldn't speak to her properly. What the devil was she coming here for, anyway? To taunt him? Was she trying to build him his own circle of hell? He was building it pretty well on his own. She looked like a kept goddess these days. Gloves, furs. Nobody would ever believe he'd seen her naked. It had been only once, the night before he went to join the regiment; they were already engaged, and he'd booked a little hotel with fake names, Mr. and Mrs. Whiteford. She'd told him off because it was too distinctive, and too like her own name; he should have used something more common, like Park, like Smith. But it's still made up, he'd said. If it hadn't been his last night, they would have quarrelled, but instead they'd had dinner, all his meagre savings spent on food and lots of pale wine, the alcohol content of which he'd doubted at first, and drunk more to make sure. He had barely eaten, too nervous about how he was holding his cutlery, and anxiously monitoring her reaction to each mouthful. Finally they had gone back to the room. He hadn't been sure if he had felt distant from her because of his nerves, or because he was preparing himself for being distant. Maybe they had never been all that close. There had been the usual sentimental business; she had cried, fat tears, and he had shown her the place by his heart where he would carry her picture. He realised that in his nervousness he had drunk rather too much, and he had to really steel himself to go through with it. But they had done it, with an amount of fumbling and blushing, and he had promised her it would get much better, when he was back. Now of course they would never get the chance—but he preferred anyway to imagine this nurse in that little hotel room now. She would have pointed out the vase of wilted flowers in the window and laughed, rather than pretending not to have noticed. She would be far more assured than Emma, far more assertive. He imagined her taking off the nurse's veil, the stiff white dress, and stripping it from her body decisively, the way she stripped a bed of its sheets. Would she ever do such a thing for him? He kept his eyes on his nurse whenever Emma visited. He imagined the nurse's chest blushing the way her cheeks sometimes did, not as if she were embarrassed but rather like her body was trying to tell her something.

No, Emma was nothing like the fleshy, real creature who took care of him, who had such strength of purpose, such certainty. He felt in his feet that same musical feeling, that twinging and twanging, a counterpoint of nerves, and he saw the doctor was standing over him—heaven help him—and he was saying that it was astonishing.

"Pardon?" Pike said. The doctor was looking around the ward as if he wanted to speak to someone else, but not finding anyone, he looked back down at Pike.

"Truly," the doctor said, "you, Second Lieutenant, are a miracle."

"How is that?"

"The infection has gone. We won't have to amputate at all. All going well—barring a recurrence of infection—you'll soon be fit for convalescence. It's extraordinary."

A miracle? Pike started trying to explain to the doctor that as a medical student he'd been told to distrust miracles, but the doctor interrupted him and told him he should rest for a while, that these things took time to process. It appeared that miracles were meant to keep quiet.

The doctor had moved on to the next patient, and Pike was left in the bed with his feet, his feet that he was suddenly allowed to keep. His body returned to him. What would Hyde-Lees say to that? It was impossible not to feel a kind of pride, pride for his sturdiness. Surely there was something in him that had caused it. Surely it was related to the fact that his brain had not cracked with what he had already seen. He would walk, dance! He could, seriously, marry this ordinary girl, he would have a real chance; after all, he did not lack charm. He had seen himself in the glass; he would never say it aloud of course, but the truth was he was a fine-looking fellow. It wouldn't be hard to get rid of the ancient, frail poet, who showed insufficient appreciation for this precious creature. Only he, Second Lieutenant Thomas Pike, knew how rare she was. He could go back to his studies, matriculate (could he?). He could become a doctor, in some practice somewhere (this part was still vague). His feet tingled and it seemed to him they were singing to him, accompanying his thinking, telling him their determination to remain a part of him. He saw her across the room.

"Hyde-Lees!" he called.

"Yes?"

She was wheeling a trolley, full of silver instruments laid on towels, and bottles of acid and water. Everything seemed to glisten suddenly, to be capable of so much.

"They're giving you more responsibilities."

She nodded at him, but she was frowning. He noticed that while she had both hands on the trolley, she also had her notebook in front of her, lying on the trolley as if to keep her company.

"Was there something I could help you with?" she asked, and although her voice was rather terse, he couldn't help but rejoice that she was looking right at him.

"You are right now addressing a miracle," he said. When she looked confused, he continued, "I'm keeping my feet. They're not cutting them off."

"Really?" she said. And now she smiled, her skin bright, her face lit up. She was delighted, he had delighted her! He was no longer a half man. She must see, too, that it would now be possible for them to get married. Who needed Emma Wetherford (or whatever-her-name-was-now), her perfect posture, her fashionable set, her cold look every time he lifted a fork to his mouth? He watched as Hyde-Lees turned away again, pushing the trolley on towards the window, and he, too, seemed to be gliding, out into the day.

———— • ————

That night she sat not far away, by the wooden chair over by the window. More relaxed about the rules, now. He had watched her take an electric lamp from the nearby table and sit on the chair with the lamp held in her lap. She covered the bulb with her dark blue veil so as not to disturb the officers, so that when she switched it on it made only a dull glow.

"What are you reading?" he called softly, but she didn't look over; it was possible she hadn't heard him at all. She was leaning back on the chair and held her book above her, tipping her head towards the ceiling.

Attraction was a kind of mystery, wasn't it? He had seen Emma talk to Major Hammond—evidently another of her worthy acquaintances—and glance back at him in embarrassment. "I am visiting a *friend*." Why had Emma been drawn to him in the first place, when she had barely ever mixed with anyone of his sort, and wasn't the type to be curious about those further down the ladder? Like most people, she was scared to look further down, in case it meant she accidentally fell herself.

They had met at Cambridge. Her brother was studying there at the same time as Pike, and Emma had been visiting Eddie. She was awfully pretty, tall and pale and upright, alongside Eddie with his severe bone structure, his cheeks hollowed out. Eddie was a genuinely kind chap, perhaps a bit too gentle for the world. They had been at a party; her brother was her chaperone. Apparently she had been taunting Eddie, who had fallen in love with a little sprig of a thing called Natasha. Emma, fuelled by port with lemon, had lunged at her brother in a way she'd often done when they were children, but Eddie had inadvertently stepped to the side at the moment she lunged, and she ended up unable to stop her momentum, flinging herself forward, losing her balance, and hitting her head on a wooden table in the middle of the party.

She hadn't screamed but landed sprawled on the floor, where she took a moment to move again. Her eyes were closed, then open. Pike approached her as she pulled her head up and glanced around.

"Easy," he said. "I'm training to be a doctor. How do you feel?"

Her eyes were very wide as she pulled herself up to a sitting position. "I'm mortified," she whispered. "Sit with me?" He paid no attention to the people who were watching them, and sat down, while Eddie stayed standing to reassure the small crowd that everything was under control and they could return to the party.

"What's your name?" Pike asked her.

She reached her hand up to her forehead to check if there was any blood. She frowned to find none. "Are you trying to seduce me?"

"I'm trying to gauge whether or not you are concussed. Today's date would also be fine."

"I'm not concussed."

"That's good," Pike said. "I'll leave you to it, then."

"Answer him, Frolly," Eddie said. "For goodness' sake."

"My name is Emma Elisabeth Anne Wetherford, and it is the seventeenth of October, nineteen hundred and thirteen," she said primly, and put her hand up to her eyebrow and winced. "No blood, then."

"You'll have a real shiner, I'm afraid," Pike said.

"It's Eddie's fault for falling in love," she said, looking crossly up at her brother.

"I can assure you," Eddie told Pike, "there is nothing here that is not my fault." He shook Pike's hand. "Thank you for helping us."

Pike turned to go, but Emma called out to Eddie.

"He can't leave," she said, "he saved my life."

Pike laughed. "Hardly."

"But you must make sure I don't develop a concussion. He must, mustn't he, Eddie? That table was a vicious adversary. Imagine what could be next."

And just like that, she and Eddie had swept him up and included him in all their plans for the week she was visiting. At first Pike had been cautious about getting too caught up in the whirlpool of this pretty, sophisticated girl—which he was, of course, immediately—but, oddly, she seemed to show signs of caring for him too. And the next summer Pike had received an invitation from Eddie to join them at the Wetherfords' country house in Oxfordshire, and he had proposed to her on the terrace, and she had wept, and said yes.

———— • ————

Silently, he pushed the covers aside and shifted his legs to the side of the bed. Hyde-Lees didn't seem to hear him. He would surprise her. He looked above, squinting to obscure the grid of white-sheeted beds, to pretend the building was once more a lovely house in Mayfair, with its violet drapes tied back from tall windows, and a large canvas with blurry Helen always on the brink of war.

He placed his miraculous feet gently on the floor to test them. The music inside them screamed. He laid them on the cold parquet for a while, waiting for them to grow accustomed, watching her rebalance the lamp carefully between her knees, holding her book with one hand, oblivious to his movements. He would just get a little closer to her.

She read under the small circle of light, one side of her face lit golden. He tiptoed, on his screaming feet, until he reached her, and still she hadn't noticed he was there. Silently he peered over her shoulder, and he could read one line:

The actual universe is a thing wide open, but rationalism makes systems, and systems must be closed.

He waited one moment and started to say, close to her ear, "What's a thing wide open?"

But she jumped. The lamp, which was balanced on her lap, fell, and the bulb smashed across the tiles.

He frowned. This was not how it was meant to go.

"What are you *doing*?" She stared up at him. Tiny splinters of shattered glass covered the floor in a loose mosaic.

"Sorry," he said.

"Stay there. You'll cut yourself. How are you even standing?"

He felt himself swaying. "I am a miracle," he said awkwardly. He found he could not move. He felt himself slither down, and he sat on the parquet, his feet out in front of him, heels cold on the floor. He could feel nothing but the pain in his feet. All the nerves in his body were collecting together to scream. There was a sliver of glass in front of him, the size of a child's finger. He focused on it. He picked it up in his fingers, and for some reason, it did not cut him. He slipped it into his pocket.

"Mary!" That bloody lieutenant. How he went on. Pike must have blacked out for a bit, woke again. Georgie was carrying something tall—a broom—and she was sweeping up the glass in a hurry. Across the room, the lieutenant had started gurgling as if he were trying to swallow something too large.

Pike winced. Why couldn't he get up? Why wouldn't his feet do what he told them? His buttocks had gone quite numb.

"Get up," Hyde-Lees snapped at him. She was sweeping the glass into a shovel. "You must get up, *please.*"

"Will you help me?"

"You seemed fine to get over here."

Pike managed to smile. He couldn't get up, but he couldn't bear to tell her. He felt warm tears clustering around his eyes and reached his hands to cover his face. He was a fool, always. He had ruined everything. She would never marry him. She was a stranger, for God's sake. She was only doing her job. The bell clanged across the room, and he shut his eyes. He heard the matron enter, the fluster of women's voices, and steps nearby.

"Come on, you idiot," a voice above him said. An arm reached down. And it was her again, it was Hyde-Lees; she had come back for him after all; her voice, even cursing him, was soft. In a moment she was holding him, she was guiding him, and because he was weak, she had her hands all over his body. He tried not to touch her any more than he had to. He clutched her arm and tried not to lean too heavily on her, all the way to the bed. He was worried what his body might do, being held like this. Her touch was everywhere. Could he stay like this? He wanted to smell her, but he could smell only his own sweat, like honey and soured milk.

TWENTY

SUMMER 1916

It was some weeks before Georgie finally found time to meet with Edmund Dulac, who was designing the ring engravings for her. They met in Berkeley Square Gardens so he could pick up the ring. She had met the Frenchman once before; he had a comfortable presence, as if nothing bad could happen to him. His drawings showed deep caves and creamy palaces, floating princes, trees like soft blankets, and peacock-blue skies interrupted by bright moons. From those drawings, she knew that he understood symbols; his drawings created not only pictures but doors that were openings to entire worlds. They had written back and forth and eventually settled on a design for the ring: an entwined hawk and butterfly, signifying the union of complexity and innocence, strength and wisdom. Inside the ring would be signs for Saturn and Venus, which not only counteracted the threat of Neptune's deception (which had refused to vanish from her horaries), but also referenced the planetary alignments at the date and time she and Willy had that first discussion of their *journey* in Olivia's library.

When she handed over the ring to Dulac, somehow it slipped from his grasp and fell into the grass. She was furious to see it vanish into the green, and she made herself stand still and feign calm as he leaned down to rake his fingers through the grass and pick it up again.

"Sorry," he said. How strange that a man so intuitive with a pencil could also be so clumsy with his hands. He picked up the ring, ripping a strand of grass with it. "You still won't tell me who it's for?"

"It's for me."

"A man's ring?"

She gave him a look that she hoped was withering. She had not thought him the type to gossip.

"You don't mind if I tell anyone, anyone at all, that I helped you to design a man's ring?" He was testing her.

"I only hope you have more interesting things to talk about."

———— • ————

An hour later she was concentrating on the mop's wet path across the parquet, breathing in the disinfected air, when a nurse arrived beside her elbow.

"I'm sorry?" the girl said, glancing between Mrs. Thwaite and Georgie. "Someone's here to see Hyde-Lees?"

Mrs. Thwaite's thin eyebrows slid up. "Are you expecting someone?"

Georgie shook her head and balanced the mop against the bucket.

"Excuse me." Perhaps whoever it was would have news of Willy. She had received only one note from him, which had been written at Woburn Buildings the day after the Rising. *My dear,* it read. *I must go away on short notice and could be gone for some time, but I will see you at the end of it. WBY*

She supposed he must have gone to Ireland, and she hoped he would be all right. They had executed the Irish rebels, and she had scanned the list of the casualties for names she knew. There was only one name she recognised, that of Major John MacBride, who had been executed by firing squad. MacBride was the estranged husband of Maud Gonne.

The matron left her alone. She had not forgotten that she'd had to reprimand Georgie for sitting down on her shift, for breaking a valuable lamp, and, worst of all, for "inappropriately handling" the second lieutenant. Pike's feet had further deteriorated following the incident, and Mrs. Thwaite considered that Georgie must be entirely to blame. "I am no longer sure I can trust you around the men," she had said. "You will no longer speak to the second lieutenant." It was, the matron told her, unsmiling, her last warning.

Georgie found that she felt sorry for Pike. She had noticed his awkwardness, how he had tried to avoid touching her as she carried him back to his bed. She had wondered what it would be like to have Willy that close, to have him that vulnerable. It seemed Willy's vulnerability was always tempered by performance, always a kind of display. There was a way in which she preferred the second lieutenant's weakness.

When she arrived out in the foyer, a nurse was walking from the operating room with bright blood down her apron. Watching the nurse from an alcove, her face rather paler than usual, was Dorothy. On seeing Georgie, she smiled and stood up straighter. "I'm sorry— I just thought I'd come and see you, just a whim—"

"I'm still on my shift."

Dorothy's face was somehow misshapen, as if her cheeks were still creased from her pillow.

"I'll go then," she said.

"You could come back at six," Georgie said. As she leaned in to kiss her friend's cheek, Dorothy's breath started to heave and catch, and she began to cry.

"Sorry," she said, "I'm not myself."

"What's happened? Are you all right?" Had something happened to Willy?

"Oh, it's—I can't—" Dorothy rubbed her sleeve across her face. "Anyway, you're still at work." She gestured vaguely into the ward.

Georgie stepped forward and put her arm around Dorothy's shoulders, guiding her towards the stairs. She had never seen Dorothy like this.

"I'll take you up," Georgie said, glancing back into the ward, "but just for a minute. There's a room we can sit in. It won't be clean, but it will be empty. Hang on." She left Dorothy for a moment, ran back to the supply cupboard, and collected a pile of white linen. When she returned, she took Dorothy's arm as if she were a patient and led her up the big staircase. They walked down the wide corridor together and turned into a small room. Georgie shut the door after them. The room had just one single bed in it, stripped. The mattress was wet. Georgie put the linen down on one corner of the mattress and opened the window as wide as it would go. She sat down on the bed and patted it for Dorothy to sit beside her. Dorothy sat. She laced her fingers together in her lap, laced and unlaced them, repeatedly.

"Sorry," she said. "I didn't know where else to go." Dorothy's eyes galloped about the room, until she gazed down into the wet patch on the mattress.

"What is it? What's happened? Come on."

Dorothy mumbled into her handkerchief and blew her nose. She looked up. "I should have married Freddie Manning! I should have married Herbert bloody Blake!"

"Oh," Georgie said. "I thought someone had died. Those men would have bored you stupid."

"Why did Ezra bother marrying?"

"What has he done?"

"He's throwing himself at—this woman. This writer—she has even come to the house. He pretends it's nothing. It's horrible."

"So Willy is all right?"

"Willy? What? Of course."

"He isn't in Ireland?"

She shook her head. "No." She wrinkled her nose. "You *have* given up on all that?"

"Of course I have." Georgie laughed. She was so relieved that nothing had happened to him, she picked up a pillow and tossed it at Dorothy, who caught it.

"Why is this wet?" Dorothy didn't wait for the answer but gazed at the pillow. "He's infatuated with her. Taking her arm, laughing, following her around. He praises every word she says and scorns every one of mine."

"Is he home now?"

"Probably."

"You should go and talk to him. I need to get back downstairs. The matron's not fond of me; she can't catch me here. I'm halfway through doing the floors—"

"I can't go back. I hate him." Dorothy threw the pillow on the bed and stared at it.

"You don't. Quite the opposite, I think."

"How can I love someone who only looks out for himself!"

"Maybe we're all a little like that." Georgie wondered if the tapping she could hear could be footsteps coming up the stairs. She moved closer to the door.

Dorothy was shaking her head and pointed to the wet patch on the mattress. "What is that?" She had once said that she would have volunteered at the hospital if she hadn't got married.

"Sweat, I think." They would smell it if it were something else. This was the room where they put the particularly mad ones, that they couldn't have in the ward. Two days before, an officer had arrived who had made a whining noise like a shell falling; it had sent several of the other men into a panic, and so they had carried him up here. Solitary, they called this room. She wasn't sure where the man had gone after that. If she were a wounded soldier, she would probably fake that kind of behaviour just to get a room to herself.

"That's disgusting." Dorothy wiped her hands on her dress.

"Well, if you hadn't married Ezra, you'd be here, wouldn't you? Making sweat-drenched beds, tipping out bedpans, swaddling infected wounds. You made the right decision. He won't leave you. How is your painting?"

Dorothy sniffed, put her hand over her nose, and offered a small cough. "You say we're all selfish. You mean that I am."

"You. Me. The nurses downstairs. The officers. The rebels. The executioners. Ezra—"

"But me especially?" Dorothy said, and recognising how she sounded, she smiled, as footsteps could be heard to pause right outside the door. Georgie lunged forward and grabbed the white sheet and shook it in the air, just as Mrs. Thwaite stepped into the room.

"Hyde-Lees."

"I'm just making this bed," Georgie said.

"No one told you—"

"I just anticipated—"

"And who is this?"

Georgie opened her mouth and shut it again.

"You can't just march about doing the Lord knows what with an unauthorised stranger. You know this bed needs to be cleaned and aired before it's made. You are halfway through a task downstairs. I will not put up with such—utter—*carelessness*. I really have no choice but to dismiss you."

Dorothy made a loud gasping noise, flourished a tissue, and blew her delicate nose, producing a squeal rather like a lapdog being asphyxiated. Georgie and Mrs. Thwaite both turned and stared at her.

"Excuse—excuse—me," Dorothy said, and she pulled a piece of paper from her pocket and waved it in the air alongside her soiled tissue. "I'm Georgie's cousin. And we—we just got news from the front. One of those telegrams. Georgie's brother."

Mrs. Thwaite stared at the telegram in Dorothy's hand, and the tight muscles around her jaw fell loose. Her eyes swivelled between Dorothy and Georgie before falling back on Dorothy's hand.

"It looks like an ordinary telegram," the matron said softly.

"It's from my aunt," Dorothy said. "She just told me. I am on my way to her now."

Mrs. Thwaite took a sharp breath in. "Your—brother—is he . . . ?"

"Killed in action at Verdun," Dorothy said with great solemnity. "She's in shock, of course." Georgie thought of her brother, Harold, who had never dreamed of going to the front, who dedicated most of his attention to the stock market, and whose shirts had started to burst around his middle. She didn't know where to look.

Mrs. Thwaite put one hand on Georgie's shoulder and another on Dorothy's, and squeezed. "I'm so very, very sorry," she said to Georgie. Her eyes were enormous. "Leave the sheets. Take as much time as you need."

Georgie was about to argue with Mrs. Thwaite, but Dorothy pressed the telegram into her hand and gave her a warning look. Mrs. Thwaite was leaving the room, gently closing the door behind her.

Once she was gone, Dorothy watched Georgie unfold the telegram. It was dated three days ago and read:

BACK THURS, PLEASE ORDER CLARET. WBY.

"I didn't want to get you into trouble," Dorothy said, returning the tissue to her pocket.

"What if she'd looked at it? What if she'd read it?"

Dorothy arched her lovely neck. "She didn't, though, did she?"

Georgie fingered the telegram. "And he is coming back on Thursday? To London? Where is he? Where has he been?"

Dorothy smiled. "He went to France, to propose to Maud."

TWENTY-ONE

On the ward, she was pouring water for the officers from a glass carafe. She concentrated on the gushing sound as the water tipped from the carafe's glass lip into the glass. She would not think about Maud Gonne. She would give up on Willy, who was conspicuous only in his absence, and his tendency to make her feel like a fool.

Two men arrived to take Major Hammond to the convalescent home. The major struggled to get into the wheelchair, but when Georgie started to walk towards him, he hissed at her. She stayed back and concentrated on pouring water for the other men. The major had never asked her name, or thanked her for tending to his wound. When he bothered to look at her at all, he stared at her as if she were a grease spot on a dress shirt.

Dorothy had gone back to Ezra. The men wheeled Major Hammond out the door. Georgie continued pouring.

When she approached Pike's bed, he was watching her. He picked up his glass and held it out for her, which made it harder for her to pour.

"Put it on the table, please," Georgie said.

He kept holding it. "I wanted to apologise."

"I'm not allowed to speak to you," Georgie said.

The lines in Pike's forehead and around his mouth seemed to have carved themselves deeper. For a moment she forgot about the glass and saw what he'd look like when he was old, perhaps living in a house somewhere, with a Labrador and a yellow-haired daughter.

"I really didn't mean to get you into any trouble."

"It's fine. Give me the glass," she said, reaching for it.

"I feel terrible—"

She reached forward and snatched the glass from his fingers, surprising herself with the fierceness of her movement.

"Are you all right?" he said, looking closely at her. "Did something happen?"

She shook her head and focused on the stream of water. The sound it made.

"Tell me," he said.

She stopped pouring. She inhaled sharply, about to reprimand him, but instead she breathed out. "I was wrong about something, that's all." She had not spilled a drop. She looked up to see Mrs. Thwaite arrive on the ward. She placed the glass firmly on the second lieutenant's bedside table and walked away from the bed.

"I'm sorry to hear it," he called after her. "I know the bloody feeling."

Georgie looked up at Mrs. Thwaite, who was gesturing to her to come over. Beside her was another nurse, wearing a bright white uniform.

"Off you go, Sanderson," Mrs. Thwaite said to the nurse, and turned to Georgie. "I'd like to have a word with you in my office."

"He keeps talking to me," Georgie said weakly. "I don't know how to stop him." She kept her eyes on the floor.

"Follow me, please." The matron walked out of the ward and down the corridor. Georgie followed her. The room Mrs. Thwaite used as an office was small. She had given up every other space she could to the officers. Sometimes Georgie forgot that this was Mrs. Thwaite's own home, that usually she lived here on her own, without her front room filled with officers, nurses, and visiting doctors. The room was rectangular and looked as though it were unchanged since the eighteenth century, except for an orderly pile of forms on the heavy mahogany desk and a series of faces staring out from half a dozen gold frames hanging on the wall. Above the frames hung a large canvas of a pastoral scene, with burnt orange and light green fields.

"Please take a seat." Georgie flattened her blue crêpe de chine veil, smoothed her apron, and sat.

Mrs. Thwaite took a deep breath. "I wanted to let you know that if you need time, you can ask. I would suggest that you go home now."

Georgie was surprised by how intently Mrs. Thwaite was staring at her.

"How old was your brother?"

Georgie had already forgotten her supposed brother. She cleared her throat, silently hating Dorothy for putting her in this position. "Twenty-four."

"My boys were nineteen and twenty-one. They were together when they died, which is good, I think. I always think it will have made it easier for them to find each other—you know—in heaven. Perhaps they have already met your brother there."

Georgie nodded. She felt a surge of hysteria rise, and patted it down. Mrs. Thwaite's conjecture was especially unlikely given that this week Harold was up at Oxford busily failing his exams for the second time. Mrs. Thwaite was staring out behind Georgie, at the wall behind her head, and her eyes were dry. Georgie sat in the chair with one hand in her pocket, pressing her fingers against her leg. She was scared to look away from the woman's face. Mrs. Thwaite's eyelids were puffed up, as if they had been stuffed with something soft. Georgie vaguely remembered hearing that Mrs. Thwaite was a widow, but she hadn't realised she had also had children, let alone sons who were killed in the war. After a minute, she broke eye contact to examine the faces in the gold frames on the wall, to try to discern which might have been her sons, but from where she sat she couldn't make out one face from another.

"The more you lose, the better you get at managing. It becomes more important to have a code to live by. I find rules to be very useful in a way I didn't before. I have to trust in God, you know, and to trust that he has chosen to give me a very hard test indeed, because he knows that I can bear it."

Georgie looked away from the faces and felt a twinge in her neck. How was she ever supposed to explain that her brother was perfectly fine, that no one had died, that her friend had made something up in fear that Georgie would lose her job?

"I'm sure you're right," she said instead.

"But no one really knows, do they? I only hope my boys are in heaven. They were rascals, you know."

"I'm sure that's where they are." Georgie didn't believe in heaven, but if she had, she would've been certain in that moment that she was not bound there herself.

Mrs. Thwaite was still talking. "It's too easy to spend all your time with the dead," she said. "That's why it's good for us to be here, I think. To look after those who are still alive. Second Lieutenant Pike looks like my youngest, you know. Oliver. He's fond of you."

Georgie nodded and smiled.

Mrs. Thwaite's gaze was steady. "I thank the Lord every day for keeping us safe, and for bringing people like you in to help us."

Georgie, digging her fingernails in her thigh, winced, and for a horrible moment thought she might laugh.

"Really," she said, "it's nothing."

TWENTY-TWO

A crash and Georgie leapt up, on her feet before she knew she was awake. Down the hall a woman screamed, once, twice, three times. The same woman? A thud, and the building was shaking, the air-raid siren blowing through the dormitory. She leapt out of her bed and ran out to the stairwell in her nightgown and slippers. Three other nurses were rushing down the stairs. Georgie could hear the landlady's voice down the corridor: "Calm, please. Order."

She waited before following the others down one flight of stairs, two, three, all the way to the bottom. In the cellar there were perhaps twenty women, all nurses, and they all stood and stared up at the ceiling, as if daring it to fall.

One of the girls was leading a prayer, but Georgie stood apart from the others. She wondered what was happening at the hospital, which was not far from here, whether the men were all right. Mrs. Thwaite would be with them. Above the ground, above the buildings, a zeppelin must be looming like a great ship of the sky. Right now, did it hang directly above them? Right now, did a man look down over the clouds, down on London? Was he poised, his finger hanging over—what was it? A switch, a button, a lever?

Vielleicht jetzt? Oder jetzt?

Another crash from above. One of the girls screamed. Georgie kept her eyes on the ceiling; if it fell in, she would see the first brick crack.

Instead the sirens stopped, and after a few minutes, Georgie headed for the stairs. One of the girls called up to her, "Where are you going?" They were all clustered together.

Georgie stopped on the first step. "I just want to have a look."

"You'll get yourself killed."

Georgie looked down at the cluster of women. Next to her, two of the other nurses were grasping one another's hands and staring up. She would not die in a basement. Maud Gonne's husband had been shot in Ireland, and Willy Yeats had rushed to her side. She would not die thinking about a man who had gone to propose to another woman. If a bomb was going to hit them, they would die whether they were in a basement or out on the street. She'd prefer to be hit looking at the sky. She ran up the steps.

When she reached the main corridor, she unhooked her blue cloak from the wall and put it on over her nightgown, wrapping it around her as she headed outside and towards the hospital.

The air was dusty, and Georgie put her hand up to shield her eyes from a thick weave of smoke. The early morning light slithered through the haze, and she could see a couple of silhouettes ahead of her, hear them calling to one another. She tipped her head back and was disappointed that the sky was empty. Some weeks back, one of the other nurses had seen a zeppelin: "slow and floating and otherworldly."

At first, beyond the smoke, Georgie could see no evidence that a bomb had fallen. But as she walked and the air cleared, she could see, a few blocks away, another thick shudder of smoke peeling off into the air. She ran towards it—until the air was filled with chunks of fine ash, and she slowed to a walk and held her hand over her mouth. She turned down an alley, and through to the main street, where the large apartment building on the corner looked as though a giant had passed by and shoved his fist down on one side.

The western part of the building had remained intact, but the eastern wing had collapsed, and the smoke was spreading from a small line of fire burning in one corner, orange-gold, greedy flames. You could see where the building should be, where the straight lines failed, where everything had turned to smoke. The road was covered with bricks, sprayed everywhere, toppled like unfinished sentences. A few metres from Georgie a crowd was gathering, an ambulance; two white-coated men were running into the smoke with a stretcher—but Georgie turned before she could see any bodies. The hospital was many blocks from here; she wondered if this was the only bomb to fall. She walked around the other side of the building, stepping over a stray brick that only minutes before had been part of a wall. Most of the bodies would be inside, underneath, crushed, perhaps some still living, perhaps some cycling through their last thoughts, staring at what had been their ceiling, brought down on their heads. How lucky not to have been inside; how blessed to be able to look across at this destruction from an unharmed, living body. Georgie took a handful of the loose material of her nightgown, creased it in her fist, and squinted against the dust and smoke. She leapt over a stray brick, like a horse clearing a jump, and started to run in her slippers, ran all the way from the building until the air began to clear, until she saw a man crossing the road in front of her.

And it was him. She couldn't mistake the walk; everyone knew that stride. She unclenched her fist, letting her nightgown loose, and waved to stop him—and his pace stuttered for a second, when he saw this dusty, oddly clad creature.

"Willy," she said, although she had never before called him this to his face. "Hello."

He stopped. "Hello, Georgie." He didn't seem surprised to see her. He kept both his hands in his pockets and glanced back over at the swathes of smoke. He seemed older, his skin looser in his cheeks, his pince-nez drooping over his nose.

"I hadn't realised you were in London." She had not meant it to sound like an accusation. She found it almost disappointing, the suddenness with which he had appeared on the street without warning, the way he could so carelessly inhabit the same world as her.

"I arrived this morning. And I'm afraid I'm already late to meet a man at my club."

"So early?"

"I've had a damnable time of it." They'd both turned to look at the collapsed building, although all that was visible now was great clouds of dust. "These raids are fond of my neighbourhood."

"But you're all right."

She was still exhilarated from seeing the building, and now him—he started to walk and she quick-stepped alongside him—one breath stumbled into the next, and the next, all caught high in her chest. She scanned the sky one last time for the zeppelin.

"Did you see it?" she said.

He shook his head. "I thought all this was quite entertaining at first, but now I've had enough." She felt as if she should stop walking a moment just to breathe, but his pace had quickened further.

"I'll walk with you. It's on my way," she lied. "I heard you were in France." As he walked, he held himself strangely, his bulk no longer pushed forward by its usual thrust from within. He stopped on the corner. He peered down as if to assess the asphalt, while tugging a handkerchief from his breast pocket.

His uncertainty made her bolder. "Is it true then, about you and Maud Gonne? Am I to congratulate you?"

Watching him, Georgie realised that the poet's habit of appearing to look into infinity could simply be explained by his being shortsighted. His mouth opened, and he made a little puffing sound, as if he were trying to produce cigarette smoke without a cigarette.

"No," he said. "There is a certain amount of politeness needed in these situations. I am fond of Maud. MacBride's head was on the chopping block. I had to support her. I proposed to her out of a sense of duty, you understand. The children need a guardian. It was more about the children. She has never had any interest in marrying me. That was why I didn't tell you." He was holding out his handkerchief like an offering. "The situation in Ireland changed everything. Maud thinks it has given the Irish cause tragic dignity."

She didn't want to hear what Maud thought. "Did you know the people who did it?"

He nodded. "One was a beautiful girl from Sligo—but she had turned very bitter. One of the men was a poet, wrote an excellent book on English prosody. MacBride—well. I'm writing about it. If only the conservatives had said they wouldn't rescind the Home Rule bill, none of it would have happened." He shook his head and looked right at her. "I went to Maud out of duty. We have a history, but there was never any real question of it going forward. I hope you understand that."

He folded the handkerchief before tucking it into his pocket, frowned at it, and pulled it out again and shook it in the dusty air. "I don't know how you keep these things neat." He sounded old, confused.

"May I?" Georgie took the handkerchief from him, folded it, and handed it back. He held it in his hand, without returning it to his pocket. What did it mean to have a history? They, also, had a history! Watching him, she was furious.

He was nodding benignly. "My dear, I've been rotten, I know, but I promise I'll make it up to you. I'm here now. I can't go to the Order tomorrow—I have a meeting—but you must come to my At Home in a fortnight. You will come, won't you?" He paused. "I will make it up to you," he said again, and looked at her with a fierceness. "All journeys have their—obstacles."

She hesitated. In a moment he had his arms around her, and although she was angry with him, she was also relieved. All of it was too exhausting.

"Forgive me," he murmured into her hair, and he kissed her hairline. She kept her eyes open and watched the dust continue to rise around them. When they broke apart, they said their goodbyes and she headed back to the dormitory. She felt as though he'd handed her a book, and she'd opened it to find each page blank.

———— • ————

When she arrived at the hospital an hour later, she found a nurse on duty sweeping up wet glass, as two carafes had smashed on the floor with the bomb's impact. Another nurse was leaning a painting against the wall, below where it had fallen. The matron was nowhere to be seen.

"I spent a lot of time examining that thing." Pike's eyes were huge, the white parts milky and lined with red veins. He was looking at the painting, which the nurse had wedged against the wall with a low table. Georgie followed his gaze.

"Do you think she wanted to go with him?" Pike said. He was staring at the canvas, with its two brown figures on the shore, and an enormous ship out on the ocean, flying crimson pennants. In the background were ruined arches covered in ivy, clouds blowing up like tissue paper.

"I'm sorry?" She was thinking of Willy, the gathered, hard wrinkles around his eyes.

Pike gestured to the painting, and Georgie peered closer. There was a small gold plaque displaying the title: *Paris Abducts Helen from the House of Menelaus, Thus Triggering the Catastrophic Sack of Troy.*

Thus Triggering. She smiled.

"Do you think she meant to go?" Pike said again. "Or do you think he forced her?"

She examined the painting. "I think those brown smudges barely look like people. I can't even tell which is which, and it's a bit of a stretch to imagine one of them is the most beautiful woman in the world."

Pike was clearly disappointed.

"You like it?" she said.

"I suppose it's become a kind of comfort. I've been staring at it for weeks. You don't ever wonder whether she wanted to go with him?"

Georgie tried to consider his question. It depended, she thought, on who was telling the story.

"Maybe the whole thing was her idea," Georgie said. "Maybe she planned it herself."

TWENTY-THREE

Back in the dormitory she replayed the moment with Willy in her mind, but too much was missing. "Forgive me," he had said. But for what, exactly? For proposing to Maud? For not communicating? For leaving her there on the street? Or for something that was still about to happen?

She tried to send her mind elsewhere. Out on the street, everyone had copies of the *Times* tucked under their arms. The war marched on, with the stretchers loaded from the cars into the hospital, with the faint rumbling of guns from the Somme that you could even at times feel in Mayfair, with the sliced meat of a private's leg severed with the bullet still in it. Not even the newspapers talked about the end of the war.

Dulac had returned the ring, as promised, with the hawk and the butterfly neatly seared into the gold, and Venus and Saturn nestled on the inside. She found she liked to look at the tiny hawk and

butterfly, liked to run her fingers over the scarred indentations. She
kept the ring in her purse. She obviously couldn't give it to Willy
unless things felt right between them. She would keep it until then.

Georgie took a car to a meeting of the Order, but the traffic
was held up by the damage from another air raid, and she was
late. When she arrived, the meeting was already in progress, so she
put on her robe, checked her pigeonhole—there was a note—and
slipped into a row near the back. Dr. Harkin, at the front of the
room at his golden podium, was speaking. "Because the aura of the
earth," he was saying, "is the thickest and most important part of
the earth as we know it."

All eyes were on him. The leader of the Order had his hood
pulled back from his face, so you could see the deep cleft between
his eyebrows and his dark, thinning curls. The candlelight caught
white glints in his eyes.

From her purse, Georgie pulled out her leather notebook, careful not to drop any of the loose pages. She settled the book on her
knee, perched her pen between her fingers, and began to take notes.

"In the fourth layer of the earth's aura," Dr. Harkin was saying,
"spirits reside who are sufficiently advanced to become teachers. They
draw their energy from the thoughts of people here on earth and
communicate through those of us who have the correct training."

Behind the podium, the wall hangings showed the tall, grey-
bricked Tower, the golden-lit face of the Hierophant, the Hanged
Man dangling upside down from a hairy rope. In between the wall
hangings, blackout blinds were fixed tightly against the windows
to ensure no one could peer in at the meeting from the street. She
noticed that while the Hanged Man's hands and feet were pale, his
face was scarlet, all the blood gone to his head.

"The seven layers of the earth are made of complex matter," Dr. Harkin was saying, "and the communicators cannot pierce through the layers perfectly. They must speak in obscure ways. They are not immune to error or confusion. You must be patient to attain the correct level in the Order, and patient when the spirit speaks. You must not let yourself be vulnerable. Interpretation takes time. Trust in Christian Rosenkreutz, our guide. Trust in Anna Sprengel, our founder."

The lecture was already over; Anna Sprengel was always the last name to be mentioned. She was the Order's founder, the Countess of Landsfeld, referred to by every new member in their first recitation: *So do I commit myself, through the ancient texts found by the countess.* Anna Sprengel was the love child of Ludwig I of Bavaria and Lola Montez, and it was she who had found the sacred writings—the very foundation of the Order—in a bookstore on Farringdon Road. Georgie felt connected to this woman, whose story allowed her to imagine that she too might be on the brink of some brilliant discovery.

She was disappointed that she had missed so much of the lecture. At the podium, Dr. Harkin nodded to his assembly, and the group began to recite the Hebrew names for God—Elohim, El, Eloah, Elah. Harkin pulled his hood back down over his eyes and walked out as the crowd continued to mumble through the names. The hat was passed around; the clanking of coins could be heard as it was shuffled between hands. Georgie threw in her usual handful of coins, although she had to watch her money now that all she had were her earnings from the hospital.

Once the chanting stopped, the silence held for a moment—a moment more—and broke. The crowds of hooded figures began

pulling away their hoods, chatting to one another, some looking
solemn, some laughing, some walking, alone, right for the door,
others hovering in clusters to speak to one another. Georgie smiled
at the members who passed her, who knew her as the Order's best
student, the friend of W. B. Yeats. She enjoyed being part of this
group as well as being separate from them. Only then did she
remember the note. She recovered it from her pocket and tore open
the envelope. It was from Dr. Harkin.

Nemo. Come to my office after the lecture.

She went up the stairs to his office, and as the door was shut, she
waited a moment before knocking softly.

"Yes."

Dr. Harkin was alone, sitting behind his desk. He nodded
to her, his face sweaty and pink. He looked like he was too hot,
but he had his robe on over his coat, and he had wrapped a scarf
around his neck. She hoped he hadn't heard about her going to
Miss Radcliffe's.

"Malaria's playing up again," he said. She had heard him boast
before about when he had contracted the disease—in Uganda, when
he was the physician to King Mutesa. It always led to the story of
how the king had decided he would murder all the Anglicans, and
how Harkin had survived only by agreeing to take three envoys to
London to meet the queen. How warmly she had received them at
the palace. But today the doctor's gaze was unfocused as he stared
out at the door.

There was no chair for her to sit on, so she stood in front of the
desk. Eventually he looked up at her from his chair.

"I asked you here because you're a fine student, Nemo."

She waited.

"You're a fine student, and I think you might become a real leader here. Have you considered that?"

She frowned. Harkin's eye was twitching, and he raised two fingers to the edge of his eye and pressed. He paused. "I've built all this. I need some help to keep it going. It's not entirely in my power to appoint you—it would be a matter for the Higher Members—but I would like you to consider putting yourself forward."

"As a leader?"

"A kind of associate. I would be grateful for the help."

"What sort of help?"

"I won't be here forever, Nemo. I need a successor. Nobody's ever done quite so well as you have in our organisation. I admire your approach, and I believe you'd be a real asset. Of course, I do need your assurance you won't dabble in anything else. No mediums, certainly. This is a real opportunity to shape the spiritual explorations of the future. Once you've passed your examination, we can move forward, if you wish it."

He stared back at her with his brow crushed, his face sweaty, and his drink half drained. She made herself look right at him, at the yellowed whites of his eyes.

"Do you wish it?"

She could not stop herself smiling as she nodded.

TWENTY-FOUR

PIKE

She had become gentler with him. Something had changed in her. Colonel Fraser had come to calling her "the second lieutenant's girl," and she simply ignored him, did not argue. Every time Pike heard this he felt a little warmer, a little more hopeful.

She came by to check on his feet.

"Do you know your Plato, Miss Hyde-Lees?"

Her head inclined slightly.

"You recall that part in the *Apology*, where Socrates decides to consult the poets, because they are clearly the wisest people in the republic? And he finds, when he goes to speak to them—" He paused, waiting for confirmation she was listening.

"That they know nothing at all," she finished for him. She did not look impressed. "And?"

"I wondered whether you'd found that to be true. In your experience."

She raised her eyebrows, and he coughed.

"I mean, your Mr. Yeats is extremely well regarded—"

"And you think he might know nothing?"

"I don't know, Miss Hyde-Lees. Perhaps to know nothing is something impressive."

"I don't think that's what you were suggesting."

"I didn't mean to offend you."

"But you meant to criticise him. You're not very subtle." She paused, and looked down the ward. "You're not entirely wrong, however. There is a blindness to him. It just doesn't seem to be any of your business."

I hope he isn't blind to something I see very clearly, he wanted to say, but stopped himself. He wouldn't let himself launch into praise of her—she was lovely, taking the world so seriously, standing with the light of the window mottled from the trees, dappling over her dress and her cheek. But he held back. He needed more time, he knew. Still, he had been told it was a matter of days before they sent him to convalescence, and then there would be no reason for him ever to see her again. Even after the lamp episode, his feet were healing fast. His body was not behaving as his mind wanted. He needed more time. He looked down at his fingers. He thought of the diagram of the human hand from his studies, the muscles stretching down like ghostly roots.

She had left now, gone to check on Colonel Fraser. Pike watched her awhile and eventually took out his book, opening the pages to where he had slipped the chunk of broken glass from the floor. He looked at it lying on the page. It was frosted, thinner than a windowpane, with uneven edges. He admired it lying there, like a tiny sword. He remembered how when he had picked it up off the floor, it hadn't cut him at all. Now he picked it up in his left hand, wrapped his fingers around it, and closed his fist.

The blood came pouring out fast, and he opened his palm to see bright red blood everywhere. It was almost a relief.

"Hyde-Lees," he called to her.

She looked up reluctantly at first, until she saw the blood. She rushed over to him.

"What have you done?"

"An accident," he said, dropping the sliver of glass onto the bedsheet and clenching his fist again so more blood squeezed between his fingers. It would be enough. He could feel the line of a deep cut sliced through his palm, and other smaller shards glancing through his fingers, furrowing their way farther into his skin. He let out a grunt. It hurt more than he'd expected. Hyde-Lees had disappeared—to the trolley—and returned with some water, which she poured over his hand, onto the floor. She had a towel and tried to mop up some of the blood, and she disappeared and came back with a pair of silver tweezers, trying to pick out the shards. But there was far too much blood.

"Don't ring the bell," he said, "please." He wanted to be alone with her.

"I have to."

"But I'm fine." He felt quite distant, however, as though he had clouds in his head. Fog. Rain.

"You did it on purpose," she was saying. "Why?" He concentrated on watching the silver tweezers bite at the cut, picking out glass as it welled blood. His eyes wanted to shut. She tweezed another thin slice of glass from his hand, frosted glass. She was gone for a moment, and he heard the *ting tong* of the bell across the room. He looked down to see bright red splashes on the blond parquet. She returned.

"Why would you do it?" She sounded very far away and was pressing a towel against his hand.

"I wanted to stay here with you," he said, and he saw Hyde-Lees's pale face as she guided his good hand around the towel. The blood turned the white towel red.

"Hold it," she said. She took his other hand in her own and squeezed. He shut his eyes.

———— • ————

When he woke, he saw Emma swoop in over him, smiling. Her manner was so easy, he was rather put off guard.

"Dear Tom, are you all right?"

"Hello," he managed to say. She was still smiling, seeming to take in his surroundings—the window behind him, the enormous curtains, the bright lilies on the colonel's bedside table—as if she'd never been there before. He tried to unblur his vision. Her blouse was a light blue grey and almost shiny, like the skin of a seal.

"Agnes Thwaite has given such a lot for the war effort," Emma Wetherford was saying. "The first time I came here, I hardly recognised her home."

He nodded and blinked. Of course he'd never seen this place before it was a hospital, not being the type to know anyone with a house in Mayfair, but the Wetherfords probably came here regularly to sip their tea and discuss their superiority to the general populace. For a moment, from within his fog, he found himself admiring Emma again, the fact that she would come over and launch into a conversation with him, that within seconds she could reference her elevated social status, flash the wedge of diamonds on her finger, and lower her slender hand in a merry wave. Like a ruler addressing one of her subjects. Not a Wetherford anymore, he remembered. Why did he still, perversely, try to please her?

"What happened to your hand?"

"An accident." He raised it in the air to prove that it was fine. Someone had bandaged it while he was unconscious. It hurt like hell, but he was still well mannered, speaking to her.

"I did not think a hospital was the place for accidents."

"My fault, not theirs." He paused. "Are your family well?"

"Yes, thank you. Except poor Eddie, I'm afraid."

"Oh?"

"The Somme. Dreadful business. Friendly fire."

"I'm sorry." He was. She had loved her brother—hell, Pike had loved him—and he was the only really gentle member of that family. "That's very sad." He felt a softening towards her, real pity. She sniffed, but her demeanour was calm. It was only now he wondered, looking at her, what he hadn't allowed himself to wonder before: Did she come back here because she wanted to marry him? Because he had touched something in her, something fundamentally good? Perhaps she wanted to divorce her titled husband and take him back after all? For what other reason would she keep visiting?

She tossed her head about, her forehead rumpled, as if she could guess what he was thinking. But it was a ridiculous idea. It was all gone, impossible; she was already married. She probably came purely out of guilt, and wanted him to forgive her. Could he?

She looked to be struggling not to cry, and he expected her to say something about Eddie, remembering that time they had met in Cambridge, when she had hit her head on that table, poor thing. Instead, she offered a strange smile. "Did you know we got engaged in the exact same place?"

"Pardon?"

"My husband and I. On the terrace. It was very odd. Before Eddie went to the front, I told him about it, and we couldn't stop laughing."

This had caught him off guard, and he did not know what to say. He skipped over their own engagement on the terrace and remembered how it had felt to receive her letter at the front—*Darling Tom, This is awfully hard for me to write* . . . He'd read it in the infirmary on that narrow stretcher, his feet scorched with pain, while the boy next to him lay dying. How long had she taken to write it? Five minutes? Ten? Even now he could recite it word for word. *I'm dreadfully sorry* . . .

"It's really all so strange, Tommy," she said now, and her tone was oddly girlish, almost as she had spoken to him in that hotel room. He looked away from her and across the room, where he could see Hyde-Lees, talking to Lieutenant Gray as she helped him to sit up and tried to coax him to drink a glass of water. He watched them closely, resisting the urge to call out to get her attention. Sanderson, the other nurse, was nearby. He felt someone touch him, and it was Emma putting her hand on his sleeve, looking down at his bandaged hand.

He looked into her eyes, their cracked blue. "How is your husband?"

"Fine."

"I'm glad you found someone so well suited to you."

"Oh, Tom—I felt so awful—"

He shifted his eyes away from her. "What are you doing here, Emma? Why do you think I'd want to see you?"

She seemed genuinely surprised at the question. "I suppose I thought we would make amends."

"We won't."

She looked confused. She took the ends of her perfectly tied scarf and pulled it slightly tighter around her white neck. She was accustomed to being vulnerable but powerful, to lowering her eyes and having everyone wait, in suspense, for what came next.

"In that case," she said brightly, as if it hardly mattered to her, "another time."

He watched as Hyde-Lees walked purposefully towards the washroom, at the end of her shift, and he glanced up and squinted at the large chandelier that hung from the centre of the room, each slender thread of strung light dripping from the ceiling.

"No. Not another time. I would ask you, actually, to get out, and to not visit me again. Anywhere."

"Tom—"

He turned his head away from her. She wouldn't understand what she had done to him, but he could at least give her a few seconds of that sense of rejection, of not being needed. He waited for her to go, and after a time, he heard her expensive shoes making pronounced claps on the parquet. Listening, he thought of the sound of a waterfall, its pearl glitter against rock. Tomorrow he would ask Hyde-Lees to visit him at the convalescent home. He was getting closer to her, he knew it.

TWENTY-FIVE

"Can we start?" Georgie was not good at pleasantries. They were, again, in the small library, with Nora Radcliffe in the middle, her mother on her right, Georgie on her left.

Nora Radcliffe looked more unwell than the last time; her skin was blotchy and her eyes kept squinting, even though the room was dark. Now they were about to begin, Effie Radcliffe was focused entirely on her daughter.

Nora Radcliffe closed her eyes.

They sat and waited. It seemed that they sat for so long that the quality of the room's light changed, grew somewhat brighter, as if the room were clearing its throat. Still nothing happened. Georgie thought of Pike's bleeding hand, of the matron's face when she had seen the blood all over the bed.

Effie Radcliffe began to shuffle on her seat, shifting her tiny derrière one way, then another, like a small child waiting for a performance, bored before the show had even begun.

Georgie had thought about cancelling her second appointment with Miss Radcliffe after her conversation with Dr. Harkin, but she was too curious. Harkin's offer was something that she wanted. Being a leader in the Order. Privy to everything. At the same time, the offer had made her nervous. She didn't fancy mediating feuds between the less imaginative of the members. What she wanted was to find the anima mundi—with or without Willy—not to deal with amateurs and halfwits, those who complained they should be able to choose the colour of their robes, or that the examinations should be made easier so greater numbers could pass, that Germans should not be admitted, or that they should update the portrait of Christian Rosenkreutz to make his hair and beard look less old-fashioned. "Even if you just gave him a homburg or a bowler hat," she'd heard one fellow tell Harkin, "he would look more like an Englishman." No, she wanted to find something real, not to organise the people. She needed to ask more about what Harkin had in mind.

Nora Radcliffe was pressing the page with her pen. Her eyelids flickered, as if she were half opening her eyes. The nib of the pen, clasped in her thin fingers, began to quiver, making tiny shudders in a half curve. It took a long time to form a single letter. The girl's wrist turned, and she appeared to have shaped a *G*.

Effie Radcliffe was nodding, rapt at her daughter's face.

The letters were coming faster, and an *E* followed.

She stopped for a moment before a *T* formed, then an *H, E*—a brief hesitation—

GETHER

Another pause as the pen hovered above the page. Then, in even larger letters, all at once:

OUT

"Who?" Effie Radcliffe demanded, her back arched strangely as she leaned over the table. Georgie clutched her fingers in her lap. The girl's hand had started to move very fast, scribbling the letters in jolts:

GET HER OUT I WILL NOT TALK TILL SHE IS GONE

A pause. The girl's hand stopped moving. The room was silent.

Effie Radcliffe had also closed her eyes. Georgie glanced at her. She waited. Nothing happened.

Georgie spoke softly. "It wants one of us to go."

Nora's mother shifted again. "Which of us would you like to leave?"

The girl's hand was entirely still.

Georgie tried once more to address Effie Radcliffe. "Perhaps you might leave us for a moment, just to see. The spirit might be referring to you."

The woman's eyes flipped open. "And why not you? It could just as well be you."

"Of course," Georgie said, trying to sound calm, while she could hear her own pulse beat in her ears. "But I am the one who is paying."

"Very well, Miss Sheldon," Effie Radcliffe said. She rose from her seat slowly and turned towards the door without a look at her daughter. As she left, the door slammed, and the two young women jumped at the sound.

Nora's eyes opened for a second and once more fell shut. But Georgie now saw, instead of a medium, only a woman irritated by her mother, who was using her position to try to mitigate her mother's influence. It was difficult to believe there were any spirits; rather Nora was making things up as she went along. It was possible, of course, that the medium's own thoughts had interfered with a spirit's communication, or that an authentic spirit might still arrive. But it did not give Georgie much hope. Why was she risking her whole position in the Order for this fraudulence? She watched the girl with disappointment. It was strange what people would lie about for money.

For Georgie the urgency had disappeared, although the girl's hand was still moving. The girl had placed the pen down on the page, and now she picked it up again in the grip she had used in the last session, so it lay between her thumb and her fist. She held the pen above the page and began to sketch. The radiator began to click, like a scatter of rainfall. The girl's hand kept sketching, in the frenetic manner of the artist, shading shapes from light to dark. Georgie could not make out what was being drawn. Her eyes drifted across the bookshelves around the walls. The books were not in any discernible order; on one shelf she recognised George Mead's *The World-Mystery*, and the novels of Thomas Hardy and George Eliot. Underneath, a collection of Hölderlin's poems, a golden-bound copy of Balzac's *Seraphita*, and a thick edition of medieval verse plays. The scratching continued.

When Georgie looked back to see what had been drawn on the page, she was surprised to see the exact image of an arm, the one with the palm facing her, and the two fingers and a thumb raised, the others curled down—the same picture that was drawn on the back of

Harkin's notes from his lecture, the same long lines of the arm, this time shaded in black. The fingers were the same, and the dimensions appeared to be identical. She pulled her chair closer to the table.

"What's this?" she said.

Nora Radcliffe's posture had changed, as though she were trying to appear very tall, her head bobbing like it was struggling to stay afloat. She was straining her entire body. The voice that came out of her mouth was not hers. It was a male voice, very low, and thickly accented Eastern European. "You received a message," the voice said from Nora Radcliffe's mouth. "Didn't you?" It paused. "It has confused you, but . . . someone is trying to get through to you. Someone wants to tell you something."

Nora Radcliffe pushed the pen against the paper. From deep in her throat came a low rumbling sound. This rumbling continued, without seeming to need to stop for breath, and she pressed the pen hard against the paper and wrote:

YOU MUST GO

"Who is this?"

There was a pause, and the hand shuddered before writing:

THOMAS
OF THE WHITE HAND

"What do you want?"

YOU MUST GO WHERE I INSTRUCTED
YOU MUST NOT LET THE SAME

HAPPEN TO YOU IT IS
A SYSTEM

"What is? What system?"

YOU ARE
CAUGHT

The rumbling stopped. The girl's hand lifted off the page.

"Hello? Please? Are you there?" Georgie said.

The girl's eyes opened. "It's gone," she said in her ordinary voice, and she looked down at the page. She glanced up at Georgie. "Do you know what this means?"

"Not yet," Georgie said. "And he's—he's definitely gone?"

Nora Radcliffe smiled at her, an ordinary girlish smile. Yes, he had gone.

Georgie would go to the reading room tonight, immediately. She was almost out of her chair. *Thomas of the White Hand.* She stared at the paper. "Can I take it?" she said.

Nora lifted her hand off the page.

"Of course," she said. She looked less tired now. Georgie took the writings of Thomas and the sketch of the arm, folded them, and tucked them into her purse. After she had paid Effie Radcliffe—and tipped her once more—she headed outside, where there was a car waiting at the curb. Initially she thought it was waiting for her, but as she walked towards it, the driver pulled away, and she glimpsed someone in the back seat, watching her. The man was straining forward to look at her. It was Dr. Harkin.

TWENTY-SIX

AUTUMN 1916

Georgie went to the reading room the next morning, and for every morning thereafter. She kept expecting to get a telegram from Dr. Harkin, but as the days went on and she heard nothing, she wondered if she might have imagined seeing him in the car. Could it have been a stranger who happened to resemble him, peering out at the road? Was it her fear that had made her imagine it was him?

At last she received a yellow calling card, announcing that her examination would be held at ten that night. She immediately wrote a telegram to Willy, letting him know the time. She had told Mrs. Thwaite that she had some urgent family business—not mentioning, but clearly alluding to, her late brother—and the matron had let her take a week off.

For the hours before the examination, Georgie went to the reading room, except instead of focusing on her examination she found herself still fixating on Thomas of the White Hand. So far all her leads were unconvincing. The first thing that had come to Georgie's mind—particularly after she'd scanned the Radcliffes' bookshelves—was the character Elfride Swancourt in *A Pair of Blue Eyes*. Georgie could remember the lovely Elfride with her *pretty white hand*. But there must be countless ladies with lovely white hands, invented by men with the Christian name Thomas. And anyway, Thomas Hardy was still alive.

Of course there was Thomas the Apostle, or Didymus, who needed proof from Christ in order to believe. Doubting Thomas, who demanded to see *in his hands the print of the nails, and put my finger into the print of the nails, and thrust my hand into his side*. This was a lesson in belief, which seemed a fitting message, the lesson being you shouldn't need proof. *Because thou hast seen me, thou hast believed; blessed are they that have not seen, and yet have believed*. But there was no mention of whiteness.

The librarian had found her a Sir Thomas White, who had dreamed about an elm, which he later saw *at his right hand* at the North Gate Oxford, after which he purchased the grounds and built the college of St. John the Baptist. But did it really count if the supposed *hand* was not a hand at all?

Finally there was Thomas of Britain, a twelfth-century poet who wrote the first version of *Tristan*, in Old French. In *Tristan*, there was a character who was known by her white hands, but they were in the plural, and the character was a woman.

And of course there was the hand which had appeared both in Harkin's writing and in Nora Radcliffe's—which Georgie had identified as the gesture of benediction. She had read that the pope's sign was invented by Saint Peter, who had intended to stretch out his palm, but because of a medical condition, he could not open his hand, and so the symbol more closely resembled a claw. But how did any of these pieces fit together? And what was the *system*? Georgie told herself all she needed was a little patience. The question of the white hand, like the question of Dorlowicz, would make sense in time.

TWENTY-SEVEN

When she came back to the dormitory, there was a letter waiting for her from Willy. She lay back on her bed to read it. It was brief, wishing her luck for the examination that evening and saying he looked forward to the chance to celebrate her victory with her. She wanted to speak to him—to tell him about her new position at the Order, and about Thomas of the White Hand. She knew she would have to give up going to Miss Radcliffe, but she wanted to talk to Willy first. She closed her eyes. After a while she thought she could hear a baby. From the stairwell, a wobbled call was echoing from somewhere. She imagined the boy—it was a boy, she was certain; he had dribble down his chin, and dark strands of hair. She swooped down to pick up the baby, but instead she woke up.

Her examination was only in a few hours, and she could hardly stay awake. She decided she would go out for a walk.

She cut back through Berkeley Square Gardens, the wet grass scattered with leaves from the plane trees, which were still dripping from an earlier downpour. It was not entirely respectable to traipse across town in the manner to which she had become accustomed, but she found that this only made it all the more appealing. She could feel pricks of the day's rain grip at her stockings. The streets were filled with dusty late-afternoon light and the trees threaded through the rectangular garden were spidery, winding their thin twigs together in a network so fine as to be almost invisible, with the little nuts hanging like bells.

She had unthinkingly walked to the hospital. She found herself looking up into the hospital windows, and she wondered how Pike's hand was. As she had time, she decided on a whim that she would check in the ward on her way past, and see if he had recovered.

Indoors, autumn air slipped through the gaps in the windows. Stepping inside, knowing there was no twelve-hour shift ahead of her, she felt lighter than usual. She peered into the ward to see the officers. The room looked the same; she was the one who felt different, as if she had become an outsider.

There was one nurse on duty, Sanderson, who acknowledged her with a nod. Georgie took that as encouragement and walked between the beds, down the length of the room. On her way back, she paused by the bed of Second Lieutenant Pike and realised that this was the first time she'd ever seen him properly asleep. His sheet was drawn up to his neck, and his arm poked out from beneath the sheet, the pale cream bandage around his hand clean. She stopped by the bed a moment, wondering how long he had been sleeping. Although flowers were scarce in wartime, there was a vase of white and pink lilies at his bedside, their raw golden stamens hanging down like greedy tongues. Sanderson was over the other side of the room, and Georgie whistled, quietly, as if that might wake him, *Daisy, Daisy, give me your answer do.* His eyelids didn't flicker.

She glanced at his head on the pillow, the straight parting in his hair dividing each dark hair one way or another, and his hair grown so long it curled around his ears, making him look almost elven. She was disappointed that he wouldn't wake up. His mouth was open and his breathing slow. He seemed too vulnerable, too open.

"Isn't it your day off?" The nurse approached her, carrying an empty basin.

Georgie nodded and stepped back from the bed.

The nurse smiled with her head on one side. "Did you ever meet Kitty?"

"Kitty who?"

"Richmond was her maiden name. She was one of the VADs." She dangled the basin in one hand. "She left, though, married a captain."

"Oh Lord," Georgie said, moving farther away from the bed, and spotting a window that was open a few beds down, she pushed it shut and latched it, with the silent implication that Sanderson should have done so herself earlier. "Don't get the impression—that's not what I'm doing. I'm not interested in the second lieutenant."

"Of course," the nurse said. "You know the blonde woman who always hovers around him? I heard him tell her not to come back."

"It makes no difference to me, honestly." Georgie looked over at Pike's bed.

"So you're only here to say goodbye, then."

"Goodbye?"

"They're sending him to Southampton. To convalesce. Tomorrow."

"Even with his hand like that?"

"Yes. His hand is fine. He missed the muscle. Cut it very cleanly. He's training to be a surgeon, you know."

Georgie nodded as if it made no difference to her. Why would it? Except that it seemed strange not to get the chance to speak to him again. Making sure that the nurse wasn't watching her, she gave the second lieutenant's arm a little shake, to try to wake him.

TWENTY-EIGHT

PIKE

They'd told him the injury to his hand wasn't serious. Would heal quickly. Once more he was a miracle, lucky him.

But he was an ungrateful miracle. He did not want to go to Southampton. He hadn't yet asked Hyde-Lees if she might visit him there, but he must. It was very strange that you could be nearly dead at the front and then a few weeks later you'd have trouble asking a girl if she would do so much as visit you.

He heard her nearby, and knew he had to do it. It could be his last chance.

She was leaning over him, and his eyes flicked open.

"Georgie," he said, before he could stop himself. (By pestering one of the other nurses, he'd learned her Christian name.)

But the face leaning over him was not Georgie Hyde-Lees's at all. It was a freckle-inflamed face with thin wrinkles, the face of an old man. One of the doctors, returned.

"Just one last check, old boy."

Pike's heart seemed to be blowing around inside him as the doctor loomed back into view. For some reason his feet felt hot. The doctor *hmmmed* in the way of someone who is trying to solve a complex problem and wants you to know how hard it is. He put his hand on the sheet and *hmmmed* again, now with his head down in his notebook. Pike thought if he ever were a doctor, he would never leave someone in suspense like this; he would always talk to his patient.

"That's it, then," the man said finally.

"Is something wrong?" Pike said. "Because you startled me just now. I didn't mean to call you Georgie."

The doctor was amused. "I've been called worse things, believe me. I'm sorry I woke you. But I'm making it official. In just over a fortnight, we'll let you go."

Pike tilted his head. "I thought I was going tomorrow."

"Not to convalescence," the doctor said. "Back to your regiment. Congratulations." He smiled at Pike, snapped his bag shut, and walked on to the next bed.

TWENTY-NINE

Georgie ate alone that evening and afterwards took a cab to the Order, getting out a few blocks early to try to get her head straight. The city felt like a stage set, as though the houses were being put up as she walked, and if she could only move fast enough, she would walk past these bits of cardboard and into nothing.

She walked as fast as she could, feeling sweat gather at the base of her back, and she reached her hand to her chest to try to stop the absurd shuddering of her heart. She figured that because the examination hadn't been cancelled, she must have been mistaken in seeing Harkin in the car at the Radcliffes'. She should have studied more, should have gone to Willy's apartment and spoken to him, so he could slip her hints about what to expect. But it was hard to imagine how it could go wrong. Compared with every other member of the Order, she was better versed in alchemy, astrology, tarot, and kabbalah. She touched the yellow card in her pocket as she walked, beginning to crumple and uncrumple it in her fingers, until it became so soft it tore.

She let herself into the Bassett Road house and peered into the cloakroom. At first she thought she had entered the wrong house. The pigeonholes had gone from the walls; the rack full of robes had disappeared; there was a faded outline where the silk hanging of the long-legged Fool had hung. All that was left were marks on the wall and a short piece of rope, such as that used to tie up a robe, lying on the floor. She walked back down the hallway, wondering what was going on. At the end a very tall figure in an ordinary brown robe was waiting for her.

"Soror Nemo," the figure said.

"What happened?" Georgie said, but the figure—it was a woman—had her finger to her lips. The woman was holding something in her other hand: it was Georgie's own robe. Georgie took it and put it on. She tied the rope around her waist, tugged her hood down over her eyes, and glanced up the stairs. But the woman pointed towards the adjoining meeting room.

"Go through."

The room was almost unrecognisable. The chairs had gone, and the wall hangings had all been taken down, revealing cheap, peeling gold wallpaper underneath. The podium seemed to have been ripped out of the floor, and where it had been was a square hole. Scattered about the floor were fist-sized spheres of dust. She heard a creak and turned around; a figure in a dark red robe was coming towards her.

From the way he walked, she could tell it was a man, and although he never played a role in the examinations, she thought it might be Dr. Harkin himself. His hood was down over his eyes and lips, too low for her to be certain. He walked around behind her and touched the back of her head, pulling her hood away roughly and wrapping something scratchy around her face, over her eyes. She felt him knotting it and she drew in breath when it caught her hair. The man finished the knot and pulled her hood down over her face. She reached up to try to release her hair, but another hand pushed hers back down. With her eyes open she could see nothing but tiny dots of light through the blindfold. She felt a jab at the small of her back, pushing her forward. She took one step, and another. Out the door. Along a corridor. She could smell ground coriander and soil. The dots of light were gone by now; it was completely dark.

The hand pushed her forward, and she lifted her foot, to find nothing in front of her. She stopped.

"Down," a voice said. She lowered her foot and hit a step below—the surface uneven—and then, below, another. She was worried she might lose her footing. As the stairwell curled around, the smell became damp—they were underground—and she could hear a faint dripping. When she reached the bottom of the steps, she felt a hand at the back of her head, fumbling. The blindfold was pulled away and she heard footsteps behind her, and she turned to see the hooded man leaving the room.

She was alone in a small room carved out of pale earth. The floor was uneven, and she could see the ill-fitting wooden door they had come through, which was raised slightly above the level of the room, and had been left open. She put her hand on the wall, which was packed earth, and damp. There were two steps below the door, cut into the clay, and the only light came from a fat white candle on one of the steps, stuck in the ground and flickering its light across the walls.

In the centre of the room was a long, thin box, a rough coffin,
beside a small crate. The coffin was made of heavy dark wood and
was propped up on two planks covered with black cloth, which
sank in the middle.

From her studies she knew that this represented the empty coffin of Christian Rosenkreutz. She would be expected to get inside.
She stepped up onto the flimsy crate and pulled open the coffin's
lid. The lid was heavy, and almost grazed the low ceiling. She managed to clamber into the box, awkwardly manoeuvring herself until
she was lying down. The box was too long for her, but rather tight
around the sides; the wood was rough, and her robe caught at her
shoulder. She reached up to free the fabric. Having never liked
enclosed spaces, she looked up at the pale ceiling, which was close
to her face. She waited.

A bell rang once, and she lay as flat as she could with her eyes
shut. She heard footsteps approach, until they were right beside her.
A creaking indicated that the lid of the box was being closed over
the top of her. She opened her eyes for a moment but saw nothing
but the lid closing over her face. She shut her eyes again.

She heard one sharp puff of breath. The candle had gone out.

She told herself to be calm, to wait. She closed her eyes and tried
to imagine she was outside on a hill, in the air. She opened her eyes.
The lid was too close for her to raise her head, and her breathing was
too fast. She frantically tried to clear out her thoughts. She could smell
her own breath, rebounded from the wood. She pushed gently on the
lid, but it was fixed above her, locked in position. And the ceiling
above. Was someone standing there, holding the lid down over her?

The bell rang three times, and a voice said, "You are in the space
between this world and the next."

She tried to slow her breathing. All she needed was to get through this. They would let her out in time. All she needed was to wait, do what the voice instructed, and she would pass the examination. But how was she demonstrating her studies by lying in a box? The harder she tried to clear out her brain, the more new thoughts leapt into her head. What if they left her in here? How would she get out?

She banged on the wood with her fist. "I want to get out."

The voice came from above her. "This is part of your test."

"Let me out," she said.

"I would stay there if I were you."

She smashed the top of the coffin with her fist. At last she heard a latch flick, and the lid lifted up.

She breathed a burst of stale air, and she leaned over the side of the coffin and vomited. A match hissed, and the candle was lit once more.

"The Higher Members will not be pleased with you." Dr. Harkin stood there, his hood pulled back from his face, looking at the ground where she had thrown up. Georgie was embarrassed. She wiped her mouth and tried to climb out of the coffin too quickly; when she dangled her foot down to find the crate, she overbalanced and almost fell on the floor. Harkin took a step towards her but did not help her. When she had recovered, she sat down on the dirty crate.

"What was all that for?" she said.

"We are testing you," he said. He was leaning against the wall, and he spoke as if he were in the lecture room, as if his words were unquestionable. "To be an associate. The Higher Members insisted. You were seen at Miss Radcliffe's. We weren't sure if we could trust you."

"So you lock me in a box? As a punishment?"

"Not a punishment. A test."

"What does a test like that prove?" She was confused, didn't understand. She felt sick, and the room smelled of vomit.

"I have reasons to do it. I need to make sure I can trust you."

She frowned. "Of course you can."

He paused. He looked exhausted; in the dim light it looked as if two enormous dark slugs had nestled under his eyes.

"There's a problem," he said. "Two weeks ago, I received a letter. Someone saying parts of the Order aren't true. And the difficulty is that—the person who wrote this letter—knows things."

"What things?"

"Well." He sniffed. "Anna Sprengel, for instance, is a—sort of composite."

"A composite?"

"A combination of several people who did exist. It was necessary to have someone as a symbol, you know." He went on. "This person found a letter from the old chief, Mathers, about Anna Sprengel, and various other parts of the Order." His voice was gentler now. "You see this has the potential to cause trouble."

"You are saying that you made her up?" Why was he telling her this?

"Mathers and I—assembled—bits—from various sources. Yes. It is part of the process, as I'm sure you understand. But now I'm being blackmailed. They're threatening to reveal all this, they want to throw me out and take over. And my members are straying. Going to mediums, finding alternatives they like better. I can't pay my bills. My main donor pulled her contributions. You saw the house; I've had to pawn the furniture. The house itself is next."

Georgie listened without really listening. She didn't want to hear it, but for whatever reason he kept talking, directing his words at her. She didn't want to hear his problems; she only wanted to be part of a system, one that was real, not invented. She wanted something bigger than this small, pitiful man, who insisted on making her listen to him. "We have an opportunity here, as far as I see it. This is a test for us—a sign that we need to clarify our teachings. It's not too late to get the members back on track. You're by far the cleverest person in the Order, Nemo. You can help me."

If she were by far the cleverest person, how hadn't she admitted to herself that *various parts* of the Order were invented by Harkin? Did Willy know this?

"Together, we can remake the origins," Harkin was saying, "and restore the Order to its old integrity. They will trust you, I think. And I will be a more attentive collaborator than your Mr. Yeats, I promise."

She wasn't sure what to say. "What about the Higher Members? Do they know about this?" She tilted her head, staring at Harkin. "Do they even exist?"

"Of course they do." Harkin was displaying a thin-lipped, awkward smile, but he looked nervous as he said it. He reached his large hand down and placed it on top of her hand. She was so surprised at first she didn't move.

"Trust me," he said. His hand felt sweaty and heavy, as if he were trying to trap her.

"Please remove your hand."

He was gazing at her, and she could see the clear sweat at the top of his forehead, beginning to soak his thin hair. She snatched her hand away and stood up, but as she did so Harkin walked around and stood in front of her, blocking the door and grasping both her arms with his hands.

"Please," he said again. "I need you to promise me." His gaze travelled down her body. It was as if he expected his desperation would be attractive to her, as if she had some responsibility to rescue him. Now she could smell him, like the sweat had broken out all over him and leaked into the air. He was still smiling at her, creases in neat half circles around his mouth.

"I've been watching you," he said, "and you'll never be lovely, but you do have something—a determination—a quality of attention—"

He was reaching up, timidly, towards her face. She summoned all the strength she had, pausing for one brief moment before she pushed him as hard as she could. She didn't wait to see if he would fall; she ran for the door, up the staircase, and found her way out of the house.

THIRTY

Once back in the dormitory, somehow she managed to sleep. She didn't wake until late morning, and when she got up, she found a letter under the door, and when she cracked the door an inch, she also saw a wrapped box that had been delivered that morning. She must have slept through the delivery boy's knocking. She brought the box inside and put it on the floor beside the bed but did not open it. Instead she sat on the bed and looked out the small square window, down over the rooftops, brick chimneys, blotchy grey and white sky.

After some time, she picked the box up off the floor and ripped open the brown paper. The box contained a bottle of brandy. The accompanying note was from Dorothy, saying that she and Ezra were going to be in London on the weekend, and had the name of a restaurant where she should meet them on Saturday night.

The second letter was a note from Willy himself:

I have been up to my eyes in work but do consider coming to see me tonight to celebrate your victory. Only if it would amuse you

*(I do not want to take you from something more amusing & be
a bore). Any hour after eight or thereabouts. WBY*

She didn't know how to reply to him. She felt disgusted at
Harkin, and ashamed of herself for trusting him. She decided
she would go back to her books. She needed to find Thomas
of the White Hand, who surely was her path to Dorlowicz,
the voice in Italy, all her questions. Surely this was not entirely
invention? She left her letters on the night table and began to
gather up her things. She would go immediately to the reading
room; she would read everything she could. She should have
got up earlier, should have left already. She would not bother to
wash; there wasn't time.

But after packing her notebook and her books, her gaze paused
on the bottle Dorothy had sent, and without thinking too much
about it, she found her water glass and filled it with brandy. Even
though the day outside was bright, the leaves out her window were
quivering, and she felt a pattern of coldness running through her.
She got back into bed and pulled the covers around her, over her
feet, up to her neck, and drank. After a while, she got up and put on
another cardigan, and then she wrapped her Order robe around her,
and she refilled her empty glass and returned to bed. She nestled
the bottle in the covers beside her. Gradually, her brain fuzzed over,
slowed, calmed. Her body began to warm.

She kept sipping from the glass, sitting in her bed in her robe,
and after some time the rooftops she could see out her window
became dimmer and began to grow dark. She wished someone
would arrive and talk to her, refill the bottle, and reassure her that
it all made sense. She thought of Gilbert, of how she'd seen drink

loosen him, stoop him, and eventually stupefy him. She imagined him swimming down in a deep pool, his strong body pushing, down, down very deep, until he found a door built into the rock. She imagined him underwater, prying open the door in the rock with his thick fingers, and swimming into an enormous room. The room was dimly lit, with bright white patterns on the walls, and chandeliers of green, interlocking lake-weed. He'd arrived at last, but he also knew there would never be time for him to swim back up.

She didn't know what time it was when she decided that she would go and see Willy. Why not just turn up on his doorstep? Why not surprise him? He had invited her. She was drunk, but she had questions for him. She did not bother to check the clock. She pushed aside the covers, placed the empty bottle in the cupboard, and went downstairs to hail a car.

———— • ————

Once in the car, she realised she had forgotten to change her clothes. Too late for that now. She should have changed the dress under her robe. Why was she still wearing the Order robe in the first place? She had been cold. She struggled to pull one arm from her sleeve, then the other. She was drunker than she'd realised. Only now she remembered that she did not have enough money to pay for the car.

The rumbling of the car's engine seemed loud.

"What's the old robe for, then?" the cab driver barked from the front. Her breath was hammering in her head and chest. Her head still felt heavy and strange.

"A—a costume party," she said.

The driver was shaking his head. The drive seemed to be taking a very long time, as though all the streets of the city had doubled, tripled, stretched interminably. How could it be they were not there yet?

"It's very late to be going to a party."

"Is it?"

"You are from one of those secret societies."

"Pardon?"

"I can tell. I see a few things, in a job like this. You know, I've been practising my own spells, honest to God, since I was a boy. Once I walked across the Thames, near Maidenhead, just four or five steps across the surface of the water."

"What happened after those four or five steps?"

"I sank."

"Ah."

"But you would go all the way across, I should think. A lady sorcerer!"

She managed to disentangle herself from her robe as the car stopped near Woburn Buildings, and she congratulated herself for getting out without stumbling. The man was smiling at her.

"You can take it if you like." She held out her robe.

"Really?" He took the cheap fabric in his arms, as reverently as if he were holding a child. She nodded, feeling the brandy rise through her nose and hoping he would not expect payment as well. She shut the car door and started to walk towards Woburn Buildings.

The cab turned back around and drove past her slowly, and the man wound down the window and called out to her.

"Bless you, ma'am. Bless you."

THIRTY-ONE

Out of the car it was very cold. She adjusted her hair and tried to pound some of the dust and dirt out of her dress. She tightened the scarf around her neck as she turned down the pedestrian walk and between the little white shopfronts of Woburn Buildings. She walked two doors down and stopped on his doorstep.

When the door opened, Willy was standing in front of her in a full-length navy dressing gown, its long sash untied and trailing behind him. She was relieved to see him. He had ink on his fingers, in black patches like a kind of scribbled code.

"Georgie?"

"Sorry," she muttered. It was the tips of her fingernails, she could feel them, they were calling to her. They were telling her to run now, singing like mermaids.

"Don't stand out there," he said, eyeing her dress. "Where's your coat?" It was a fair question. He held the door open for her; it seemed to dangle on its hinge, and she thought she could smell the inside of the coffin. She tripped on the step and stumbled forward, and for a mortifying moment she thought she would fall and keep falling, that the ground was not solid at all but rather an enormous hole. But she didn't fall. And he hadn't even noticed; he was already leading the way up the stairs. Now his steps stopped and he turned.

"Are you all right?"

She nodded, took the next step, then the next. Although she was concentrating on each step, her boots fell heavily.

His voice drifted down. "Try not to wake the landlady."

When she arrived at the top of the stairs, he was already holding the door open for her.

"I should tell you," she said, picturing her words like a smooth silver slide into water, "I have been drinking."

"It's two o'clock in the morning, my dear," he said. "I would be rather surprised if you hadn't. It's quite late for ringing people's bells."

She had already forgotten that she had rung the doorbell. She thought he had come down because he had sensed her somehow; he had known she was there. The fact that she had rung the doorbell was a disappointment.

When she walked into the apartment, he handed her a glass.

"It's empty," she said.

"I thought I'd put some water in a carafe of some kind. Hang on one moment. Or would you like some tea?"

Water, tea, it all seemed wrong. This was not what she was here for. He noticed her expression and disappeared into the kitchen, and she heard water running.

"And congratulations!" he called from the kitchen. She said nothing.

The room had orange walls. Lurid, sickly walls he had chosen. She wondered what it was he had been doing before she arrived. He looked very awake given it was two o'clock in the morning. She was facing a dark green chair with stuffing coming out of both arms. It looked like an ungainly man, trying for an embrace. It disturbed her. She stayed standing.

Willy reappeared with a carafe and filled the glass with water. She watched it pour, watched the bubbles flatten, and looked back at him. Wasn't she in love with this man? And here he was, pouring her water at two o'clock in the morning. She wondered why she wasn't more pleased.

"Is that all right?" He seemed anxious, almost excitable. "Please, sit." He directed her to the green chair. She regarded it doubtfully, but decided she might sit so long as she didn't touch the chair's arms. He smiled at her as he sat in the chair opposite, which was a little higher than her own. He looked to her, at this moment, like a wild version of someone's father. In the low light his blue dressing gown was like a bright animal skin.

"My dear, I'm so glad you've come," he was saying, but as soon as he said it, he stood up again. "In fact," he said, "let's have a splash of claret." He disappeared back into the kitchen. She sipped the water, which was lukewarm, and held it in her mouth before she made herself swallow.

While she waited, she examined the print on the wall in front of her. It was a Blake print that she recognised: the earth pale, flames red, sky deep blue. It was the circle of hell for those who had sinned because of lust. Above a blue-clad body, a blazing round of light held an image of an entwined couple within. To the left of the light, so many bodies rolled around naked, writhing, eyes black and hollow, all imploring to be let out. This was where Paris was, and Dido, and Helen. She wondered, somewhat nervously, why Willy would choose it for his wall.

"You will come to my At Home, I hope," he called through to her from the kitchen, his voice muffled. She couldn't see through to the kitchen, but he continued to call out to her. "It will be quite a gathering, I think." She'd forgotten how he opened his house to entertain. It was difficult to imagine this room filled with friends and strangers.

He reappeared with two large glasses of dark red wine, and handed one to her. She glanced down at the book on the table in front of her; it was Flaubert's *L'éducation sentimentale*, although she knew that Willy could barely read French.

"This is congratulations," he said, raising his glass to toast. "I've no doubt you'll surpass me any day now."

Georgie did not lift her glass. "Dr. Harkin said that it was all, all the origins—Anna Sprengel, that was all—made up. All a lie. He said he wanted me to help to rebuild it."

"All that again."

What did he mean, *again*? "He claimed there was a letter—from Mathers—"

Willy was nodding. "Yes, yes. There was a letter like that. Did the rounds years ago. They burned it, but I always thought someone must have made a copy." He looked almost pleased to have antici-pated it.

She was confused. "What happened?"

He leaned back and patted his hair, the grey streaks bright in the lamplight. "There was a reshuffle. There's always a bit of fabrication in there. Of course the traditions are true. It's just the stories that are crafted around them someone always toys with. You can't worry too much about it. As you know, we can only access it through symbols." He saw her expression and smiled. "There's no such thing as a flawless institution, is there?"

"Why didn't you say something?"

"What would I have said? There's been infighting as long as there's been an Order. Someone will push Harkin out. Never mind. He'll replace Harkin's stories with his own. It hardly matters. We know the parts of the Order that are worth something."

"Do we?"

"A little interpretation is not so bad. Did you really think it was all true?"

Georgie was embarrassed. "It throws many of my findings out."

"We will draw up new charts." He moved to the edge of his chair. "It's an opportunity."

She was conscious of him close to her. Part of her wanted to get even closer, to dissolve herself in this other person, but the other part was agitated. She had studied so hard for the Order, without realizing what it was exactly. He was meant to be the gullible one.

But he was still talking, not seeming to notice she was unsettled.

"We should ask Nora Radcliffe's spirits! They have taught me all kinds of things. And now you don't have to worry about Harkin giving you a hard time, you can go to her too."

Georgie forgot herself and pressed one of her hands against the chair's stuffing. The chair's arm felt damp and coarse and she quickly removed her hand.

"But I did go to her. I told you already. I've been twice." She thought of the ring in her purse, how it was meant for him. Would she ever be able to give it to him? Had she been wrong about this too?

"Of course you did. My apologies. My brain rather goes to gooseflesh in the evening. Or rather, the early morning." He paused. "I don't usually get visitors at this hour, you know." His chair seemed to slide across the floor of its own accord, closer to her own. "But now you're here there's something else we need to talk about," he said. "Something even more important than the Order." He gave her a long look and a half smile, knowingly flirtatious. "Something we haven't had a chance to talk about in a long time."

She looked at Willy and remembered Harkin's thin face, looming near her own. Why couldn't Willy tell she didn't want to talk about this now? Why couldn't he tell she was too agitated?

"Georgie?"

"I haven't seen you in weeks."

"I get this nervous illness sometimes." He put one hand on his stomach, but in the same moment he took it away and reached for her arm. His dressing gown had slipped away at the neck, revealing a little flesh below his throat, puckered in layers. She looked back at him, confused by this familiar creature in his long gown. She stared at the folds of his neck. Wasn't this exactly what she wanted? Behind him, William Blake's muddle of bodies soared together, the breasts the same double curve as the bottoms, all swirling nauseatingly.

"Georgie?"

She reached her free hand up to her collarbone, and held on to it like it was the rung of a ladder. She felt a queasy pressure, of wine and brandy squeezing through her nose.

Willy was still smiling. "You can rest here. Sleep it off. Please, child, stay awhile."

She particularly disliked the word *child*. "No, I won't."

"What's wrong?"

"It's simply not good enough." She got up from her chair. "You need to do better."

"Georgie—I know you're tired—but don't leave, please." He followed her towards the door.

"Good evening," she said, and walked slowly down the stairs, letting her boots thump on every step.

THIRTY-TWO

It was only when she was outside that she remembered she had no money to get a car, and that she would have to walk all the way across town. She couldn't go back to his apartment, so she started to walk. It took a long time, and the streets, like her thoughts, repeated themselves. When she finally got back to the dormitory, she went to sleep and didn't wake again until the afternoon. When she woke, she wrote a note to Mrs. Thwaite. In it, she claimed that *recent events*—again an implicit reference to her brother—meant she was still not ready to return to the hospital. The lies spilled easily. Second Lieutenant Pike would have already left for convalescence, anyway, and she struggled to see the point of going back. She would ask her mother for money. Mrs. Thwaite responded by return post and said they were short-staffed but would try to manage without her. She should take the time she needed.

She also had a telegram from Willy, who had written, simply: *I WILL DO BETTER.* She propped the note up on her bedside table. She would go to his At Home, arrive before the guests, and they

could have a proper conversation. She would make her own decision. In the meantime, Dorothy had asked her to meet her and Ezra
tomorrow night. That would distract her. She remembered an old
poem of Willy's:

Sweetheart, do not love too long:
I loved long and long,
And grew to be out of fashion
Like an old song.

Why did she love him? He had initiated her into the Order. She
still remembered his voice from that first night of her initiation. *So
do I commit myself.* She had gone to his lectures, she owned all his
books and had read them until lines from his essays and plays and
poems circled in her head of their own accord. He was a brilliant
poet. She loved his mind. They had work to do together.

Now she had her days free to work, but Harkin's lies and her
conversation with Willy meant that she struggled to trust what was
in front of her. She still hadn't found any real leads on Thomas of
the White Hand. Her next appointment with Miss Radcliffe was
not for five days. Nelly sent her a small amount of money, but told
her that she would not send more. Without her shifts at the hospital, this was a serious problem. She walked between places rather
than taking a cab, and she ate at cheap teahouses, but even living
frugally she wouldn't be able to subsist for long. Something needed
to change, but she could not work out what.

That night after she got back from the library and was lying
in bed, there were steps up to her dormitory door. A banging. She
heard the handle turn. She didn't want to open her eyes.

She opened them. It was a young boy, no more than twelve, standing in the doorway of her room.

"Excuse me, miss. I'm sorry, miss. But there's a call for you on the telephone."

She pressed her head with her hand, felt the angles of her own face. "The telephone? Who is it?"

"They won't say, miss."

The boy must have been one of the servants' children, drawn the short straw to go and bother one of the VADs. Irritated at the disturbance, and still half-asleep, Georgie considered telling the boy to go away, but she realised it was the middle of the night, and no one would call at this hour without a very good reason. Could something have happened to Nelly? She shooed the boy away, got up, and put on her robe, making her way to the stairwell. She ran down the stairs so quickly she slid down the last three, and would have fallen if she hadn't gripped the balustrade. The boy, who evidently had got only so far as the bottom of the stairs, laughed at her. She ignored him, just carried on through to the corridor, feeling the cold wooden floor through her slippers.

She pressed the metal receiver to her ear.

"Hello?"

But there was no sound on the other end. She looked around for the boy, but there was no sign of him either.

"Hello?"

She could hear something. A faint scratching, perhaps. She tried once more. "Is someone there?"

"There are plenty of people in the world, Miss Hyde-Lees." It was a very strained voice, and it was hard to tell if it belonged to a man or a woman.

"I beg your pardon?"

"There are plenty. So why do you have to pick the wrong one?"

"Who is this, please?"

"For the love of God," the voice said, "pick another. Let him go."

There was a loud click, and the call was disconnected. She waited, in case the telephone would ring again, but it was silent. She realised she was cold, standing in the hall, and she turned to go back to bed. She took the stairs slowly, letting her slippers fall heavily on the tiles. Was the phone call meant to refer to Willy? She didn't understand it. When she got into her narrow bed, she felt alone, shaky, unable to settle her thoughts. It took a long time to get back to sleep.

The next morning someone knocked on the door of the dormitory, an authoritative knock. Georgie waited a moment before answering. When she opened it, she was surprised to see Mrs. Thwaite.

"Hyde-Lees," she said. "I'm afraid we need you."

THIRTY-THREE

Without her, Mrs. Thwaite explained, they simply did not have the nurses to keep the hospital afloat. Lieutenant Gray was still unwell, Colonel Fraser's condition had worsened, and another of the nurses had fallen ill. Georgie agreed to come at once.

When she arrived at the hospital, the men were pleased to see her and welcomed her by name. Colonel Fraser cheered for her, and Second Lieutenant Pike—whom she was very surprised to see— called across the room that he, particularly, had missed her terribly, that he had thought she was never coming back. There wasn't time for an explanation as to why he was still there. There were floors to mop, and Georgie found she'd never felt so enthusiastic about washing a floor in her life. With this singular task, her brain cooled off, levelled. The ability to run a mop along the floor, and see the floor shine clean and wet, demonstrated a kind of logic, a system. Even Mrs. Thwaite seemed lighter than usual, coming in often to walk between the beds, exchange words with the officers; even she could be heard laughing at an officer's rumbled quip. Why had Georgie found it so hard here? Yes, the men were not well, some had gory wounds to show for it, but it was an honest place. Everyone was doing the best they could. Sometimes that was crying or screaming. Sometimes it was cracking obscene jokes. But no one was pretending. No one had made any of it up.

Although she wanted to talk to Pike, she had to do the floors quickly and keep a close watch on Lieutenant Gray, whose night terrors had apparently gotten worse. The lieutenant had a gunshot wound in his calf, and Mrs. Thwaite told her that the night before, he had torn his own wound on purpose, ripping open all the doctor's stitches with a pocketknife. They had confiscated the knife, and Mrs. Thwaite said they wanted to take him to the upstairs room, but they did not have an extra nurse to keep him under surveillance. For the moment, he must stay on the ward.

As soon as Georgie had finished mopping, an officer she didn't recognise called out that he needed some water. She poured him some and checked again on Lieutenant Gray, who for the moment was still sleeping. She was also required to sterilise the newly arrived Captain Markham's wound. And so it went, for the next three hours—she was leaning over men, refilling cups of water, adjusting a blanket, washing a wound, nodding, coaxing them back into sleep, it was all right, they were safe, not at the front, in London, in London.

Often after their dreams the men couldn't go back to sleep, and all she could do was sit with them, and try herself to stay awake. Too often the officers' dreams were like viruses; they spat up blurred horrors. She had read Dr. Freud's book which suggested the repetition of trauma was a way of mastery. Keeping up the vigilance you had failed earlier. Calling the terror to you, to try to master it. She tried to see this in the men. But what she saw was so far from mastery, or even the attempt to overcome. All she saw were minds torn open by shock, stuck in the moments that had broken them. When Lieutenant Gray woke, he once more called her Mary and hissed obscenities at her.

———— • ————

In her dinner break, she quickly changed her clothes and went to meet Dorothy and Ezra at a cramped restaurant near Soho. The place was dark, but as it was unseasonably warm, the windows had been flung open, and the streetlight pooled on the bright blue linen tablecloths. They both stood up and kissed her. She was relieved to see them looking the same: Dorothy with her large eyes that embraced you in a single glance, Ezra with his untameable hair like a dark halo. For some reason she thought they would be changed somehow. They had already finished eating, and gave the impression they had been sitting and drinking awhile. Although Georgie had not had dinner, she eyed the fine crumbs left on the tablecloth and found she didn't want anything. She was already aware that she would soon have to return to the hospital, and she felt alert, as if she needed to be on her guard.

"What would you like, madam?" A waiter had appeared at her elbow.

"A glass of water."

Ezra shook his head. "What? Absolutely not."

"I can't drink, I'm on shift."

"Oh, just a tipple, darling, come on." He held up his glass. "It's been a long time, you must indulge us. *We* are drinking. She'll have a brandy Alexander."

"Very good," the man said, glancing at Georgie.

"All right. One. But only one."

"Georgie has an imaginary brother to mourn," Dorothy said, smiling.

Ezra did not ask what this meant, but picked up a small cluster of pine needles from around the candle on the table, and thoughtfully pulled it apart, extracting one of the needles, inserting it in the far corner of his mouth, and proceeding to chew on it.

"How is the hospital, anyway?" Dorothy said, ignoring her husband.

"All right. Saving me from myself."

Ezra nodded and explained to her that he had been working, and also trying to fix the unfixable *Poetry* magazine, and sometimes he attended the loftiest of circles where everyone was an amiable imbecile . . . but really the war had stopped poetry everywhere— undigested war being no better than undigested anything else. Dorothy was clearly not listening to her husband, which made it more difficult for Georgie to pay proper attention.

"There's no time for anyone to digest," he was saying. "None of the London poets are worth a damn apart from Eliot and our old Eagle."

The waiter returned with her drink, and Ezra stuffed a few more needles in his mouth and turned to Georgie, two needles hanging from his lip like a farmer's boy chewing on a piece of straw.

"How is all that, then? The great romance?"

Dorothy gave him a look. Ezra gave the impression of standing on the edge of a building, tilting, tilting, waiting to see if anyone was concerned by his behaviour, if anyone would leap in to try to save him. He also gave the impression that if you did try to save him, he would turn around and laugh at you.

Georgie shook her head and stared into her drink. It had a brown glow, as if it held a fire inside, and when she sipped it, the taste was strangely greasy. "Even I've given up on that."

But Ezra was insistent. "But how are we going to fix his poetry? I saw it in your voluptuous eyes, my dear, that you wish to steer this great man onto a better course. For all of us."

"Ezra," Dorothy said at last, "it's not her problem."

"But it is *everyone's* problem to save poetry from a fate of coarse melodrama, of crushing boredom, of great, wasted gifts. Besides"— he turned to Georgie—"he was talking about you last week, George, and he called you gentle, and very clever, and—I am not making this up—a 'barbaric beauty.'"

Georgie looked away, embarrassed. She put her nose in her drink and drank. Still greasy. She tried to think of the hospital, tried to think of clear, basic tasks.

"I believe in everyone having their heart's desire at the earliest opportunity," Ezra was saying, looking at Dorothy.

"I think his poems are getting better," Dorothy said.

"They're not," Ezra said.

"Perhaps we could ban him from using the first person," Georgie said.

"Oh, bloody good Lord in heaven, no. Not that."

"Why not? Perhaps he needs to think differently about the role of the personal."

"But most great poetry—truly great poetry—has been written in the first person."

"Who says that?"

"I do. Because it's true. Of the last—well—two thousand years or so. The third person sometimes works. The second is horribly wooden."

"What about Lord Byron? What about Milton?"

"As I say, it sometimes works. And as with all rules, there are millions of exceptions. Also we can't hold up Byron or Milton as an example of anything but obtuseness." He looked bored.

"Ezra misses Stone Cottage," Dorothy interjected. "He is talking to you like you're Willy."

"I am not. I am talking to her like she is herself, which is how she should be talked to. And I detest the country. I only ever went out there for posterity."

"And still, you miss it. You miss him."

Ezra turned to Georgie. "My wife doesn't listen to me."

"It sounds like she listens more carefully than you want her to."

Ezra sniffed and turned away from them both.

Dorothy said, "Well, what would you suggest to fix him? In your infinite wisdom?"

He turned back. "Me? Nothing. It's in my interest to let him wither into foolishness."

"You don't believe that," Dorothy said flatly.

The waiter was coming back, and Ezra ceremoniously spat what was left of the needles into his palm. "Dorothy and I have done what we can. It's up to you now. This is your voyage of discovery, your journey into the underworld. It's your own great poem to be written. Shall we have another drink?"

"Yes," said Georgie.

——— • ———

She was tipsy by the time she got back to the hospital, but she believed she could hide it from the men. Mrs. Thwaite had gone upstairs to sleep. In her tiredness, she started to imagine things: she saw Willy again, on the street after the raid, and for some reason she was chasing him up the dusty street, but every time she grabbed his shoulder, he turned around with another face, that of Lieutenant Gray with his face half blown off, or Mrs. Thwaite with her look of disbelief, or Second Lieutenant Pike with his curved hair like owls' horns.

Pike himself was in his bed, staring up, still awake. When she approached, he eyed her with suspicion.

"You left us," he said. "Where did you go?"

"Does it matter?"

"It does, yes."

In the bed next to him, Colonel Fraser laughed. "He's been desolate without you, Hyde-Lees. You must promise never to leave again."

Georgie smiled, as if this were a joke. She did not know what to do with Pike, who was looking at her with such intensity she had to look away. What could she possibly say? What had she ever thought of this man? Hadn't he been just one more body in a bed?

"What about you?" she said. "I thought you were leaving."

"There's a story to that one."

"I have to stay near Lieutenant Gray."

"Well, you know where to find me." He was smiling now. "Hyde-Lees, have you been drinking?"

She didn't answer.

"You have! I won't tell anyone," he said, "but I'm glad you let yourself do something. You take life too seriously."

"I must go and check on the lieutenant."

Pike nodded, still smiling. She left him.

Lieutenant Gray was still sleeping. She stood by the bed, watching his chest collect his breath, and dispel it.

She wanted another drink. She walked out to the nurses' lockers and foraged through the other girls' things, to see if she could find anything. Finally, stuffed in the pocket of a cardigan in a bag, she found a miniature bottle of whisky. Quickly, she unscrewed the lid and drank. She hid the bottle under old newspapers in the rubbish bin and returned to the ward. There were only a few hours to go. The room smelled of fresh linen and a large vase of lavender sprigs that one of the officers' wives had brought in. By now even Pike was sleeping, his mouth open, letting out gentle snores. The newspapers were spread about the beds, and you could almost imagine that this was just an ordinary group of people; if it weren't for the lined-up beds, the white sheets, the bandages, the blood, and the missing limbs. If you just replaced the medicine bottles with champagne flutes and blurred your vision, it could be the end of a large party.

She sat down on a stool facing the silver trolley; her sleepy eyes drowsed across the neatly stacked instruments, the gleaming bottles and basins, and she leaned her stool against the far wall, and dozed.

——— • ———

A man was calling to her.

"Nurse." A thin voice. "It's the lieutenant, Nurse." Georgie stood up fast, shook her drowsy head. It was still dark, but fine hints of light were peering through the curtains. Almost morning. She walked over to the lieutenant's bed and saw the young boy's body half spilled out of the bed, one arm dangling down. She reached up to help him back into his bed, but she realised that the lieutenant's blanket was wet. She thought at first he had wet himself—in the darkness, everything was black or grey—but she slowly realised that the blanket was soaked through with blood. She reached to touch the boy's wrist, and his skin was cool. There was blood on her fingers, and she rubbed it against the cream blanket.

"He's dead," the man in the bed next to him said.

"Just sleeping," Georgie said, wondering why she bothered to lie. The blood had soaked everywhere, and she could smell it, fleshy and metallic. She leaned over the boy and found that his fingers still clutched a silver scalpel that he must have taken from the trolley and used to slice his own chest open. How could he have done such a thing silently? Without waking anyone? Her eyes were adjusting, and she could see the boy's eyes. They were open, staring out. She gripped his wrist; he was definitely dead. The ward was still silent, but at the same time she could hear a high-pitched hum in her ears, a kind of not-hearing, her brain trying to block this out.

And someone was behind her. She turned around fast. It was Pike, out of bed and standing beside her.

He saw the officer's body, and looked back at her.

"Help me," he said. Together, they lifted the boy's body back on the mattress. She went to get a clean blanket, shook it out, and covered the body up to the neck. Pike reached up to close the boy's eyes, with the confidence of someone who had done it before.

She realised she had blood all down her uniform, and Pike was also covered in blood. She realised, with surprise, that she was weeping. Pike put his hand on her shoulder. She pointed towards his bed, to indicate he should return there, and she went over to the bell and rang it. It was a relief to hear it ring.

She walked over to the trolley to wash her hands. She assembled what she needed in front of her: a jug, a basin. She thought she heard someone behind her, but when she turned, there was no one there. She upturned a bottle of water into the basin, felt the liquid chugging out of the glass. She washed her hands, dividing the world up into live and dead. *Hands, live.* But was water alive or dead? Once more she heard someone walking, but this time it was Mrs. Thwaite, looking down the two lines of beds.

"What is it?" The ward seemed quiet, sedate, as though nothing had happened.

"It's the lieutenant," Georgie said. "I left the trolley out." She moved away from the bed and gestured to the blood down her uniform. Mrs. Thwaite inhaled sharply. She hurried over to the boy, and was silent. She crouched beside him for a moment, crossed herself, and then stood. She wheeled the bed out of the ward, into the storage room. The men were waking up but had caught the sombre mood. Georgie followed the matron out. Mrs. Thwaite pulled a screen around the bed.

"I need to go and make a telephone call," Mrs. Thwaite said. She pointed Georgie towards the stack of nurses' uniforms and walked back out through the ward. Georgie took a clean uniform from the top of the stack and went out to the washroom. The uniform was too big for her, but she changed into it. Not knowing what else to do, she put her bloody uniform in the rubbish.

Georgie was still in the washroom when Pike appeared. His feet were so much better, she realised, he walked naturally. Behind him, the morning light was coming through the windows.

"You shouldn't be in here."

"I wanted to check on you."

His eyes looked at hers as if he were trying to skin her, trying to see underneath to her blood, bones, guts. How strange it was for him to look at her like this. She wondered how it was that she was looking at him. She could hear Mrs. Thwaite's voice from down the hallway, and seeing she was coming this way, she pushed Pike, quickly, back towards the ward. He held her hands a moment, and obediently slipped back behind the curtain, disappearing only just as the matron entered the washroom.

"Nurse," the matron was calling. "I need to speak with you."

Mrs. Thwaite hadn't seen Pike, who would be on his way back to his bed. Georgie began to roll up her sleeves, which were too long for her, and the matron walked over to the window and retracted the blind. She wondered how the officers would deal with the news of the first death on the ward. She supposed they were used to death. The morning light poured in now, and the sky was bright blue.

Mrs. Thwaite turned back to Georgie. "A man is coming to take the body."

"I shouldn't have left the trolley out."

"I should have stayed up myself," Mrs. Thwaite said. "But there is something else."

"Yes?"

"Your mother just called."

Georgie looked up.

"She wishes to speak with you. She would like for you to call her back."

"Thank you." But why would the matron deliver such a message personally? There was a notebook for recording these things.

Georgie turned back towards the beds, but she was aware that Mrs. Thwaite was still standing there. "I wondered," the matron said quietly. "What was your brother's name?"

Georgie turned.

"Your brother who was killed. What was his name?"

"Oh," Georgie said. "Harold."

"Harold Hyde-Lees?"

Georgie hesitated. "I mean . . ." Georgie reached her hand up to her face and rested her cheek in her hand for a moment, desperately trying to think, as Mrs. Thwaite was standing across from her.

"Your brother is at Oxford."

"I'm sorry. It wasn't my idea."

The matron was staring at her.

"Mrs. Thwaite?"

"We will not provide you with a reference."

"No."

"I know you had hopes of going to the Foreign Office. There is no question of that."

"Yes." She looked down at her hands.

"You are dismissed. Please leave the premises now, and clear out your dormitory by evening."

THIRTY-FOUR

PIKE

Pike had stayed close to the curtain and heard the entire exchange
before he crept back to bed. Everyone was distracted; Mrs. Thwaite
was supervising Georgie as she collected her things, and escorting
her out of the building. He didn't get a chance to speak to her; he
had planned to tell her everything, about how they were sending
him back to the front, about how he adored her, about how, if he
came back . . . but he had been thrown by the exchange he'd just
overheard. To invent a dead brother—that was a horrible thing,
bizarre. Who hadn't lost something real in this war? How many
men had he lost? Eleven, twelve? And Mrs. Thwaite herself had
lost both her sons, for God's sake. He supposed Georgie Hyde-
Lees wasn't who he'd thought she was. It seemed she was more
the object of his invention. Perhaps it was Emma he'd loved all
along; perhaps Hyde-Lees—Georgie—had been only a shield. Or

all of it had simply been his own invention. Perhaps he loved no one at all.

Still, by the afternoon he wished someone were there with him. It was better to have someone on your mind, on the edge of your vision, no matter who it was. They were coming down between the beds to load him into the car, to take him away. He was sitting on his bed, trying to take all his surroundings in, so he could recall them later. He stared down the room to the painting of Paris and Helen, which had been hung back up on the wall in its original position. He didn't care what Hyde-Lees had said; to him, it was still beautiful, the pair of them waiting, enthralled, for the ship to take them away. Of course, the Trojan War would not have really been started by two lovers waiting like this, so patiently on the shore. There would have been violence, rape. Anxiety would have led to anger would have led to brutality. In reality, no one got the chance to wait patiently; people were wrenched around by circumstances out of their control. But he liked the story the painter was telling. Even though it would lead to the biggest war the world had ever seen, it still presented a story of something sweeter, something more romantic, than ever happened in life.

"Second Lieutenant," one of the men in uniform said.

Pike rose and saluted.

"Good to have you back," the stranger said.

THIRTY-FIVE

Someone had shifted all her things out into the corridor of the dormitory. Outside the door of what had been her room was a pile of unpacked clothes. She tried the door, but it had been locked.

Embarrassed, she knelt down and started to fold the clothes and place them inside the empty suitcases that had been dumped beside them. She quickly hid away her undergarments. Now and again a girl would pass by and lower her eyes and pretend not to see her. She didn't blame them for wanting to disassociate themselves from her disgrace. One woman hesitated beside her and said, "Excuse me?" but Georgie waved her on wordlessly. She couldn't speak to anyone.

In amongst her clothes, Georgie found the old telegram she had received. *IT DOES NOT END WELL.* So far it seemed accurate. She had seen the way Pike looked at her as she left the ward; he must have overheard them. Once she had finished filling the

two suitcases, she carried them down the stairs. She kept her eyes
on the ground.

She had no choice but to go to the telephone and call Nelly to
ask her to come and meet her.

Down the phone line, Nelly's voice sounded far away. Georgie
said as little as possible. Nelly responded that she was rather busy
with a lecture she was organising and she was getting ready to go
down to the country, but if it was really urgent she supposed she
might be able to come to meet her. Georgie replied stiffly that she
would be grateful for that. She would not cry. She hung up the
phone and tried to pull herself together. With the last of her money,
she paid a boy to carry her suitcases across to a tea-shop. She sat in
the tea-shop and waited for her mother to arrive.

Although it was supposed to be nearly winter, it was an air-
less afternoon, as if the city were an enormous room they were all
trapped in. A man sat nearby in a perfectly respectable grey suit,
smelling of mothballs and sweat, as though he hadn't changed his
clothes in weeks. His smell made her swallow. She moved her chair.
She ordered tea, although she knew she would not be able to pay
for it until Nelly got there. She imagined a tube running down
the centre of her body, through her head, down through her neck,
stomach, and down to her bottom, and this tube was filled with
gunk, and whorls of dust.

Nelly took a long time to get there. For a while, Georgie
feared her mother would not come at all; could they arrest her,
she wondered, for not being able to pay for a cup of tea? Georgie
had not told Nelly the whole story; how could she? She hadn't
mentioned her dismissal, only said that she was finding the hospital too much.

When she arrived, Nelly kissed her daughter's cheek. As she joined her at the table and noticed her suitcases, she radiated *I told you so* but did not say it. She poured the tea so slowly, it was as if she were tickling Georgie's brain with a feather. Georgie tightened her fingers around the handle of her cup.

"In my house," Nelly said as she lowered the milk jug, "you will need to abide by my rules."

Georgie nodded.

"No mediums. No poets. You can stay with us in Montpelier Square and we will go down to the country together. We will get you that position at the Foreign Office and you can commute." She finished pouring with a flourish. Everything had gone her way. But the very mention of the Foreign Office made Georgie place her teacup too heavily in its saucer. She could not get that job now, not without a reference, not with Mrs. Thwaite ready to tell everyone she was a liar. And back in Sussex, Nelly would not let her go to mediums or to see Willy. Whom could she go to for help?

The first person who came to her mind was Nora Radcliffe. Could Georgie go to her one last time, before she went to her mother's? She watched her mother dip the teaspoon into the tea, agitate it, and remove it. Her actions were meticulous, almost proud.

"We have decided to go down to Sussex on Monday," Nelly said, having deemed the tea appropriate to drink, "given the circumstances. It's all arranged."

"Why?"

"Darling, you can't have failed to notice. The raids are getting worse."

Georgie shook her head. There had been the usual sirens, but Georgie had stopped listening for them, and it had been a long time since she had picked up a newspaper.

"Hundreds of civilians have been killed," Nelly said, sipping her tea and gazing at her daughter.

Georgie considered her. "Really?"

Nelly looked at her sadly, pitying her. She pointed at a newspaper on a nearby table, and as Georgie reached over to take it, Nelly gave her a look as if to say, *Do you believe me now?* Georgie skimmed the article. They had just had the worst air raid of the war, it said. She glanced at the date and remembered that Willy's At Home was tomorrow night. Couldn't she delay her departure, go to the Radcliffes' now, find a way to stay overnight in London, and make it to the party tomorrow? Wouldn't that mean she could then clarify things with Miss Radcliffe, and straighten things out with Willy for good? Once she had sorted out her affairs, she would be ready to go and stay with her mother, even if that meant she had to go down to the country. For the moment, she could leave her suitcases with Nelly.

"I've just realised," Georgie said, replacing the newspaper on the table, "I'll have to stay somewhere else tonight."

"Where?"

"With Dorothy," she said smoothly. And why not? "She is going to help me finish my translation. I'll come down to Sussex on the train. Perhaps you can have your boy take my cases." She gazed down into her tea, the deep brown surface rippling slightly as a hansom cab clattered by outside.

"I came all the way over here." Nelly was annoyed, but Georgie didn't feel like apologising. *You could have been nicer to me*, she thought. *You could have let me do what I wanted.*

"I'm grateful," she said instead. She drank a slug of tea, and another. "I wonder also if I might borrow a little money. I will pay you back, of course."

Nelly silently withdrew a pound note from her purse and placed it on the table. Georgie picked it up. They both looked out the window towards the empty street and said nothing. After a minute, Georgie took the opportunity to excuse herself, kissed her mother on the cheek, and stood up quickly. She left her empty teacup on the table.

THIRTY-SIX

Out on the porch of the Radcliffes' house, two men were wheeling a large wooden bookcase towards the steps, preparing to carry it inside. Effie Radcliffe was watching the men when she turned and noticed Georgie.

"What on earth are you doing here?"

"I'm here to see Miss Radcliffe."

"We are not expecting you."

"It will only take a moment." Georgie walked on the other side of the men with the bookcase and through the doorway. Effie Radcliffe followed her into the foyer.

"Excuse me," Effie Radcliffe said. She was wearing one of those dresses many of the women were wearing at the moment, baggy and drop-waisted, and in a particular shade of milk chocolate that, while *en vogue*, looked good on no one. "You can't just walk right into our house."

"It's important," Georgie said. She was trying to keep her voice calm, light, when every part of her body felt like it was straining to keep itself together, to cling to the semblance of respectability. "I'd watch those delivery men. The small one looked like he might topple over. Is that bookshelf of any value?"

"I'm going to have to ask you to leave."

"Is she up here?" Georgie pointed up the stairs.

Effie Radcliffe fluttered her arms helplessly. She was not going to grab Georgie, but she appeared to be uncertain what else she could do. "Rogers!"

"I'll only be a moment," Georgie said, and as the butler came out to see what his mistress wanted, she ran up the stairs two at a time and walked down to the end of the hall, where the door was slightly open and mumbled a little against the doorframe in the breeze. She opened the door, and there was Nora Radcliffe, sitting at a desk in the middle of a lot of open books, the skin between her eyebrows knotted.

The girl leapt up from her chair when she saw Georgie. She gathered up some papers as if to hide them away, but in so doing she knocked another stack of papers towards Georgie, who knelt down and picked them up and, without looking at them, passed them back.

"I need your help," Georgie said.

"Mine?" Nora Radcliffe took the papers and wedged them under a book, while Georgie pointed to a leather chair in the corner, from which she wouldn't be able to see the contents of the desk, which appeared to be making Nora nervous. "May I?"

"Of course." The girl dragged her own chair away from the desk. She pressed her dress down with her fingers and glanced at the door. She seemed desperate.

"I'm not here to try and trip you up," she said, trying not to notice Nora Radcliffe's nervousness. "I just thought you might know more about something that's been worrying me. You see, I got this telegram, and this phone call, and I don't know—"

At that moment the door opened, and Effie Radcliffe stood there, triumphant, with the butler behind her. "Remove that woman," she said, pointing, as if she were straight out of an amateur theatre production.

"Mother," Nora said, "it's all right. She's just here to ask a question."

"I don't care. She can't come into our house uninvited. Before long we'd have every madman and his daughter—"

"She is my friend," Nora said.

"I don't care if she's your uncle. We did not invite her in."

The butler hovered nervously, clearly wondering how he was going to evict a lady who appeared to have no intention of leaving.

"Please," Georgie said. She stood up from her chair and took out her purse, from which she retrieved the pound note. She held it out in front of her. "I realise this kind of—consultation—comes at a price."

"Well, I never," Effie Radcliffe said. "She thinks she can buy us off." She snatched the note and backed away from the door, and while she did not shut it, she could be heard retreating down the hallway. Nora stood up and returned the door to its earlier position, not quite closed, shuddering with the breeze. "I am so sorry," she said. "She means well, but she doesn't understand—"

"It's fine."

"You were speaking of a telegram."

"Yes. Unsigned. And a telephone call. All warning me to keep away from someone."

"Who?"

"They don't specify. Someone who is lying to me."

"Oh?"

"A man," she added. "I thought they must be about a recent experience, about somebody who lied to me, but it doesn't fit. I wondered if you could help."

Nora walked over to the window. "Honestly I am having trouble hearing anything of use," she said. "All the dead from the war are getting louder. I can only hear a rush of sound, hardly any individual voices—and when I do hear an individual voice, it's almost always a soldier, who doesn't seem to know he's dead, calling out a name, over and over. Often they just call *Mother*."

"Have you heard anything from Mr. Yeats?"

"You mean Mr. Smith?" Nora smiled. "He is all over the place, Mr. Smith."

"I expect the telegrams are somehow to do with him. And I wondered"—she turned around—"what it is he might have told you."

Nora stiffened.

"You see," and Georgie leaned forward, surprising herself with her confession, "it was thought, at some point, that I'd marry him. And now I don't believe that will happen at all. But I am still getting these hostile messages. And I just want to understand it. I just want to know what to do."

Nora walked back to her chair and sat down.

"I'm sorry," Georgie said. "I'm asking too much. I just didn't know who else to ask. Everything has gone rather wrong." She was horrified to find that she might cry. She reached a hand up to her cheek.

Nora watched her. "Here is what I know," she said slowly. "Mr.—Smith—is torn between three forces. The cat, the hare, and the dog. Three women, I think. He doesn't know which one to choose. As far as I can tell—we talk in symbols, of course—he was going on a journey, over the water, to make a proposal to the—the dog. It was unlikely, from the stars, or indeed from anything that Mr. Smith says, that she consented. So it is unlikely that he will be connected to the dog. In which case he will decide between the cat and the hare." The young woman pressed her fingers to her lips. "I assume you are one of these."

"Yes."

"I should not have told you all that, of course."

"I won't tell anyone. I am rather bored of it, to be honest. Sometimes I wish he would find an elephant or an albatross and marry it instead."

"But perhaps your telegram came from—one of—the others."

Georgie stood up. "Yes. Thank you."

Nora stood up too. She was reaching into her pocket, and she passed Georgie a handful of coins.

"This is all I have," Nora said. "But please take it. Mother shouldn't have taken all that money."

Wanting to refuse, but knowing that she would need it, Georgie took the money. She wasn't sure what to say.

"I do want to help," Nora said. "If you ever need—to come again, please do." She smiled tightly, looking out beyond the door. "I will tell Mother I invited you."

THIRTY-SEVEN

The-cat-and-the-dog-and-the-hare. The-cat-and-the-dog-and-the-hare.
Maud and Georgie and a third. Tomorrow she would go to the At
Home and settle this. She was determined. The cold air tumbled the
bottom of her coat, her lapels, her hair.

But tonight, where would she go? It was too late to call Dorothy,
and besides, Georgie was still angry with her for lying to Mrs.
Thwaite, for starting all this.

She had thought of trying to smuggle herself back into the dormitory. But the doorman would surely know not to let her in, her
old room was locked, and all the girls would have seen her today
in the hallway. Now if anyone caught her, they could report her to
the police. The only other place she could think of to go to was the
Order. The front door of the Bassett Road house was never locked.

She was in no hurry to get anywhere. She walked all the way
across town under a heavy grey sky. She saw a group of children

begging on the edge of Hyde Park and did not meet their eyes; she had nothing to give them. She passed them in a blur of blue and grey ragged clothing. *The-cat-and-the-dog-and-the-hare*, she repeated.

There was a chill, the cool air rushing up her nose and into her ears and mouth. Sometimes she imagined them all, years from now, all old and poor, walking around this city as abroad everyone still killed one another from holes in the ground. A soldier had told her that at the front early on, the Belgians had had an advantage over the Germans until the Germans piled up their own corpses and hid behind them, shooting at the Belgians from between the German bodies. Still, some people insisted they were not sending a whole continent of men out of their minds. That there was some way forward after this.

When she got to the large white house, she saw a For Auction sign on the lawn. It was arranged, then. Still, she went up the steps to the front door and found that it was open. Inside, the house was silent. She hoped there would be no one there.

The house had still not been cleaned, and was emptied of most of the furniture. The dark mahogany staircase looked lonely. At the foot of the stairs was a box, with various items of clothing. She picked up a single red cushion, and underneath found a robe, black with a white cross at the breast, to mark the Hiereus. She shook out the robe and examined it. In a pocket she found a couple of coins, which she put into her purse. The hangings had all gone, as had any other evidence that the building had ever housed a magical order. Inside it looked more suburban and ordinary than ever. It was hard to imagine any spirit had ever entered its doors, that any magic had even been thought of in these rooms. As she stepped, the floor groaned under her, but there was no answering noise.

She went upstairs, carrying the cushion and the robe. Each stair creaked painfully under her steps.

She let herself into Harkin's office. It was completely bare—the desk had gone, and the books; only the built-in bookshelves remained, clean of books. A piece of cloth was wedged in the window, presumably to stop up the draft. She raised the window and pulled the cloth out. It was one of the scrunched-up hangings from the walls, of the Hierophant. She shook the hanging out and laid it out on the floor. The Hierophant's hands were both raised, the same as on her major arcana card. On the hanging, the right hand was making the gesture of benediction. She would usually think this was some kind of sign, but now it seemed like empty coincidence. The cloth was thin, but it was all she had, so she lay on top of it, using the cushion as a pillow, keeping her coat on and layering the robe on top of her like a blanket. She thought it would be impossible to sleep.

She woke in the morning with the light milkily entering the windows. Her neck and shoulders ached. She saw there was blue ink spilled over the floor which she hadn't noticed in the dark, and that she had stained her coat and her dress. Only then did she notice that there was a woman standing in the doorway. The woman's hair was sleeked down, her skirt and jacket impeccable, and she was staring at Georgie as if she were vermin.

"What are you doing here?"

"I—I was told I could come."

"By whom?"

"By Dr. Harkin."

"He has given up this house."

"Ah."

"The mad are no longer welcome here."

"I'm not mad."

"You are trespassing. I will telephone the police."

"I'm already leaving." Georgie picked herself up and left the robe lying on the floor. She walked out past the woman, feigning a dignity she did not feel.

Once she was safely outside, she went to find a tea-shop, where she could sit and have a pot of tea. The coins she had were just enough, if she gave no tip, for a pot of tea and a telephone call. Seeing her coat and dress marked with ink stains and her hair frizzed around her face, the proprietor eyed her warily, and stayed close by as if at any moment she might do something inappropriate. But once he heard her speak and saw she had some money, he brought her a pot of tea and left her alone. The tea was warm and strong. She raked her fingers through her hair and wondered what it was she should do with herself. The party was tonight, but how could she turn up like this? When she stood up from the table, the proprietor was relieved to see her go.

She used the telephone in the hallway to call Dorothy.

"Where are you? Nelly called for you."

"What did you say?"

"I said you were sleeping."

"Thank you."

"What are you doing?"

"I need to come over."

"Why?"

"They found out about Harold. At the hospital."

"Oh. Right."

Georgie felt a moment of panic. "I don't have any money for a cab."

"I can pay when you get here." Dorothy told her the address.

———— • ————

When she arrived, Dorothy was waiting outside on the curb to pay the driver. She said nothing about Georgie's appearance, just ushered her inside and up the stairs. Ezra and Dorothy's apartment was small, not in a desirable part of town; the young poet didn't make much in the way of a living. He was out, and Dorothy gave Georgie a towel and encouraged her to wash. When Georgie returned, Dorothy did not offer any apology about the story of the deceased brother, or even ask her what happened. They kept to safe topics at first, of Rothenstein's new work, of Marinetti's lectures, and of Dorothy's new pictures, which she showed to Georgie, all of a similar cubist bent that seemed more interested in adhering to intellectual ideas than struggling with the strange contradictions of human existence. But all this dancing around was making Georgie feel more desperate.

"Do you think you might have something for me to wear?" she said suddenly.

"For what?"

"For Willy's."

"You're going?"

"Of course."

"But you're not still hoping—"

"Of course not."

"Georgie—"

"Actually, I met an officer in the hospital."

"Really?"

"A medical student. He's very handsome."

Dorothy raised her eyebrows, and walked through to the bedroom, where she opened the wardrobe. Georgie listened to the squeak of hangers shifting across the metal bar, and the clunk as the hangers bumped into one another.

"He's sweet," she added, "and age-appropriate, of course."

"You might be able to make this work," Dorothy called from inside the wardrobe. "It's too big for me. You can keep it if you want."

She re-emerged with a dress on a hanger.

The dress was black. It was a rough silk which was too dressy for the occasion, and it cut off just above the ankles, in the newer fashion. Georgie's ankles were her least favourite feature, being rather puffy and pink, as if her skin had been splashed with boiling water.

"I can't wear that."

"I don't have anything else that would fit."

Georgie frowned at the dress. Dorothy made no move to leave the room, so Georgie pulled her own ink-stained dress over her head with her friend standing there. She felt awkward, and involuntarily held her arms tightly across her chest as she stood in her petticoat.

She tried to pull the black dress over her head, but it felt small, and she got so stuck Dorothy had to help her. There was a sharp ripping sound, and as Georgie pulled her head through the hole in the neck of the dress, she gave a brief sob.

"Not bad, actually," Dorothy said. She had obviously noticed Georgie's distress, and patted her friend's arm. She led her to the mirror and disappeared from the room.

It was too dressy, yes, and her ankles did look puffy and awful, like a sick person's. But perhaps no one would look at her ankles. She was also not wearing the right shoes, but Dorothy's feet were far longer and slimmer; nothing could be done about that. The overall effect was not so bad that she wouldn't go. It was never her looks that people had been attracted to anyway, she told herself.

Dorothy returned with a brandy bottle and two full glasses.

"What was it that tore?" Georgie said.

Dorothy closely examined the dress. The hole was just under the armpit.

"Barely visible," Dorothy said encouragingly.

"Well, I can't take it off now, anyway," Georgie said, taking the glass and drinking. "I'll probably never get it off. What will you wear?"

Dorothy smiled and sipped. "I'm not going."

"What? Why not?"

"I'm not in the mood."

"Is it Ezra? Is it that woman again?"

Dorothy shook her head.

"But I thought we would go together."

Dorothy shrugged. "Ezra and I quarrelled. I promised he could go on his own."

Georgie hesitated.

"Don't worry," Dorothy said, "I'll lend you the money for the car." She held her glass up, as if she were offering a toast.

THIRTY-EIGHT

As she had time while she was waiting for the car, Georgie briefly stepped into a scruffy department store, passing by the store clerks and locking herself in one of the dressing rooms to assess herself one last time in the mirror. Immediately she wished that she hadn't. At the last minute she had borrowed a coat from Dorothy, and in the mirror now it looked terribly naive, the way the lips of the pockets slightly turned out, as if they were little tongues lazily protruding from mouths. She took the coat off, but she knew she had nothing to replace it. She wished she had borrowed one of Dorothy's shawls instead. She put the coat back on and resolved she would take it off as soon as she got in the door. Yes, that would work. And the dress would have to do. She turned in the mirror. *You are being an idiot,* she told herself. *This will do fine. Not only do you not especially care what he thinks, he doesn't care for things like dresses anyway.* Although he likely did, of course, being so concerned with what he wore himself. He strutted, Willy did. She didn't strut, and certainly could not strut, particularly with this dress and this coat. It was a difficult thing to explain away in a conversation. *I ruined my coat and my dress and so I borrowed these! I know they are a little odd-looking!*

"Miss? Are you all right in there?"

Why was she so nervy, so irritated? She patted her hair, the frizzed parts like wild entwined cobwebs in the light. It didn't matter. If you were beautiful, you looked beautiful; if you were middling, you looked middling. She would not pretend she could change this; she didn't want to appear to have tried too hard.

"Miss?"

"I'm all right," she called through the door. She put her coat back on and pushed her hands in her coat pockets. She checked her wristwatch and confirmed what she already knew: she was late. She had planned to be there early, but now she would arrive in the middle of the party. She smiled at the reflection in the mirror, and the reflection smiled back sceptically.

———— • ————

"We'll get there, lassie," the driver said, lifting a cigarette to his mouth as though it were a flute and he were playing a lullaby. He seemed amused by her agitation. After they had driven through a few streets, she realised she was sweaty, and her armpits gave off a strange reek that she didn't recognise as belonging to her.

"You can stop here," she said, and the driver peered back at her.

"You sure? We're some way off yet."

"I'm sure." After paying him with money that Dorothy had lent her, she launched herself out of the car. She walked slowly past

Endsleigh Gardens and down the Euston Road, hoping the breeze would dry the marks under her armpits, neutralise the smell, hoping her heart might lighten, might stop making itself known. How she hated herself for all this fussing; it would be fine, she knew, once she got there. *I don't even mind what happens*, she told herself fiercely, as she crossed the busy Euston Road and turned into the narrow alley to Woburn Place. At the doorway, a tall, elegant girl was standing in a slim green coat, shielding a cigarette with her hand as she lit it. Georgie walked past her and went on through the doorway.

THIRTY-NINE

Upstairs a large crowd was already gathered, scattered about in clusters. Someone was changing the gramophone, until the notes of Chopin's nocturnes trickled into the room. She stood apart a moment, looking for Willy.

"How lovely you look!" It was Olivia, Dorothy's mother, and she embraced Georgie. She smelled of cold lemons and some kind of pickle. Georgie followed Olivia to a circle of people, standing with their drinks and talking. Someone handed Georgie a glass of Chianti. She still could not see Willy. And although Olivia was always clever and witty and particularly skilled at bringing out those qualities in those who barely possessed them, to Georgie the conversation seemed to stroke over everyone's lips, without pausing to gain any substance: there was a play that two or three people had seen which was neither good nor bad; Rothenstein was preparing another exhibition, said to be similar to the last; and someone's boy was home on leave from the war, and it was said he'd started writing interesting poems. Georgie kept scanning the room for Willy, but she couldn't see him anywhere.

Ah, there he was, emerging from the kitchen and taking his place near the middle of the room, flanked by four or five others, who were all watching him, bemused by his usual performance of playing the Great Poet: commanding, clever, in control—so unlike when she'd seen him on the street after the uprising, or the old man she had visited the week before. This was the Willy she had fallen for: the performer, and seeing him she wanted to be close to him again. From across the room, she watched him for a moment throwing his hands about as if to conduct his audience, playing his voice like an instrument, with artful decrescendo and sudden crescendo. She came a little closer, her elbow jostled by a man, who did not turn around. "At the last session," Willy was saying to the little cluster of people, "even Leo spoke to me."

A bearded man looked up at him. "Is that someone you know?"

"My daemon. Leo Africanus. He is a fourteenth-century Moor."

The man suppressed the smallest of smiles. "Really?"

"He speaks to me in Italian."

"How extraordinary."

Georgie knew the stories of Willy's daemon, whom Willy had once admitted to her he'd likely got from an encyclopaedia.

A tap on her shoulder and she turned to see Ezra beside her, his hair flushed up around his head like a peacock. He had a wine bottle in one hand and sloshed more Chianti into her glass, until it was comically full. As she sipped it, Willy noticed her, midsentence, and while he kept speaking to his audience, he winked at her. Ezra pressed an unlit cigar between his lips and spoke out of the corner of his mouth. "Where's my wife?"

"She's not coming."

"Really?" He seemed neither disappointed nor surprised, but took the cigar out of his mouth.

"I thought you knew."

"She said she wouldn't, but I never know what she'll do. What about you? You're not leaving already?" He was wearing that lazy smile, and it wasn't till he gestured with the cigar that she realised she'd forgotten to take off her coat. She shrugged it from her shoulders and held it for a moment, awkwardly, at the collar, before Ezra reluctantly took it from her and walked it across to the coatrack. On his way back to Georgie, he swerved away to speak to the tall, pretty woman who had been outside earlier.

Georgie looked around the rest of the crowd. She recognised maybe half of them. Rothenstein was over by the window talking to someone Georgie didn't know, and nearby, Jelly was laughing with her sister. Olivia was in a group of men, who rotated about her as if she were the centre of an atom. Willy—where had he gone? He was just breaking away from his own group, and heading to the kitchen. She followed him.

He was collecting a couple more wineglasses, which he balanced between the fingers of his right hand, when she slipped into the kitchen behind him. He turned and she saw there was a small white mark on the lapel of his velvet jacket, and she reached up and brushed it away.

"Salt," he said, licking his finger and pressing it to the faint white trace. They smiled.

"My dear," he said.

It had seemed they had so much to say, that now she couldn't think where to start. He held up his hand with the glasses.

"I should deliver these," he said. She followed him out of the kitchen and back to the small circle who were waiting for him. He handed the glasses to two women in the circle, and to Georgie, he said, "You will absolutely not believe what I've discovered, Georgie. I have just been explaining"—he was speaking to the group, through her—"it is a *machine*." He raised the bottle and poured wine into everyone's glasses, leaving hers until last. "A machine that communicates with the dead," and he smiled directly at her. "Now it's not perfect, not all worked out, but we are going to go and test it—small numbers are better, I think, so as not to confuse it. Perhaps you can come with us?"

"Quite unbelievable," said one of the men, with the faintest brush of irony.

"And where is this machine?" Georgie said to Willy, whose eyes were very bright. "Who does it belong to?"

"The fellow's name is Wilson. He is a solicitor, needs money, a patron, you know. Out at St. Leonards-on-Sea. So you see, I am an emissary of sorts." He winked at her. Georgie smiled back, and as someone tried to push past her, she took a step backwards and walked right into the girl whom she had seen outside before, who was dangling another cigarette, this one unlit, from her fingers. She was very striking.

"They will kill me for this," the girl said to no one in particular.

Georgie felt someone tap her elbow, and when she turned around, a pale man addressed her nervously.

"Excuse me," he said. "Aren't you Nora Radcliffe?" The man held his head on an exaggerated tilt.

"No."

"Oh." The man's head jolted upright. "I thought you were." He started to point across the room, and stopped. "Never mind." He laughed. "Forgive me. I am in a muddle. I am Henry Poddle. I am Henry Poddle in a muddle," he declared. He reached forward and whispered, "Please shake my hand so I don't look more than 80 percent idiot."

Georgie shook his hand, and told him her name.

"Oh, Miss Hyde-Lees! Of course you are! How do you do?"

Georgie had turned back to the circle, where the tall girl was now in close conversation with Willy. The girl was dark-eyed, with a half smile that suggested she had heard it all before.

"It's a pleasure, Mr.—uh—Poddle," Georgie said, "but I really must—"

"There you are, Ernest," Poddle said, as Dr. Harkin appeared from behind Georgie. What was he doing here? He was well dressed, and looked more relaxed than usual, probably drunk.

"Look what you found, Henry. May I present Miss Georgie Hyde-Lees? Miss Hyde-Lees, this is—"

"I know," Georgie said. She had no intention of spending any time in the company of Dr. Harkin, or his fumbling companion. "If you don't mind—" She looked back to where Willy had been, but he had disappeared, and the tall girl had disappeared too.

"What an interesting outfit." Dr. Harkin was surveying her from head to toe. "It's a pity Poddle here isn't the kind of journalist who describes the way the society ladies dress, because this would merit an entire column of its own. Is there someone you are trying to impress?"

Georgie ignored him and turned to Mr. Poddle.

"You are a journalist?"

"I am writing a literary profile of Mr. Yeats," he explained, scratching his white-blond hairline, where the skin was already pink.

"I haven't heard your name before."

"I'm new in London."

"And you have an interest in mediums?"

"Oh, no. It's only for the profile. I'm always telling him"—this with an elbow jab at Harkin—"that mediums are a bit like boy sopranos. They have a very short season, I mean. They sing such lovely songs, and everyone crowds around to listen, and then something in them breaks and no one ever wants to listen to them again."

"Of course," Harkin interrupted, "Nora Radcliffe is different. That's what everyone says. She genuinely speaks to spirits. Wouldn't you say, Miss Hyde-Lees?"

He was testing her, but she didn't know why. His usual hesitations had vanished; he was acting as he did when he stood at the podium at the Order, as if he knew more than anyone else in the room. She turned to look around at the guests, until she saw Willy re-emerging from the kitchen with the young woman, and the two of them standing in consultation together.

"You don't know who that is, do you?" Harkin saw her watching, and sipped his drink to hide his smile.

"Should I know?" Georgie said lightly.

Harkin laughed. "Perhaps you could share with Henry here your own thoughts on The Astonishing Mr. Yeats."

"I thought it was a literary profile."

Poddle was shuffling his fingers in the pocket of his jacket. "I am interested in the whole gamut, Miss Hyde-Lees. Don't you agree that his work of the nineties was better? That it was moving, in a way that the new work is disjointed and trying too hard? There is vanity in the new work."

"There's vanity in all work."

"Yes, but," and Poddle nodded to Willy across the room, who was addressing the young woman, enumerating some point on his outstretched fingers, "it needn't be quite so *apparent*. It becomes disconcerting. Don't you think?"

"I think he's wrenched his new work into the world he actually lives in. I can't wait to see what he does next."

Dr. Harkin smiled, not taking his eyes off Willy. "Neither can we."

"You really must excuse me," Georgie said.

———— • ————

She left Harkin and Poddle, and approached Willy and the young woman. Standing in front of them, she felt as if the floor were higher where they were; they both had to look down at her. She felt herself to be rather wide as well as short, and self-consciously raised herself up slightly on her toes, and flattened her stiff black dress with her fingers. Willy's eyes flashed over her before turning to the young woman.

"Georgie is an accomplished occultist and astrologist. She thinks it's madness that I go to mediums in Soho, and I think it's madness she stays away. But you haven't met? Really? Georgie Hyde-Lees, this is Iseult Gonne." He paused. "Iseult is a gifted scholar and translator, currently working on Péguy's *Le Mystère de la charité de Jeanne d'Arc*." His French was cumbersome as always, and his enthusiasm in his introduction seemed somehow embarrassing, as though he were drooling on the floor in front of them.

"A pleasure," Iseult said, with the word *pleasure* loose in her lips.

Georgie took a gulp of Chianti and began to cough.

"Are you all right?" Iseult said. She was willowy, thin enough to be almost unhealthy, and her pale face glowed. Her eyes were dark, with reflected triangles of light. Georgie nodded, swallowed, and tried to clear her throat.

It was Maud Gonne's daughter. Of course. The one they talked, at times, about him *caring for*. Georgie had always thought when people laughed about Willy *caring for* Maud's children, it was because Willy was only ever interested in Maud, and not her children at all. But now she could see the irony was altogether different. It appeared he might be far more interested in Maud's child than Georgie had ever considered.

"We have just been talking about my most recent communications with the machine," Willy said. Iseult glanced at Georgie and raised an eyebrow, to convey her scepticism on this subject. Georgie smiled and looked around her, at various people who were in their own conversations or half listening to theirs, all smiling and drinking and talking and nodding. This was what they all expected from Willy Yeats, flights of genius and flights of nonsense. He was too susceptible to ambitious American poets, to pretty French Irish girls, to conniving schemers from St. Leonards-on-Sea. This was why he had needed her: because she could direct his mind better, stop it floundering. But now it seemed clear she wouldn't get the chance.

He was still talking and Georgie was struggling to listen. Iseult Gonne! Not enough to be in love with the same woman for thirty years, but now to go and start courting her daughter! Just standing there, Georgie felt humiliated. She wanted to leave the conversation but could not see how, and the girl was staring at her in a needy way. She tried to look breezy, unsurprised, aware of Harkin's mocking eyes on her. The ridiculousness of it! Did Willy even know how absurd he was? She could tell someone else was watching, and she turned for a moment—whoever it was would also be witness to her stupidity—but instead she saw, under his black curls, Ezra. And he was focused not on her but on this girl, this girl, almost as tall as Willy but slim as a child. Georgie stared down at Iseult's sleek bare ankles. Iseult was half smiling at her. She had steel to her, along with that glow of the damp-eyed ingénue. Perhaps an ingénue always had a little steel to her, aware of the kind of power she had.

Willy said, "Iseult may come and live in London."

"How *wonderful*," Georgie heard herself say. Why hadn't Dorothy said anything? She looked up and saw Dr. Harkin. He raised his glass to her.

"Finally," Willy was saying, waving at a man who had just arrived, who was removing a high-collared coat that could have been a bearskin. "I must say hello." And he left them alone.

Iseult had turned to Georgie but said nothing.

Georgie breathed out. "You—you are a—translator."

"I am not so good." Her French accent was tinged with an Irish lilt.

"He suggests otherwise."

"He is a poor judge, in this instance. You can see that. He's—not objective."

"I think I know what you mean," Georgie said, "but I'm sure you're wrong. The thing is," and in spite of herself she relaxed slightly, talking about Willy's quirks, "he's not generally misguided in terms of work, as far as I can tell. He makes mostly sound editorial decisions. Yes, he publishes his friends, but they are never terrible. You must be good."

"He is—not consistent."

"Not always. But no one is. He is worse when it comes to spirits, I think. He is too hopeful."

"Here, I think he is also hopeful."

"Well." Georgie looked over at him, and back at Iseult. How pretty she was! How delightful and foolish a little tale it was. How she, Georgie, did not appear in it at all! Across the room Willy had thrust an arm around the fellow's shoulders, having apparently forgotten about her and Iseult for the moment. Iseult's eyes were intent on Georgie. They were so large Georgie could see the white all around each of her pupils.

It was impossible not to admire her. "And does he have reason to hope?"

Iseult looked down. "I am very dependent on him; it is awkward."

"I see," Georgie said, not entirely seeing. Iseult turned to watch Willy and the other man for a moment, seeming not to notice that Ezra was still staring from the other side of the room. Iseult's face was still lovely while it scrunched in confusion, her eyes flicking from Willy to Georgie with intensity.

"If I said no—and then he married someone else—I would hate it. It's awful of me, I know. But I can't get it right. I don't want to lose him, but I also don't want to marry him, you see? Really, I am a *beast*." She pronounced this word at the front of her mouth, as though with a lisp, and when she blinked, tears gathered at the bottoms of her eyelids. She reached up to wipe her eyes and made a funny coughing sound. This was why people said *beautiful creature*: because there was something almost inhuman about this kind of beauty, something vulnerable and clean and glorious. The girl was wiping her eyes with her sleeve.

Georgie felt sorry for her. This girl was telling her everything, was displaying the kind of honesty of which Georgie herself was hardly capable. Who would she tell all her feelings to? Not Dorothy, not Nelly, not Willy—and certainly not to a stranger.

Across the room, Willy was oblivious; he had his hands up, he was talking animatedly to the man with the bearskin coat. Iseult was looking at the floor. "I do not know what it is that I should do." She paused. "Do you think you will get married?"

Georgie was surprised by the question, and found herself nodding. "I am engaged to an officer."

Iseult looked up. "An officer! Really?"

"A medical student. But right now an officer."

"And do you know for sure, then, that this—officer—is the right person?"

Georgie nodded. "Absolutely. When it's right, you know."

What kind of game was she playing? Iseult nodded sadly, and lit another cigarette. Whether she was aware of Ezra's particular gaze was difficult to tell, but she looked both radiant and uncomfortable.

"They will kill me for this," she said again, lifting the cigarette, still like a child. "They hate me smoking, he and Mother. I don't want to make them unhappy."

"I get the sense that the longer you draw all this out, the unhappier you'll all be," Georgie said, and sensing there was someone behind her now, she added, "Hello, Ezra."

"Georgie," Ezra said, taking two quick steps forward and kissing her—it seemed, only because it was now necessary to turn and also kiss her lovely companion.

"I must go and telephone Dorothy," Georgie said, although everyone must have known that the apartment had no telephone. Iseult didn't look at Ezra but instead reached in to press Georgie's wrist with one of her slim hands, as if to take her pulse.

"Thank you for listening to me," she said.

——— • ———

Georgie strode towards the window and stood on her own. Across the room, a woman and a man had started dancing. Beyond them, Georgie recognised the figure of Mrs. Radcliffe, Nora's mother. She was talking loudly, her arm raised in the air, one finger pointing up. Georgie watched her for a moment, and remembered something.

There was a part of the story of *Tristan*, written by the poet Thomas of Britain, where the protagonist, desperately in love with his Iseult, meets another woman. The other woman is called Iseult of the White Hands, and because the first Iseult—the Irish girl he knows and loves—is already married to his uncle, he proposes to this second Iseult instead. He goes on to marry her. It isn't until the night of their wedding that he realises he has done this only because he wants to be with the first Iseult. He can't bear to touch Iseult of the White Hands. She loves him, and he will not touch her. They are both inconsolable.

This was what Nora Radcliffe had meant by inventing Thomas of the White Hand. She had meant to point to the fact that Willy had approached Georgie only because she was a substitute

Iseult—an Iseult of the White Hands. That he'd never really love her. At that moment Georgie was certain there was no spiritual communication in what Nora had written—there was no spirit of Thomas communicating from the dead—it was Nora herself, having heard Willy go on and on about his romantic predicament, the-cat-and-the-dog-and-the-hare, trying to communicate to Georgie, in some clever way, that she was destined for disappointment. And Georgie, despite her supposed intelligence, had missed the message. She had not been able to decode it, and had come to this party to see it play out for herself, to be humiliated. She thought of Nora's pale, whimpering face as she wrote down these messages from "Thomas." All that posturing, when she could have just told her in plain speech. All that shuddering and pretending, that whimpering and moaning and taking her money, when she could have just said a few words—*I think Willy is in love with Maud's daughter*—and released her.

Her whole body had gone oddly rigid. Across the room, the dancing couple were curling their bodies around each other, twirling and spinning, and a space cleared around them as people watched. Georgie watched too, unable to unstiffen her shoulders, her neck. The male dancer curved his back until his fingers grazed the floor. As he flipped back up again, the woman tossed one of her legs in the air, rested her heel on an invisible point in the air, and brought her leg back to the floor. They were smiling, confident their bodies would do what they asked, confident they could let themselves go. When the music concluded, the dancers stopped and embraced, and there was a clatter of impromptu applause. Georgie couldn't loosen herself; the more she tried, the tighter she felt. She didn't clap, and felt unkind for not clapping. She turned away and right into a small crowd, which included Mrs. Effie Radcliffe, who at that moment pointed right at Georgie.

"See! Look! Turned up unannounced at my house, demanding an audience with my daughter." A cluster of people were looking curiously at Georgie. "Not only that, but when I confronted her, she tried to buy me off."

"I say, is this true?" Henry Poddle exclaimed with an eagerness not common among literary journalists. Effie Radcliffe was nodding her head and affecting a look of grave injury. Georgie looked around at her sudden audience.

"Just came right on in," Effie Radcliffe was saying.

"I offered money," Georgie said quietly, "because you generally charge for an audience with your daughter. I offered money, not a small amount, and you took it."

"Only to save you the embarrassment," Effie Radcliffe said.

"I wasn't embarrassed."

Another gentleman, perhaps trying to defuse the conflict, said, "Your daughter must be a real marvel."

"She is the best in London," Effie Radcliffe said, "just ask Mr. Yeats. Most people have been very respectful of her talent."

Mr. Poddle was nodding and scrawling notes in a small square notebook. What was it that made Georgie so angry with this awkward, fawning man, and this foolish, blustery woman? Why couldn't she simply block them out and go and find people she thought sensible? For some reason Poddle particularly enraged her; she felt so furious with the weak words he spat from his pale lips, his round shapeless chin bobbing up and down, his fat-coated jaw like a misshapen glob of butter.

Georgie looked to see what Willy was doing, but he'd disappeared again. No, there he was, by the window with Iseult, his body leaning towards hers, his hand resting very near hers.

Why had she come? Why hadn't she listened to Dorothy?

"I have lived in that house for twenty years," Effie Radcliffe was saying, "and never, ever, have I had a near-stranger just admit herself without invitation. The most dreadful manners."

"At least," a familiar voice said, "it proves her talent." It was Dr. Harkin, joining the circle, smiling broadly at Henry Poddle.

"Except," Georgie said, knowing that Harkin was baiting her, but unable to resist, "it doesn't prove that at all."

"I beg your pardon?" Effie Radcliffe's voice raised, and she stared at Georgie. "What are you trying to imply?"

Dr. Harkin continued to smile, and Georgie tried not to look at the notebook still clutched in Henry Poddle's hand.

"Only that my turning up at the door doesn't prove a thing," Georgie said. "It merely suggests what I said at the time. That I wanted to speak with her."

"Are you questioning her talent?" Effie Radcliffe said. Someone was trying to take the woman's arm, trying to calm her down, but she shook him off.

"Your daughter is a clever young woman," Georgie said. She paused. "But I'm not convinced she can channel anything aside from her own brain. She has a good brain. I am more interested in that, than in any ostensible talent. Increasingly I do not think she has any kind of channel to the spirit world. I find her rather a skilled manipulator."

Effie Radcliffe's voice had leapt up a register. "You—insult—our integrity! You are—desecrating our livelihood!"

"As I see it," Georgie said calmly, "there is nothing to desecrate. I consider that you in particular have very little integrity to insult."

Effie Radcliffe looked as if she might hit her. It was only then that Georgie saw, just beyond the circle, that Nora Radcliffe was standing there, listening to every word. She was staring at Georgie with a look of complete astonishment. Dr. Harkin was standing not far from her, smiling. Effie Radcliffe's face quickly eclipsed her view. "You are vicious! Simply vicious!" She reached up and Georgie felt something slap her across the cheek.

"Ladies, please!" someone shouted. Georgie rushed her hands up to cover her face.

"This is exactly why we should never give them the vote," someone else called out. From nearby there was an odd shrieking noise.

"What in God's name was that?" someone said.

"Why, it's my boy soprano impression," called Henry Poddle. "End of Miss Radcliffe's career. The final notes."

FORTY

When she opened her eyes, the world had shrunk to a bubble around her, a thick soap bubble she couldn't see out of. Her cheek stung, and she kept her hand over her face. She walked over to the coat stand, and in the half-light she could just see, under the stand, the grotesque chair with the stuffing coming out of the arms, as if it were stuck in the process of vomiting parts of itself. A part of her wanted to crawl into that chair with the stuffing and not look up again until everyone had left. Someone was walking over to her, trying to talk to her, but Georgie quickly retrieved her ugly coat and hauled it around her shoulders, hiding inside it and making for the door. She glanced back a moment and thought she saw Willy hold up his hand as if to stop her. His expression was uncreased, innocent. Beside him, Iseult had her back to Georgie, her stance as casual as a dancer's.

Now she was rushing, down the stairs, out the door. As soon as she got outside she stopped just beyond the doorway and she waited to see if anyone might follow her.

Outside, she had trouble breathing, urging herself not to cry. She thought of Lucy beating the rugs on a day with no wind, so that the dust clouds rose and hung heavy on the air. She thought of her own body powdered to dust.

Why had she answered Harkin? He had wanted to humiliate her, and he wanted to destroy Nora Radcliffe, and he had very neatly managed both, with the help of the vile Poddle to write it up for whatever trivial gossip rag he wrote for. There was no doubt in her mind that a man like Poddle had not written a "literary profile" in his life.

It was cold. She was close to where the hospital was, and to where the bombs had fallen, in Gray's Inn and Kingsway, where still more might be falling, like tiny stars spraying across the city. She would have welcomed a bomb to gulp her down right now and stop her thoughts altogether. She thought she could smell rotten flesh, but it was probably just someone roasting meat in another building. She waited, watching her breath puff out in front of her.

She heard someone behind her, and turned. But it was only a stranger, a woman coming down the steps and walking off into the night. She watched the woman pull her coat up around her ears, in a protective act. The woman glanced at her, and Georgie remembered the shocked look on Nora Radcliffe's face, and Iseult Gonne's back to her. Georgie pulled out a thin book from her purse and, under the darkened lights, squinted to try to read the words as she walked away from the house. She walked, not thinking where she would go. She kept reading as she walked, trying to coax the book into speaking to her, as if there were a person beside her, neither a man nor a woman, just a shape, calmly saying, *Our lives are like trees in a forest. The maple and the pine may whisper to each other. . . But the trees also commingle their roots in the darkness underground.* She saw a cab but she did not hail it. She tried to think of roots—meeting under the ground, recognising one another, merging together—but instead imagined curled, tangled worms, trying to strangle one another, long hairs that could slice open skin. Her palms were damp, and her mind was bitter, and guilty, and all her own.

FORTY-ONE

She walked all the way to the station, and once she got there, she discovered there was no train for Sussex for nearly four hours. She walked back and forth along the platform in the dark, watching the dirty trains pull in and out, avoiding the gazes of the men who were on their own, who watched her closely. When one of them tried to speak to her, she uttered nonsensical syllables at him and turned away, as if she could not speak English. She sat and waited.

She slept on the train, and when she got out at the station, she began the long walk to the house, following her mother's instructions, looking out over the long glowing yellow fields with green peering out from under. When she arrived at the large white house with ivy dripping down its facade, she stood awhile out by the woodpile. Blood was tumbling in her head as she walked to the door.

She knocked at the door and waited.

Her mother opened the door and tried to embrace her. Georgie avoided her, walked slowly straight for the stairs, and shut herself into one of the rooms.

FORTY-TWO

When she got up, the house was empty, and Nelly had left a note for her outside her door:

We have gone out to the Hendersons' until late afternoon. Make yourself at home.

She felt a mixture of anger at her mother for leaving and relief to know that she had gone. She went downstairs and stood in the kitchen staring out. The woods ran right in front of the house. Outside, through the grid formed by the kitchen window—past the one drip of white paint frozen on the glass—it was almost completely fogged over; she could see only the thin slice of lawn just in front. Beyond was entirely white.

She had organised for the maid to pick up a stack of vile gossip rags in order to find the one that Henry Poddle wrote for. She pieced through them slowly. Sure enough, there was a column, under the name GH Chest, which read as follows:

Last night was last act for medium Nora Radcliffe, whose
fraudulence was exposed by a Miss Georgiana Hyde-Lees. Miss
H-L, who had arrived at the event resembling an overfed
black crow, was doubly rewarded for her efforts with a nasty
slap from the medium's mother, and a painful jilting from her
imagined betrothed, WB Yeats.

All eyes are on WBY these days, who at 51 is feverishly chasing
an alarmingly young girl-child, who must be no more than
20 and the daughter of his great love. Reverse-Oedipus? Has
someone sent for Dr. Freud?

She crumpled up the paper and threw it in the fire.

An overfed black crow. It didn't matter. People didn't read this
stuff, and when they did, they dismissed it. Still she felt the gritti-
ness of shame, and each time she thought it might have lessened,
she felt it shift and dig inside her, as if her body were a bag filled
with sharp objects.

The door was propped open, and Georgie stepped outside. The
leaves were crunched brown, the air tinged with ice.

Although she wore only slippers, she walked out towards the
edge of the woods.

She walked away from the houses. While the day was bright,
the woods were much darker, as if she were entering a faery story.
Under the trees it felt closer to evening.

There were certain things she had not let herself think. The fact
that her father had died, in a stranger's home, on his own, his brain
wiped clean: she had wanted to add to that story, to make some

sense of it. She had accepted she wouldn't speak to him again. He was gone. But on the other hand, when any spirit spoke to her, she *was* in a sense speaking to him; she was speaking to the same place he had gone to. The same place everyone would go when they were dead. When she imagined that man on that boat in Italy, she had proved this to herself, even if since then she had never found evidence of this name *Dorlowicz*. She was willing now to accept that this word was probably one she had made up, just as Willy had made up his daemon, just as Nora had made up Thomas. With that one scene, that one word, she'd proved to herself there was such a thing as a memory without a body.

It occurred to her only now she hadn't needed much to convince herself.

And now the evidence was against her. The Order, invented. Nora Radcliffe and her stories. Shaking hands and mirror writing. That moment on the boat in Italy; why had the man's Italian been at the exact same level as her own? Why had he not used grammatical structures she herself would never have used?

It would appear there was no shared memory at all. That every soul was just a temporary, lonely anomaly.

The trees were still, implacable, unconcerned with her mind's flurries. What was the point of thinking any of it through?

She didn't want to die either. She didn't want her thoughts and memories wiped, dissipated, dispensed as nameless atoms. She had thought she could speak to the dead, and this was proof they were all safe from oblivion. She had thought she could marry a famous poet, and they could speak to the dead together, and their lives would also be kept safe inside their studies and his verses—but this had been wilful ignorance, both believing in it and believing in him.

Now she had seen the untruth of it all, she could not make herself unsee it.

And she was ashamed. Dorothy and Nelly had known all along that all this was nonsense, and how cruelly she'd rejected them for their shallowness. How quickly she had let Nora Radcliffe take advantage of her. How stupid, how naive, how painfully she had been taken in, believing that Willy would marry her. How eagerly they had all praised her cleverness, and how clearly she had proved otherwise.

She kept walking. Eventually the trees gave way to a small sliver of a lake, surrounded by a clearing. The water was shallow, and she noticed at the water's edge a swan and her cygnet, foraging in the grass. The cygnet was making frantic, furtive gestures in the green, its beak spotted with mud. The young bird was not much smaller than a newborn human baby, but covered in soft down, like a teddy bear. Georgie stopped and watched. The bird straightened up, trying to use its wings—tiny, useless-looking triangles—to balance, and revealing its grass-covered chest. The mother stretched her neck casually, as if to yawn.

Georgie stood and watched. The birds did not notice her. And if they had, what would it matter? She turned and went back to the house.

FORTY-THREE

When she returned, there was a letter waiting for her in the hall-way. It announced a new meeting of the Order to be held that afternoon to assess the current situation, *in the wake of the departure of Dr. Ernest Harkin.* Georgie returned the letter to its envelope. She would not be going, but she was pleased to hear they had got rid of him. Her mother was waiting in the conservatory for her, with a magazine lying beside her and a tall glass of lemon juice in her hand. Georgie focused on the pale swirl inside the glass, the one stray pip at the bottom.

"Darling. I'm so glad you saw sense."

"Pardon?"

"You know I was silly enough to marry the man I fell for, and I spent twenty years suffering the consequences."

"I wouldn't describe myself as 'silly.'"

"I didn't say you were. But we all do silly things."

"I'm not sure I did."

"It's all right to sometimes be wrong—"

"I'm comfortable being wrong, when I am wrong."

"You don't consider you were wrong, then, to fall for such a philanderer?"

"He isn't a philanderer."

"Ah."

"He was just confused about what he wanted." She felt stuck, as if she had to argue her case but didn't know how. All she knew was that she would not let Nelly near her, and any argument against her was better than none.

"But you had the sense to change your mind."

"Not really."

"You haven't changed your mind?"

Georgie focused on the toe of her shoe. It was slightly scuffed, the black leather shaved down to brown. "I don't know."

"I take it back, then," Nelly said. "You haven't seen sense at all. But I'm glad he's out of the picture."

Georgie didn't look up from her shoe. "Please don't."

"Don't what, darling?"

"I wish sometimes you'd trust me to do the right thing. I'm not an idiot."

"I do trust you, darling. No one is saying you're an idiot. But no one is right all the time."

"Not even you."

Nelly paused, and said calmly, "Not even me. Tomorrow Henry and I will go up to London for the day. Perhaps you might come with us and meet with Freddie at the Foreign Office?"

"No." Her panic rose. How could she tell her mother what she had done wrong, how she'd lied, how she'd no longer be considered for such a job? "I want to stay here. I have my own work to do."

"You can't stay forever, Georgie."

FORTY-FOUR

AUTUMN 1917

It was sometime at the beginning of autumn that Georgie woke in the late afternoon, dressed, and went down to the kitchen. The enormous plane trees nodded to her out the window, their trunks grey and, in parts, scraped down to gold. A gardener was fussing out by the herb garden.

Everyone was out. Nelly and Henry had gone up to London and would be back later that evening. Lucy had left to see her family for the afternoon and would be back in the evening to fix Georgie's supper.

Out past the garden, the next-door neighbour's house seemed to be sprawling especially to catch sun, its four grids of windows with their bright white sills alight. The wind was getting up, rumpling the trees. The gardener was slowly settling on his old knees in the garden, his hands encased in black gloves and his back to the wood.

It wouldn't be too bad to live alone. No one to try to change, no one to try to talk around. She had been able to imagine it before.

But now she could hear someone knocking at the door. She frowned and walked back to the bedroom, and quickly got dressed.

From the bedroom, she tugged back the curtain and checked out the window. The trees were shifting around like giant hands, grasping at air. While someone knocked on the door downstairs, under the trees, she could see another man, standing at the end of the path beside a car that was waiting at the curb. This man was all in black, not moving. She supposed he was the chauffeur.

The other man, who had been knocking, had stepped away from the front door to glance up into the upstairs windows. He couldn't see her. She didn't wave.

He was calling for her from outside the house. Georgie watched him for a moment longer—an officer. She had not recognised him at first; it was still strange to see him upright, moving forward so effortlessly. The car still waited by the curb like a crouched animal. She turned and took the stairs two at a time.

"Hello." Second Lieutenant Pike called to her from the doorway. He looked nervous, standing in the doorway, clutching his officer's cap in both hands.

"What on earth are you doing here?" Georgie said.

"I'm sorry," he said. "I needed to speak with you. It's important."

He stood stiffly, his cap in one hand. There was something about him that seemed very far away. His frame, not especially tall, fit neatly in the doorway's frame, and he gazed over the empty trellises that climbed up the house's brick facade. "Nice place," he said.

"It's a summer house."

"It's hardly summer."

"Not really, no."

"It's very—big."

"Shall we walk?"

Georgie led the way out the back gate and wandered down the path towards the trees. She was walking behind him and found herself admiring his functioning legs. The miracle. The hospital seemed so long ago.

Neither of them said anything. The afternoon sky was white, with the sun streaming through, as if it were wincing.

Only now she realised what his uniform meant.

"You've been back?"

"And I'm going again. On Wednesday."

"Oh." She didn't know what to say. She remembered what she'd told Iseult at the party, and blushed. He was so young and handsome, moving around so easily. She couldn't imagine being engaged to such a man. His expression had loosened somehow, freed up, since she had last seen him. Even though uniforms these days seemed like death sentences, they still held something hopeful about them in their stiffness, their correctness, their suggestion that there was some order to the world.

"I suppose we did too good a job then. Looking after you."

"It seems so." He smiled.

"You don't want to hide in the basement?" she said. "Till the war's over?"

He fiddled with the edge of the pocket on his uniform. "No. But—there's something I need to tell you."

"Oh?"

"That is—did you ever get any telegrams? Strange ones?"

Georgie stared back at him.

"Well, it's a very odd thing. I don't know—if you remember there was a girl who came to visit me. Emma Wetherford is her name, or it was, although I don't know if you ever knew it."

"I remember. The one that hung around."

"Exactly. It turns out she was quite unhinged. Her husband says sometime after the wedding, she started saying strange things, acting oddly. She had a kind of a collapse. I think the death of her brother, and the decision to marry, broke her, somehow. And the thing is"—he looked up now, into the trees, and squinted—"she told me she wrote to you. She had decided that you were in love with me."

Georgie gave a little snort of surprise. "Really?"

"A little unlikely, I know."

She smiled and he went on, "Although, I mean, you lock animals in a cage, and eventually they mate."

"Pardon?"

"Never mind." He was looking at his hands.

"I wasn't in any cage."

"You sort of were. And we definitely were." He paused. "Forget it."

"She is all right, then?"

"Not really, no. They sent her to an institution. They don't think she'll ever recover."

So it had been nothing to do with the Order or Willy after all. Georgie remembered that last day at the hospital, moved to say something, and stopped. She was trying to think of an excuse, a defence of the lie she had told about her brother, but couldn't. They walked in silence. The sun was slipping behind the white layers of cloud, and pricks of rain were beginning to fall.

"Oh, come on." Pike was looking up at the sky. "Give me a bit more time." He turned back to Georgie and smiled. "Your ghosts are not co-operating."

It occurred to her that he had not only come to her about Miss Wetherford's strange telegram or to speak about the hospital. He was here for something else.

"They're not mine," she said, turning back towards the house.

"Let's get under those trees. It's not so bad."

"We can talk back at the house."

"Wait—" He took her hand gently and pulled her towards him. Puzzled, she focused on the scruffy soft hair above his lip. She could smell him, human and used, and although she was now half aware of his intentions, she was still surprised when after a moment of hesitation, he put his arms around her. His uniform was awfully rough. He pulled back slightly and tipped his face towards hers as if inviting her to kiss him.

"Really?" she said, trying not to laugh.

"Why not?"

She had not properly kissed anyone before. It was awkward, but all right. Afterwards he leaned his face into her hair. "You were very good to me."

"I wasn't."

"You didn't pretend anything."

"I never do," Georgie said, remembering herself. "Let's go inside." She wasn't sure what he meant to do next. As they walked back, he swung her hand back and forth in his, as if he were a child.

They sat for a while inside, looking out at the rain coming down over the woods.

"Look what you've done," she said. Somehow, since just a few minutes before, the situation between them had changed. She found that when she looked at him, she had to look away, but soon afterwards she had to look at him again.

"What?" he said, watching her and smiling, and starting the process over again. "You didn't think it was like this before?"

"It wasn't." It was like they were playing with magnets. She kept shaking her head. "You need to get your car."

"Georgie—" he began, but she interrupted him.

"Just try not to get yourself killed." She stood up, to stop him from saying anything more. He stood up, too, and backed away, still waiting for her to say something, but she wouldn't.

"Georgie—" he said again.

"Goodbye, Second Lieutenant." He rushed forward and kissed her one more time, and she kissed him back, before they both pulled away and he turned to go.

The door clunked behind him. She sat back down and waited. Her body was like an open fire, crackling and spitting.

———   •   ———

A few minutes later, she heard the rattle of the door again, and she jumped up and rushed into the hall. But it was only Nelly.

"What's happened?" she said. She walked in and put her hand up to her daughter's forehead. "Do you have a fever?" She looked concerned. Georgie shook her head and, on a whim, embraced her mother.

FORTY-FIVE

Over the following days, Georgie wondered where Second Lieutenant Pike was, what he was doing. In France somewhere, fighting in some field-turned-mud. She wished she had asked him what it was like, so she could imagine it better; she wished she had asked where he was going, even though he wouldn't have been allowed to tell her. She shouldn't have rushed him to the car, although she couldn't think what else she would have spoken to him about. She didn't think she wanted to marry him, and still, there was something tingling about the whole thing, something prickling, not entirely unlike when she saw something out of the corner of her eye. She was reading less about magic these days, and more about other wars, and the ways in which they had ended. This one would end too.

She often went out into the woods. The trees were spindly and brittle, rather like coded messages, curled into a language she couldn't read. Tonight they seemed like warnings, except that she remembered her brain was interfering, trying to make them legible, trying to make them into messages. They meant nothing, she reminded herself, as she returned to the house.

Back in her bedroom, she poured herself a brandy. Nelly had talked about returning to London, so Georgie decided she may as well help the servants and start to pack up a box of books. Spine after spine. She took her time placing the books beside one another, ordering them from thinnest to thickest. Downstairs, someone was knocking at the door. She heard Lucy open it, heard some muffled voices, and the thump of the maid's footsteps on the stairs.

Lucy stood in front of her, out of breath. "Mr. Yeats is here."

Georgie looked up. "I'm sorry?"

"Mr. Yeats is at the door."

Georgie frowned. She drained the brandy glass, pulled the scarf from her hair, and ran her sleeve across her face.

"I'll come down," she said.

FORTY-SIX

Willy lowered his head to get through the door. He had never been the person of his poems, not really, had too much pride, which sat so much more awkwardly in his body than in his stanzas (not that his poems were free of bravado, but they could attain a fluidity that the man never quite managed). Nelly had followed him into the living room, and Georgie stood up as they came in. He greeted her.

"You can leave us," Georgie said to her mother, and Nelly, looking at Willy, did as she was asked, although as she left the room she glanced back twice. Willy was about to take Georgie's hand, but she pulled it back. For a moment he hovered, troubled, but she gestured for him to sit down.

"Tea?"

He shook his head and sat down. "I'm sorry it took me so long to come."

"It was the long route. Bloomsbury to Coleman's Hatch via France and Ireland."

He laughed, but didn't seem able to properly smile. "Is it too late? I thought—when you didn't reply to my letters—"

Georgie frowned. She hadn't got any letters; Nelly must have taken them. But she didn't say anything to him. She watched as he nervously raked his mass of greying black hair through his fingers.

"I really don't think I've known my own mind. I am a Sinbad—who after all my misadventures—has finally gained sight of port. Here. With you."

Georgie looked out the window, at a sky that was still a crumble of greys, light shuffling into darkness. She felt too much towards him: frustration, anger, a kind of fierceness. What had happened with Iseult? she wondered. Had she turned him down? She remembered the hawk and butterfly ring, which she had taken from her purse and wedged in the bottom of a box of books where she had hoped to forget it.

She spoke levelly. "You're very late."

"Oh, Georgie." He stopped a moment, not certain whether this was to be taken as encouragement. "You are in my blood, really; I always seem to return to you. We have a life of study ahead, don't we? I—I brought you something." He produced a satchel, which he opened with much ceremony, and pulled out a small white bag marked with soil. He pulled out of this bag, and placed before her on the table, what looked like a handful of dried grass, some twigs, a pebble, and two tarnished coins. He looked down at them as if they were enchanted.

"It's the seisin," he said. She waited for an explanation, while he stroked the small stone. "The symbols of possession. For the tower. Perhaps you know I've bought a tower? At Ballylee, only six miles north of Coole. This is," and he pointed to the items on the table, "two florins from the sale of a fallen tree; a handful of thatch from the cottage; some strands of grass from the field; and a stone from the tower wall. Has anyone ever suggested you might live in a medieval tower! A little damp, perhaps, and still in need of some renovations—a roof, for instance—but I have a man working on it now. I've always said it is really no use unless I have a wife, and I want so very much for that to be you."

She glanced behind him, through the window into the woods. Dorothy had written to her about this tower. *Apparently it is so damp it has a river on the first floor. Water pouring off the walls. He calls it Ballylee. We call it Ballyphallus.*

"They were just going to lock it up, let it go to ruin. I'm certain it dates back to the Normans. The Normans had form, don't you think? You are not saying much."

She swallowed. "I am just—what should I say? Recalibrating?"

"There's a winding stair. And on one wall, the head of a gargoyle. You will fall in love with it." He pulled his hand through his thick hair again. He stopped and met her eyes. "You will come and see it, won't you? Wouldn't you like to?"

She would, wouldn't she? She'd been waiting for this moment for so long that it didn't really feel as if it had arrived. It felt too casual, too improvised, and her body was accordingly unworried, did not seem to remember what the stakes were. She remembered Second Lieutenant Pike's scratchy uniform in her fingers.

"Are you still chasing that machine?"

"No. It was nonsense."

Georgie smiled.

"You knew that already, of course. That's why I need you. Part of why."

She nodded, feeling herself coming around. He shifted his chair closer to hers.

"Before we get carried away," he said, "there is one other thing I must ask you. That is, you remember Iseult?"

Georgie stiffened, nodded.

"I must take her on as my ward—because she is vulnerable. Her stepfather was violent, her constitution is poor. Her mother won't have it any other way. How does that sit with you?" His knee was almost touching hers. Georgie was still for a moment, and Willy pushed his knee until it was against her leg.

Georgie dragged her eyes up to his. "What does that mean? She would live with us?"

"Not necessarily. Just that I would be responsible for her, in a sense."

Responsible was not the kind of word she readily associated with Willy Yeats. But she supposed she needed to trust him. It still felt very unreal.

"Fine," Georgie heard herself say. "I like her."

"Good." He laughed, his face bright. "I received a note from Nora Radcliffe—she has stopped giving sessions, but she sent me a letter, saying I should let the evening star rule. There was a sketch, of a cat on a rug by the fire, and I knew it meant—I should come to you. That you would still be here."

She wished he hadn't shared this image of her as the domesticated house cat, a world away from the wild hare. Still, Georgie thought, dear Nora. Still trying to help in her own way after all that had happened. She looked back down at his long legs next to hers, the boxy structure of his trousers' creases.

They sat there a little longer, looking at each other uncertainly. Georgie looked away, focusing on the bits of grass on the table.

Willy said, "Did you hear how Harkin lost the leadership?"

Georgie shook her head.

"Vote of no confidence. For the moment, the leader is Miss Stoddart. Of course Harkin insists she's corrupt."

Georgie flushed her hand through the air as if to say she didn't care for any of that.

"Let's leave that for now."

He nodded. His bulk was solid and his outline clear. "Shall we go and ask your mother?" he said.

She nodded, and he jumped up. But he stopped, as if he'd forgotten something. He sat back down, and pulling the chair closer to hers, he leaned forward and kissed her wrist, moving to the inside of her elbow, and raised his head to her cheek, and now—glancing at her as if for permission—he kissed her mouth. It was strange to have a different mouth on hers. His lips were thinner, his mouth drier, and he tasted of soil, of vast, closed-up rooms blowing open.

FORTY-SEVEN

As soon as he'd left, Nelly sat down opposite her daughter.

"You can't be sure."

"I am."

"He seemed—almost strained, when I spoke to him."

"I think he wants to get the marriage part over. It's not really his style. I think he just wants to get on with being married."

"That's not normal, Georgie. This should be the best part."

She cast her eyes around the stray boxes, one stack of books, a ball of thick string. "I wouldn't accuse Willy of normality."

"You know what I mean."

"I don't, actually."

"How will you have time for your own work?"

"It's our work. We have the same work."

"But if you marry him, it will be his work. You will be a glorified secretary."

"What is this 'if'? I am marrying him. We are as good as married."

"I don't think you understand."

"Why did you take those letters? That he sent to me? They were mine."

Nelly winced. "I was trying to protect you."

"I don't need protecting from myself."

———— • ————

Two days later she went to London to meet him at Woburn Buildings. When Mrs. Olds let her in, she walked through the rooms on her own. If they kept the flat, she would replace almost all the furniture; she would put one of those potted aspidistras by the desk. She saw the old chair in the corner—unchanged, spitting its stuffing—and laughed. She would keep it, she decided. She couldn't quite believe this was her life, yet.

"Is that you?" Willy said, and he came out, took her hand, and led her through to the bedroom. It was breezy outside; the curtains were shuffling in the breeze.

He came and pressed his hand to his own chest. "My dear girl," he said, and she wondered when she might ask him not to call her *girl* or *child*. He kept his hand to his chest and came forward and started kissing her. It was pleasant. She supposed soon she would forget the soft fuzz above Pike's lip.

Willy was directing her towards the bed, and she walked over and sat on the edge of it. She found herself wondering: Was there something perfunctory about this? Was there something missing? He hovered above her, still kissing her, and she unbuttoned the top button of his shirt, the second button, and ran her hand across the skin of his chest, loose like a rhino's; she lay back on the bed, and as he kissed her she thought for a moment of his other women, of Olivia, of Maud, even Iseult. Had they all lain here? She gazed up at the cracked ceiling and thought of them all, on their backs, gazing up at it too, these beautiful, clever women who'd shared this bed.

"We will get a new bed," Willy said, as if reading her mind. He fell on the bed beside her and propped himself up on one elbow like a much younger man.

She laughed. "I don't mind," she said, because she really didn't. She was wondering if she would need to remove her long dress, if they were going to do this now. "I like it." Her dress was hitched up above her knee, but she left it. She was trying not to seem nervous.

"You are too good," he said, and he put a hand on her shoulder. "What do you think of your name?"

"Pardon?"

"Georgie, I mean. If you could change it, would you?"

She stared back at him. "I haven't really thought about it."

He waited.

"Are you trying to change me already?" She extended her leg and looked down at it, her shoes still on. "We're not married yet." He looked at the length of her leg as if studying it, as if there were something he was trying to interpret. He disentangled himself, stood up, and went to the window. After a moment he turned back to her.

"We'd better go down to lunch, darling."

FORTY-EIGHT

She walked back towards the station alone, and she was in an alley not far from the hospital when she heard a few people call out from the street. She was still thinking of Willy's hand on hers through the lunch, of the pale yellow wine. She looked up and there it was: a giant ship, from below, more grey than silver, the curve of it like a pregnant belly.

A zeppelin! It passed by silently, slicing through the cloud, before it vanished back into cloud. She had never seen anything so impressive. So industrial, but also so graceful; a heavy body driven by a human through the sky! It made you think of Zeus, coming down. How could the air stop such a thing from falling? And just like that, the giant, sky-gulping beast had gone. No one around. She wanted to see it again. She stood there, head tipped back, desperate for it to come back.

She was aware that she still hadn't given Willy the signet ring. She wasn't sure why, beyond the fact that she hadn't felt it was the

right time. She loosened the scarf around her neck, walked out of
the alley and back out onto the street. She tipped her head back
to look once more at the sky. But it wouldn't come again. It was
unclear why no bombs were dropped, why it had merely slid by. The
afternoon resumed as usual. The light had grown yellowish, a glow,
as if the heavens were nauseous.

FORTY-NINE

Georgie and Willy were married in the Harrow Road Registry
Office in Paddington on the morning of the twentieth of October,
with Nelly and Ezra as the official witnesses, and Dorothy as the
wedding party. The ceremony was over in a few minutes.

Later she would hardly remember the day itself. In the morning, because her fingers were shaking—less a tremor than a violent
twitching—she couldn't tie the ribbon she'd planned to put in her hair.
She wanted to look casually beautiful, thrown together; the event was
unimportant, they'd agreed, compared with what came after. Nelly
had insisted on pinning a spray of lavender to her daughter's breast,
which seemed all wrong to Georgie. But she didn't argue; in fact, she
could hardly say a thing. For breakfast, the maid had made her boiled
eggs—a special find, given rationing—but she hadn't boiled them
for long enough, and the whites were that pale, almost translucent
texture, the centres of the yolks lukewarm. It was a waste, Georgie

thought, and she ate them anyway. Afterwards she could remember the taste of cool yolk on the back of her throat.

And then they were married. Their honeymoon plans—France and Italy—were quashed by changes on the Western Front. Stone Cottage had already been booked. So the day after the ceremony, after dropping by Woburn Buildings, they headed out to the old golfing hotel on the edge of Ashdown Forest.

FIFTY

PIKE

The place had been pretty before, you could bet on it. Now it was only mud. He wished that his tin hat had a bigger lip, to keep out the falling dust. It all got in your eyes, and in your mouth, and in your ears. He did want to stay alive, which was interesting. There were two boys with him, young boys who had not known each other before (the War Office had learned it was better for strangers to serve together) but now were inseparable. Barker was more of a soldier, decisive and quick, whereas Hamilton—who was Pike's aide—was one of those absolute softies, the kind who would have irritated Pike in peacetime but whom he found he pitied in wartime. Hamilton was a thin boy with gigantic watery brown-yellow eyes like a puddle, who had a gentle soul and feared everything. Barker was taller and heavier, and tended to shield Hamilton from danger. They were chatty, sweet boys—not especially intelligent or gifted, but so very much themselves that Pike admired them and envied them their closeness. Most of the men cradled their photographs, told you of their families, their wives and mothers and sweethearts, but Barker and Hamilton were more likely to pour you a drop of the whisky they'd saved, and play gin rummy, and invent gossip about the other boys in the regiment. They didn't like being soldiers, but they weren't yearning for elsewhere.

The Württembergers always bombed promptly on schedule, and once the morning raid was done, the unit's new commander announced he was sending some men over the top. Barker was one of them. Hamilton clutched his arms around his own chest. The men lined up and Hamilton stood close to Pike, who waited a moment before he called the order.

As soon as the men's bodies appeared above the trench, the shooting started. Shouts were heard as the bodies went down. Hamilton tried to look up to see what was happening.

They didn't hear the shot, or Barker's particular yell, but only one man returned, running like hell; it was a miracle he didn't fall into the trench. The man was not Barker.

Hamilton's eyes looked like they would burst open. He found his voice. "I have to go, sir, I have to."

"No, Private—" But the boy already had a foot on the ladder.

"Hang on." Pike rustled in his pocket for his handkerchief. Like everything, it was muddy, but it still had white patches. "Wave it in the air."

The boy showed a glimmer of doubt, as if he had only just realised the risk.

"Or stay," Pike said. Hamilton looked like a boy trying to pluck up the courage to ask a girl to a dance, not deciding whether or not to risk dying on a muddy field. "Right," Hamilton said. His posture was unnaturally upright. He climbed the rungs quickly, reaching up with his hand and beginning to wave the little flag, like a child trying to get attention.

Pike watched the skinny boy clumsily clamber over the top, raise the grubby handkerchief above his head, and disappear out of sight. There was no shot. The whistle of a shell exploded down the line.

A few minutes later, a muddy outline appeared. Hamilton was back, hugging another body to him. Barker's body had been torn open by shrapnel, and a long welt down his left side had turned much of him inside out. His face was half gone. Hamilton stood at the top of the ladder holding the body and would not come down. Pike climbed up the ladder and coaxed Hamilton into letting him help to carry Barker's bloody body down the ladder. He laid the body in the mud. When Hamilton reached the bottom, he embraced the body and said in a warm voice, "Here we are." He no longer seemed aware of anyone around him. He lay down in the mud and settled Barker's ruined body on top of his. They were blocking the way through the trench, and over the top, and Pike should be telling Hamilton to clear the way in case anyone needed to get through. But he did nothing. Hamilton placed his hand on what was left of Barker's bloody cheek, and leaned over and kissed his mouth. Pike turned away.

It was afternoon in the trenches. Evening light spilled down, yellow, the sun's last argument for the day. The water that pooled up between the mud turned silver. No man's land was puddled with holes seemingly filled with mercury. Pike scratched his head under his helmet, his hair still wet. He had been waiting for his madness to flick on, like an electric light, or the way someone switched on the wireless, filling the room with voices and static. He would like to slice open a part of his brain and fill it with static.

"Well," one of the other men said quietly to Pike, glancing back at the dead boy, still seated on Hamilton's lap. "I suppose they got what was coming to them."

Pike laughed, and the other man laughed too. To think they'd once believed in wrongdoing and punishments! An eye for an eye! Here, the best men took a bullet no differently from the bastards. Even that was wrong; you didn't take the bullet. The bullet took you.

No one was surprised that within a few days Hamilton was dead too. You got to know how these things worked. They assigned Pike a new man, but this one was all saluting and yessirs. The man—his name was Everton—was determined to show everyone that he was the most professional soldier of all. He spoke of fighting for the king without irony. Nobody liked him.

"A letter came for you, Lieutenant, sir." Everton passed it down to Pike. The envelope had already been opened by the censors. Pike pulled out the single page and tried not to read it too quickly, tried to ration out the pleasure of it. Perhaps he could read it one line at a time.

> *Dear Second Lieutenant Pike,*
> *Thank you for your letter. I hope you are safe. They claim the*
> *end of the war is nigh—don't they always—but they may even*
> *mean it this time.*

The handwriting was blue, a round, casual scrawl, not fussy, and although he was trying not to read it all at once, he gulped down the words too quickly. Her initials were in the right-hand corner in blue. *GHL.*

> *I write because—and you'll hate this—I had a dream. You featured alongside a tower (a symbol of profound change). I don't know if this will mean anything to you but I expected it wouldn't hurt to pass it on, even if you do not believe a word of it. (Even I have grown more sceptical, would you believe.) Perhaps you have told your fellow officers of your ghost-mad nurse you met while you were in the hospital.*
>
> *I hope you will come and see us when you are back. I wanted to let you know that I am to marry the mad poet after all. It will be done by next week. Do come and visit us when you are home.*
>
> *Yours affectionately,*
> *Georgie Hyde-Lees*

He folded the letter and handed it back to Everton.

"They're going over the top now, sir," Everton said, his face so pockmarked, tiny caverns and gullies, like someone had etched at his skin with a metal tool.

"Coming," he said.

FIFTY-ONE

From their room in the hotel, she could look out over the forest, sparse with drifts of mist knitting the trees together. Although it was still only afternoon, it was already dark. There was a storm forecast, said to be bad. The proprietor claimed it was meant to be one of the worst England had seen in years. But perhaps it would be exciting, perhaps it would distract him.

"Maybe we should go out before the rain," she suggested. "A bit of air might help."

"I couldn't." Willy cradled his stomach with both his hands. He had sat by the window ever since they arrived, at the smallish desk with only one chair, and had pulled out some papers in front of him. He had not said a word to the proprietor, not glanced once at the bed, but pointed where the cases should go and sat down at the desk, his large body drooping over its smallness.

"You go, if you want," he said to her now.

It was his stomach, he said, all twisted around itself; yesterday on the train he'd said it was probably something he ate, it couldn't last. But it had lasted, it had lasted all day yesterday and all day today, and it was only when he looked down at the loose manuscript he had brought with him, and pieced through the pages, that his fingers did not shake. In fact, a strange smile kept creeping onto his face when he looked at those papers, but the smile was awful. It was a smile for himself and not for anyone else, a fool's smile. She wanted to yell at him, *I know you aren't happy, I can see you're not*, but she didn't, just looked back at the smile and waited for the moment it would change into something calmer, when he would invite her to meet it with her own.

There had been a letter waiting for him when he arrived, and he had taken it from the proprietor without a word, removing his hand from his stomach and placing it in the pocket of the black coat which now hung over his chair. He must have read it when she went to the lavatory, but she did not ask who it was from. She decided she would check the next time he left the room.

For the moment, she opened her suitcase and looked down at the clothes she had packed. She wondered if she might change now. She had her green dress, which she was going to save until tomorrow, but perhaps now, given Willy was feeling so poorly, perhaps this might distract him, perhaps it would coax him away from his desk? Perhaps he might forget long enough to have a drink, to come to bed? They had still not actually done what married people did; he claimed he was too unwell. Now as he remained hunched over his pages, Georgie took the green dress into the lavatory and changed into it. She left the door open, in case he might turn around and happen to glimpse her, his new young wife, in a state of undress.

"Perhaps I will get the doctor," he said, not turning around, oblivious to the fact she had even left the room. "This is unbearable. I haven't felt anything like it for years."

"I can call if you like," she called back.

"We'll wait," he said. "See if it settles."

Georgie pulled the new dress over her head—it was clinched slightly just below her waist. She tugged it down and stared at herself in the mirror. The line at the top of her cheeks was bright crimson, and even her nose glowed red. She thought of her father, whose cheeks also raised red like this, and tried pressing her cool fingers to her cheeks. She thought of Iseult Gonne's slim arms and fingers, her creamy skin, which did not matter, because it was only skin, and Willy had not married Iseult. She stared at the glass, through which her own eyes were such a lovely yellow green. They deserved to be looked at. They demanded it.

When she returned to the room, Willy still had his back turned to her, and he had begun to write. She stood there for a while in the dress, waiting for him to notice. When he didn't turn around, she considered going back in and changing again—it seemed silly now, to have made the effort, and what would she wear tomorrow? But instead she made herself sit down, at the table, a newlywed in a new green dress, and waited for the brandy to arrive. When it did, Georgie paid the woman and asked Willy if he would like any. He said, without turning around, "A little, perhaps. Would it settle the stomach, do you think?"

Georgie brought a small glass to him at the desk, and he looked up and said, "Thank you, my dear." He pointed in front of him, to where she should place the glass. If he noticed her dress, he said nothing.

She returned to the table and poured her own glass, which she drank quickly. She poured another. If she leapt around like a lunatic, would he notice? If she took off all her clothes in the middle of the room, would he even bother to turn around? He said he was sick, but was it possible he was just regretting the whole thing? But no, he was sick, really. And when you felt truly unwell, it was hard to be careful about the feelings of anyone else. She needed to be patient.

She stroked the bodice of her green dress with her palm; the rough raw silk. It was wasted on him. "Are you hungry?" she said.

"Oh, I couldn't eat," he announced to the window. "It's the nature of these things. It will just take a little time. If you wanted to go down, have something—"

"Did you want to go down?"

"Oh, not me, no. I'll stay here. Darling."

She went over to her suitcase and, under the dresses, found a book, dragged out a chair, and faced away from him. She tried to concentrate on the text.

After a while, she heard him scrape his own chair back and stand up. He was facing her, holding the letter in one hand: "I must tell you. I have had a letter." As if she hadn't been there when it arrived, as if this were a surprise to her. *I have had a letter.*

"Oh?" she said. As he stood there, looking down at her, for a moment she wanted to reach out and touch him, touch his hand, here, move her face against his hip—wasn't that what a wife did? But instead she got up from the table and poured herself another glass of brandy.

"Who is it from, then?" She tried to keep her thoughts still. He held the piece of paper by its corner, as if afraid of what would happen if he held it properly in his hand. He unfolded the page and held it up to show her. His hand was steady. Georgie walked over and took the other corner, but he did not let it go. She read what she could:

I burnt your first letter: it made a very ghostly little flame . . .

Georgie looked at him, and he snatched the paper up and laid it face down on the desk. "She's wishing us well," he said. "She says a new condition—an abruptly new condition—is bound to have a little of the fearfulness of a birth."

But the birth of what? So he had been writing to Iseult about this "condition," and called it fearful. She thought he might reassure her, even embrace her, but instead he shuffled his body towards the lavatory, with an awkward, sickly smile.

A wet rope of cold was weaving down her back. As soon as he closed the lavatory door, Georgie went over to his desk and looked to what he had scrawled on the page:

I can exchange opinion with any neighbouring mind
I have as healthy flesh and blood as any rhymer's had,
But O! my Heart could bear no more when the upland caught
the wind;
I ran, I ran, from my love's side because my Heart went mad.

The rope down her back pulled tighter, twisted, and she tried to walk it out of her body, paced down the room, reached her fingers around to touch her spine, but her back felt like a stranger's.

She had reread *Tristan* before the wedding. There is a moment after Tristan's marriage when Iseult of the White Hands is out walking with her brother, and water splashes up her thighs, and she laughs. She says this water has come higher up my thigh than my husband has ever touched me.

The bell rang, and Georgie went to the door. The proprietor stood there, the lines in her face deeply embedded, as if a child had sculpted her face from clay.

"Yes?" Georgie said, with more authority than she felt.

"Just arrived." The woman handed over a telegram and tried to peer past Georgie for a glimpse of the famous poet. Georgie did not move from the door.

"A pleasant night? You got enough blankets?"

Willy emerged from the lavatory and returned to his seat by the window, without looking at either of them.

Georgie kept her eyes on the woman's face. "Actually, we might like a little more brandy."

The woman's mouth twitched into a smile, and she nodded and turned away.

"What was that about?" he said from the window.

"Telegram."

His eyes lit up almost cruelly, and he stood up from his chair and held out his hand. She waited a moment, watching his face, which was so hopeful, so expectant, before she shook her head.

"It's for me." It had been redirected from Nelly's address in Sussex, forwarded to Kensington, and forwarded again from there.

It was from the hospital. The return address said Mrs. Agnes Thwaite, 27 Berkeley Square. Georgie tore it open. The creamy paper was damp from the rain. It read:

LT PIKE KILLED IN ACTION.

She dropped it, and it floated, settling near Willy's chair, but he did not stoop to pick it up. He didn't notice it was there at all.

She stared at it. *Pick it up*, she thought. *Pick it up.*

Willy didn't move.

Pick the damn thing up.

Willy turned around. "Did you say something?" His left arm was once more wrapped around his stomach.

Georgie walked over and bent down to pick up the bit of paper herself. She took her ugly coat from the hook, wrapped it around herself, and slipped the telegram into her pocket. She glanced back at the weak creature by the window. *Husband.*

"I'm going out."

She didn't wait for a reply, just let herself out. Her last glimpse of him was of his shoulders crushed together, like an old priest after the congregation's gone, wrenching out another sermon.

FIFTY-TWO

The storm was as bad as the newspapers said. In the morning, they would see massive trees uprooted, wrenched out of the ground as if the soil had rejected them. For now, it was dark and the rain came thwacking down, slanting from what seemed like all directions. The wind shunted the trees and made them creak to the point of cracking.

She ran. The ground was soft, the trees sparse; she'd have to work to get herself lost. Branches cracked under her thin shoes. There was no way he'd follow her. He probably wouldn't even notice she'd gone.

The bottom of her dress was already sludged with mud, the green soaked and spattered in brown. She would ruin it, but that no longer mattered. She checked behind her—she could still see the chimney of the hotel. Perhaps someone from under the ground would take pity on her, reach up and drag her under. Maybe someone would push her all the way down to hell, and she could ride the

monster Geryon around its circles, clutch his rump, watch the rise
and fall of his wings.

The wind was building, lifting, and as she slowed to a walk, the
trees shuddered above her. She wanted to speak to a stranger. She
wrapped her arms around herself. Behind her, the chimney of the
hotel had gone. But you couldn't get lost here; when she walked up
this next rise, she'd see the hotel again behind her, and she didn't
need to see it to know he was there, sitting at the window above the
heath, no doubt fixated on the words on his page, deaf to the wind
playing outside the window. He didn't care that she was out here;
perhaps he wished she'd be crushed under a falling tree, so that the
mistake of their marriage could vanish.

And Second Lieutenant Pike was gone. He would never turn up
again at the house in Coleman's Hatch, never walk along that path
with her, not quite talking about the future. Thomas Pike with his
feet all fixed. He'd once been engaged to a girl. That was the best of
it, she supposed, one paltry moment with the rain falling, a glass of
pink champagne in your hand, and your best shoes in the muddy
grass. You never realised it was your best moment, until nothing after
it quite compared, and then you were trampled into the mud yourself.

She tried to direct her thoughts, but her brain hated anywhere
she tried to send it. The woman who ran the hotel squinting at her.
Willy with his pretty poems and his audience of admirers. Iseult
Gonne with her immaculate cheeks. Second Lieutenant Pike with
his body gone.

Think of a stranger. Now the rain was tapping, slipping through
the foliage, like an audience's first trickle of applause. The ground's
surface was turning slick, and she stopped on the path.

She would leave him. It had been a mistake. She had to leave.

Georgie smoothed her dress with her hands and looked up through the dripping trees. She could leave. It would be all right. She could go back to her mother's. As she watched her dress's bodice dapple from pale to dark green, the sound of the rain grew louder, the clap of hundreds of thick, uneven drops as they met the heath—as if all through the auditorium, the audience members were rising from their seats, applauding, as the actress emerged for the curtain call, finally able to play herself.

FIFTY-THREE

When Georgie returned to the room, he was still seated by the window with his back to her. He heard the door and turned around, and all he could do was nod to her, and she didn't nod back. Her ruined dress was dripping onto the floor; she lifted it a little—its wet, muddy weight—and dropped it again. She was pleased to see a puddle forming at her feet.

"You went out in that," he said finally. She wasn't sure if he meant the dress or the weather. He didn't get up. He had put on his heavy coat inside to keep warm.

Why had she fallen in love with this man? Why had she married him? Had she always thought he could give her something he was never able to give? The rain was slashing the panes, and the brick seemed to be breathing, cold air slipping in the gaps around the windows. She thought of Saint Peter, with his mangled hand, making the sign of benediction. Surely that was what Harkin had meant: we can only do what we can; our bodies and our minds are not made for anything pure. That a blessing is a kind of contortion.

She would sleep here tonight and leave in the morning. She felt calmer now she had decided. All his actions proved that it was the right course. She walked into the lavatory, wrapped a towel around her dress, and returned to the room. She edged closer to the gas fire.

The second lot of brandy had arrived, and she poured herself a large glass. She had seen the proprietor at the door when she came in, and avoided her look—it would make a good story, Georgie knew, the famous poet and his too-young wife, already flailing on their first nights together. *Worse than if they'd been married for fifty years already*, she'd say. *Seemed like they couldn't stand the sight of each other.* The story would be much improved when the gossip spread that they'd been divorced after only two days of marriage.

She was soaked through, but she could feel her body heat trying to leak into the wetness, to force her wet clothes to warm.

She sat herself at the table with a notebook—intended for the final version of her Pico translation—and shivering, she placed the little broken candle in front of her. Taking a flint, she lit the candle, leaning its thin frame in a candleholder so it stood on a slant, a tiny flicker of flame. She ripped a page from the book so the cream wax wouldn't drip directly onto the table. She picked up a pen and began to write.

"I am writing too," she said.

He didn't look up from his paper. Why should he? Georgie wrote faster, scribbling off the edge of the paper. She ripped out a page, screwed it up, wrote another. Willy kept his eyes down, probably plotting out half-rhymes and stresses, probably tracing the lines of Iseult's delicate collarbone, her huge eyes—

Georgie pressed so hard she tore the paper.

She ripped out this page too, and looked over at him. He didn't seem to notice she was there.

"I feel like," she said loudly, "we've lived through all this before. Don't you?"

He looked over at her; he no longer concealed the fact that his eyes were wet with tears, the lines of his forehead all crumpled together. He seemed as if he were becoming less and less substantial, sitting there, as if he were growing into a ghost himself. He turned to face her, and spoke with his eyes lowered.

"I am worried," he said, but she ignored him; she kept writing; she started a new page, writing fast. "I am worried I may have made—"

"Something *is writing through me*." She ripped out another page, started a new one. She didn't bother to shut her eyes. She was determined to make him listen to her. Now he stood up and walked over to her. He peered over her shoulder, and her writing slowed, grew more concentrated as he approached.

With the pressure of her pen, she ripped the page again:

WHAT
YOU
HAVE DONE

"Who is it?" Willy said, staring at the paper. "Who is speaking?"

"I don't know," Georgie said.

IS RIGHT
FOR BOTH THE CAT
AND THE HARE

Willy was silent, standing over her and waiting for the words to form from Georgie's pen. His body pressed in closer to hers as he leaned over, and he stared as her hand shifted across the paper:

YOU WILL
NEVER REGRET
NOR REPINE

He put one arm around her shoulders. "Who am I speaking to?" he said again.

THOMAS

"Thomas," Willy said. "Thomas who?"

THOMAS OF DORLOWICZ

Georgie pressed the pen harder into the page. Behind her, bent over like an elderly man, the poet had started to stroke her hair. She felt his cheek against hers. He whispered, "George, my darling, darling girl. You will not believe this. You simply will not believe it."

FIFTY-FOUR

Once she had stopped writing, it seemed as if a different man stood above her.

"Is he still there?" He was hovering over her, one hand clasping her shoulder. She shook her head and put down the pen.

"He's gone." She returned her hands to her lap and looked up at him.

He reached down and kissed her, and would not stop kissing her, and his hands travelled across her neck, her shoulders, her breasts.

"How did you do it?" he asked her, and she pretended she did not know what he was asking. She was exhausted, and glad to finally have someone else prepared to look after her. He took her hand and led her through to the bedroom, where he stood in front of her and, for a while, just stared at her. Georgie felt somehow outside herself, somehow operating both in this room with her poet husband and some miles off, as if she had deposited the book of her brain in a library, or into some other layer of the earth.

"May I?" He addressed her nervously. He gestured to her dress and she nodded. He unbuttoned the back of the green dress, gently, and peeled the wet silk from her body. She pulled his dry shirt over his head. He pressed his palm on her bare back and she turned around and kissed him, and her hands were all over his loose skin. She felt as if she were drifting back down into the room, like her split selves were coming together. He was disentangling the dress from her legs, and as she edged herself under the bedsheet, he slid in beside her and touched her, which he knew precisely how to do, just where his fingers should be, and just how they should move. It was a relief.

When it was done, she got up and brought the bottle of brandy and held it out to see if he would drink from the bottle. He drank, and she did too.

"It was like something I had lived through before," he said. "It was so strange when you said it. It was exactly how I felt."

FIFTY-FIVE

The next morning she woke up with a headache and Willy sleeping beside her. She got up. The rooms were quiet. Out on the table, the words from Thomas of Dorlowicz were still sitting there, looking decidedly worldly, in her own handwriting.

She wrapped herself in a dressing gown and let herself out the door quietly so as not to wake Willy. She had planned to go to the proprietor to enquire about breakfast, but when she got downstairs, she went to the external door instead and stepped outside for a moment. The wind was still blustering, unsure from which direction it was coming or going. Everywhere there was evidence of the storm: large uprooted trees, fat roots wrenched out of the earth, a chaos of mud and branches. One tree had fallen and broken the fence around the hotel garden, forcing the dirty white pickets to the ground. It reminded her of the tumble of bricks from the zeppelin raid near Gray's Inn. She walked a few steps down the path. The wind was searing cold and strong, as if it were determined to clear everything away.

Back inside the hotel, she located the proprietor and ordered for tea to be brought to their rooms. The proprietor considered her, seeming disappointed by her calm delivery, her clear gaze. She was looking for signs that Georgie was rattled, but Georgie only stared back at her.

"Please leave the tea things outside the door," she said. "I'd prefer you didn't knock, as my husband is still sleeping."

"Certainly, ma'am." The woman was still watching her as Georgie took the stairs up two at a time and headed back to their rooms. When she entered the bedroom, Willy was sitting up with his eyes open.

"I worried you'd gone. Escaped me."

"It's a little late for that," she said, smiling. She took off her robe and slipped back into bed beside him.

FIFTY-SIX

SUMMER 1918

Willy worried that it would be too bleak for Georgie to visit the tower over the winter. She had never been to Ireland, and still had seen Ballylee only in a photograph. But once the summer arrived, Georgie and Willy travelled to Galway, and because the tower wasn't yet habitable, they stayed with Lady Gregory at Coole. Willy was clearly nervous about what Georgie would make of it. He had appointed an architect, William Alphonsus Scott, but he was not in the least reliable, and with all the materials that were still being tracked down—timber for the ceilings and floors, iron fittings for hearths and hinges, and a new roof to be arranged—the actual renovations had still not yet begun.

But Willy needn't have worried. They arrived in the afternoon when the light was a deep yellow. They had passed many ruined towers on their way, all standing since medieval times, but it was

Ballylee that seemed to Georgie unlike any of the others. It seemed sturdier somehow; it had a face, a dignity. A small cottage was attached. As you approached the tower, you crossed a short stone bridge, across a river whose banks were bright white with mayflower. And all this was theirs. A stares' nest at the top of the tower was busy, the slim black birds swooping about on their own errands. Georgie stood beside Willy and stared up.

Eventually he took her hand and led the way inside.

When she first walked up the winding stair and saw the four floors of the tower, she was already filled with ideas of how they would furnish it. She decided that for the entire week they were in Galway, they must spend every day here, and stay until they lost the light. The tower was empty, the windows still clear of glass, all the walls and floor bare stone. The roof was only sparsely thatched, so if it rained, the rain would fall right through the roof and flood the bottom floor.

On the first night, she finally gave him the ring which Dulac had engraved. He spent a long time examining it before he slipped it on his finger, and promised he would never take it off.

During that week, it didn't rain. Georgie and Willy sat together in the same window alcove as the wind blew right into the tower, and they looked down across the river and the trees, talking about how they'd furnish not just the tower but the adjoining cottage, and what poems he would write here, and which spirits they would speak to. Sometimes they walked outside, down over the bridge, and off into the trees, and on one particularly warm day, they went down to the river and dipped their feet in the water. Their week was filled with plans and imaginings.

On their last day at the tower, she summoned Thomas of Dorlowicz as it was getting dark. Georgie sat cross-legged on the cold stone floor and wrote in the notebook Willy had brought. The darkness was coming quickly, so it was difficult, particularly for Willy, to decipher what was written.

"Will you always come to us?" Willy said.

I WILL NOT ALWAYS BE NEEDED

"The two of us will manage on our own?"

NOT TWO

"Why not?"

THERE WILL BE AN HEIR

They had not thought to bring a candle, and as the darkness came, it seemed the darkest she had ever seen. Neither of them could read the pages anymore. As Willy sat beside her on the stone floor, it seemed the air was alive, that so many stories were within their reach, that they were at last inside the anima mundi. It seemed they were surrounded by voices, neither dead nor alive, coming from the stone, from the blank windows, from the cottage and the bridge, each voice interrupting the others, all straining to be heard. Although they knew they would miss dinner at Coole and this would annoy Lady Gregory, Georgie spread out a blanket on the top floor of the tower, and painfully and awkwardly, but amidst much laughter, they made love on the stone floor.

FIFTY-SEVEN

They were both nervous about the pregnancy. It was her third after two miscarriages, and she struggled to believe this one would be any different. It was clear that Willy wanted to help her but he didn't know how. She felt as if her body were being taken over by something out of her control. The spirits—Thomas had been joined by another spirit who went by the name of Ameritus—had promised Willy that the boy would be healthy. The spirits promised a perfect heir. But Georgie kept having nightmares. She was certain something was going to go wrong. In one nightmare, she went into labour and gave birth to nothing. In another, she realised her pregnancy was something she had invented, and she had to go to Willy and tell him that it had all been a lie.

They had moved to Oxford, to a house on Broad Street they had let because the tower still wasn't ready. Every time they received another letter about Ballylee, Georgie snatched it up to read it. She had become obsessed with the tower's progress, sure it was linked to her own state, sure that the tower's renovations reflected the creature growing inside her. Scott, the architect, had fine ideas but was very slow, his updates were sporadic, and he was known to be a drunk. He engaged the local craftsmen, and had acquired wrought-iron hinges from the blacksmith at Liscannor village on the Clare coast, and beams and planks and old paving stones from Lord Gough's disused mill, and it was his idea to use the mill wheel as a hearthstone. But although she waited, and although he'd promised, she had heard nothing from him on the final designs.

The builder, Rafferty, did write, but his reports were mixed. Two weeks before, he'd said he had finished building the chimneys and the fireplaces, and installed the eaves. This week, he had made the castle windows and he was planning to stay overnight to plaster the cottage. But there had been heavy rains overnight, and in the morning he had found the hall and the first floor of the tower flooded. The cottage was only one and a half inches higher than the waterline, and the yard was three feet underwater. She was certain that all this meant there would be something wrong with the child.

Willy was working on a poem, and when he was at his desk he seemed happiest, having made some change that felt significant. She was pleased for him but envied him the escape. She had read a first draft over his shoulder—it was about the last stages of the war, the turmoil of the Russian Revolution and the continued conflict in Ireland—but she felt that when she spoke to him about her thoughts on the poem, he seemed distracted. She thought it would be better if the poem reached beyond the war—its effect seemed limited by specific lines about the Germans arriving in Russia—but either he didn't agree with her, or he wasn't listening to what she said. She felt agitated; there was not enough connection between them. She felt as if she were merely a vehicle for a baby. She wanted him to touch her.

"I want to go back to Ballylee," she said.

"We can't, of course."

"I have to."

"Darling, it's practically underwater. And you are due in six weeks."

"I want to go."

"Perhaps we can ask Thomas for advice?" Willy said. "Perhaps he might lend another perspective?"

"All right," she said. But she kept putting off asking the spirits anything. She claimed that they wouldn't come. She said she was too unwell.

———— • ————

A week later, Georgie had two letters. One was from Rafferty, saying that he hadn't been able to do any work on Ballylee for a full week because of the flooding. The other letter said that Scott, the architect, had caught a chill at Archbishop Walsh's funeral, contracted pneumonia, and died. She shut herself in the library and read, tried not to think about the tower or the birth, and to remind herself whatever was happening with her body, her mind was still her own. She read a newspaper article about how Sinn Féin was growing more popular in Ireland, even with many of its members in jail. She wanted to talk to Willy. She was about to stand up and head upstairs to find him, but at that moment, Willy walked into the room. He came in and sat across from her.

"I need to speak to Thomas," he said. He handed Georgie a pencil. "Thomas, are you there?"

Georgie gave in. She stood up and walked over to the chair where she usually summoned the spirits. Willy followed her. As soon as she sat down, he began to address Thomas:

"I've decided to dedicate myself to your writings. To write down all the things you say."

He waited. There was a pause before the reply came.

THAT IS NOT OUR PURPOSE. WE HAVE COME TO
GIVE YOU METAPHORS FOR POETRY

"But I want to write a book with your teachings," Willy said, "so that the world can learn—can know—all this is real."

WE DO NOT NEED YOU FOR THAT

Willy shuffled uncomfortably in his chair. She thought of the poem he was writing, and of the flooded tower.

THE GREAT WHEEL IS TURNING. THE CYCLE OF
TWENTY CENTURIES IS ENDING. CHRISTIANITY
ONLY ONE TURN OF THE WHEEL. DO NOT ONLY
LOOK AT NOW AND THEN. LOOK AT THE CYCLE.
LOOK AT WHAT'S TO COME

"But what is to come?" he said.

NEW ERA OF DISTRUST AND DESTRUCTION. DO

NOT NEGLECT THE MEDIUM. DO NOT FORGET
THE 6TH SENSE. THE MEDIUM NEEDS ATTENTION
OR WE WILL NOT RETURN

The sixth sense was the sexual, an area which Willy occasionally needed to be reminded was essential to continue spiritual communications. She put the pencil down, opened her eyes, and looked straight at her husband. "I'm going to bed."

"I want to make some more notes," Willy said. "I'll be there in a moment." His eyes were wet—he was excited—and he leaned down to kiss her gently. He picked up the notebook she had been writing in and tucked it under his arm.

Georgie went upstairs to the bedroom. Willy was not listening to Thomas either. She didn't know how to make him listen. She put her hand on her pregnant belly, this part of her body that no longer felt like hers, that now belonged to her son. Again she had the sense that something was going to go wrong. She wanted to call downstairs to Willy so she could tell him she felt afraid, to ask him to reassure her. But she was worried that if she called him, he wouldn't come; she was worried he would stay downstairs with the scrawlings of Thomas, and that this would be worse than if she didn't ask at all. Instead, she rubbed her neck, which at least she still recognised as her own. She got herself ready for bed and wondered if Willy would come to her, but by the time she lay down and closed her eyes, he still had not come. Much later she woke when she heard him come in, the soft thud of his steps around the room, before he slipped under the sheets and wrapped himself around her.

———— • ————

The following evening she found a new draft of the poem on his desk. The ending read as follows:

> *The darkness drops again; but now I know*
> *That twenty centuries of stony sleep*
> *Were vexed to nightmare by a rocking cradle,*
> *And what rough beast, its hour come round at last,*
> *Slouches towards Bethlehem to be born?*

She returned the page to the desk. She was already flooded with dark images of the birth; she found the imagery disturbing. She put her hand once more to her stomach. At the same time, she could see that Willy had listened to Thomas, and what he had written was good, far better than the poem she'd read back at Stone Cottage. Things would be better when her son was finally born.

FIFTY-EIGHT

It was not until the labour was over, and when the nurse called out her congratulations, that Georgie realised what it was that had gone wrong. The baby was a girl. For a moment, she was horrified— the spirits had clearly promised a boy. But when the nurse placed the baby in her arms, Georgie stared into her eyes and found that she could manage, that she didn't really mind so much. Even Willy, when he arrived at the nursing home within the hour, declared that, despite all the promises to the contrary, he was glad to have a daughter.

FIFTY-NINE

She had expected Nelly to arrive all afternoon. Georgie had looked forward to showing off Anne again, who by now had a slick of thick black hair, and large dark eyes that stared silently at what went on around her. She even had six words, which she deployed very carefully, watching how you reacted, as if she weren't sure if they meant what she thought.

There was no sign of Nelly. She was still not there at five o'clock, and the nurse had to put Anne to bed.

"Why can't she do as she says?"

Willy tried not to smile at her usual frustration with her mother. "There's probably some holdup in London."

"She's doing it on purpose. She knows you're going to Dublin, so she's waiting for you to leave so she can have Anne all to herself." Georgie had also wanted to show Nelly the house, which everyone agreed Georgie had furnished beautifully, despite their constrained

finances. It had been some consolation to Georgie that she'd managed this, given the endless delays with the tower's renovations.

She considered Willy, with his book on his lap.

"Why aren't you packing?"

"I couldn't find my suitcase."

"Did you think it would find itself?"

He smiled at his own incompetence, placed his book aside, and
stood up from his chair. Standing, he looked at her. "Perhaps you
have seen it somewhere?"

She had not noticed before they married the extent to which
he couldn't manage his own affairs, the extent to which women
like Olivia and Lady Gregory had always stepped in to help him
with practical matters. He seemed to find his own ineptitude
charming.

She went downstairs, found his case where he had left it behind
a chair in the parlour, and started to drag it across the room. He put
his hand out.

"Darling, perhaps, before I pack, we could consult with them
one last time?"

He meant Thomas, Ameritus, and the others. She shook her
head. "Of course we can't. There's no time." The spirits had been
rather defensive after Anne turned out not to be a son, but Willy
had forgiven them. They said they could never predict things with
true clarity. It was possible they had been misinterpreted.

"But it will be a whole fortnight." He had to go for Abbey
Theatre business, but he didn't like to be away so long.

"Nothing would come now even if we tried. Please just pack so
we can get you on that train."

"And you will go and see Iseult?"

"Of course I will."

"I'm so glad you two are such good friends."

She began collecting together the books from his desk and handing them to him.

"Thank you," he said, taking the books, placing them on the bed, and kissing her. "What would I do without you?"

"You'd miss your train," she said.

———— • ————

There was still no sign of Nelly when he left for the station. After he left, she sat by the window. The clouds were heavy cream with a puffy underside of deep grey. Anne was asleep in the nursery.

She had got what she wanted. She had, in a way, been more right than anyone.

What was strange was that even though she never could have married a man like Thomas Pike, she still thought of things she might say to him. She might explain, for instance, the way all lives were a kind of compromise, and the one that she had chosen was right for her after all. She would show him this house that she had furnished, she would show him Willy's latest poem, and most of all, she would show him Anne. But why did she wish to show him anything? To defend her decision to marry Willy? Was she imagining an intimacy she and Pike had never had? Was she confusing him with the spirit she mustered to guide Willy through his anxieties? Although she used Pike's first name to talk to Willy, she didn't feel that he—that young officer in his narrow bed, or walking with her in Ashdown Forest—was speaking through her. Someone might be, maybe, but not him. Sometimes she pictured his body in the process of being blown to bits, in a shower of mud and skin, blown into the air. Sometimes she wondered what was kept from that moment. An image of the lady Emma's pale throat? Those crisp sheets Mrs. Thwaite always insisted they pull sharply to smooth a crease's hint? That blurry canvas of Paris and Helen, waiting on the shore?

She entwined her fingers together and looked out the window. The sunset seemed ridiculous, as if it were old-fashioned somehow, like an old textbook depiction of heaven. The knock on the door surprised her. She remembered Laura was in the parlour, and she sat back down and waited.

It was Nelly, at last. She had been delayed, she was dreadfully sorry; she was dying to see little Anne. Almost as an afterthought she swooped in to hug her daughter, in a surge of perfume and soap.

"She's sleeping in the nursery," Georgie said, leading her through to the baby's room, and at the same time staring at the way her mother's face had fallen in slightly more since she had seen her last, the way the skin pulled down as if filled with fluid. She was tired, she said, so many delays, and even first class had been stuffy and smelly. In the nursery, Anne was sleeping, but when she heard Nelly chattering, the child woke up and began to cry. Nelly reached in and picked her up, but she cried harder.

"Come on, Anne," Georgie said, rather desperately. "It's your grandmother."

"She looks exactly like you," Nelly said, seeming unworried by the rising screams as she cradled the red-faced child. "Exactly as you did." She glanced at her adult daughter and smiled at Anne. "Could be the same baby."

"I think you should put her back," Georgie said, stopping herself from reaching for Anne, but Nelly shook her head and walked around the room with the baby screaming and pushing her tiny fists into the air.

"She's fine," said Nelly, face to face with the baby. "Just a little growly, aren't you?"

"Give her to me," Georgie said. She took Anne, tried to soothe her, and called for the nurse to come back. She hustled her mother out of the room, and Nelly led the way out into the hall.

"I'm sorry I didn't come earlier," Nelly said. "The trains—"

"It's fine," Georgie said. Nelly had to have it her own way. She was looking around with a calm expression but didn't say anything about the house.

Out the window the sunset had gone; the sky had turned dark blue and would soon be black. Nelly looked back towards the nursery, where the crying continued. "She's a very dear thing."

Georgie smiled. "Yes. Willy has written her a poem."

"How useful."

Georgie ignored this.

"Are you taking Anne to Galway?" Nelly said.

"As soon as the renovations are finished." She glanced at her mother. "It's perfectly safe."

"It's so remote. And there's so much unrest. Surely you could wait till she is older—"

"It's important for us to go."

"It's not your country."

"It's Anne's, and Willy's, and it will be mine. It will only be for the summers. You can visit us." She wouldn't come all that way, Georgie was certain. She had not told Nelly that all the money to renovate the tower had come out of the savings that had been released on her twenty-fifth birthday. She refused to give her mother any more reason for disapproval.

Nelly was watching her closely. "Are you enjoying marriage?"

"Yes," Georgie said. It was true enough. She had given up trying to explain to anyone what it was like.

SIXTY

It was a relief to go down to London for some days, to spend some time away from Oxford, and leave Anne with the nurse. The train was on time, and Georgie was happy to sit back and watch the world flash by. It was a gift not to have to take care of anyone for a few hours. She brought along Willy's poem for Anne, in which he solemnly instructed their young daughter not to end up like Maud Gonne:

> *An intellectual hatred is the worst,*
> *So let her think opinions are accursed.*
> *Have I not seen the loveliest woman born*
> *Out of the mouth of Plenty's horn,*
> *Because of her opinionated mind*
> *Barter that horn and every good*
> *By quiet natures understood*
> *For an old bellows full of angry wind?*

Georgie herself had kept quiet when she read the poem, and resolved that she would teach her daughter that having her own opinions—whatever they might be—was to be applauded. Anne would never be mad like Maud. Georgie would encourage her to be as noisy as she wished. Reading the poem again, she supposed she herself would never escape the Gonne women; they were knitted into her victory.

She walked from the station to the small tea-shop, tucked away in a leafy courtyard, where Dorothy was sitting under a tree, with a teapot already waiting. Dorothy leapt up and embraced her with a surprising fierceness.

Georgie laughed nervously and sat down. Dorothy was already lifting a flask from her bag.

"Not for me," Georgie said. "I'm not quite well." Without meaning to, she raised her hand to her stomach. She hadn't told anyone yet, worrying it might amount to nothing.

"Not again?" Dorothy hesitated, unable to hide her disappointment, but she made an effort to smile. "How marvellous. Well. We should celebrate." She tipped some of the flask into Georgie's cup. "Ezra might drop in, too. He has gone to someone with a proposal for a magazine. We thought we might get some money out of it."

Georgie eyed the teacup and wondered if her stomach would settle. She raise the cup to her nose, sniffed, and took a sip; the alcohol was strong. She took another and returned the cup to the table.

"How is Anne?"

"Good. I left her with the nurse."

Dorothy was not much interested in children, but she tried for Georgie's sake, and she had at least acted pleased with Anne when they had brought her to London the first time; she had held the child and pronounced her lovely.

"And you're already ready for another?"

"I suppose we are." Georgie was more relaxed about the prospect of pregnancy than she had been, knowing how it had gone with Anne, knowing not to make any promises in advance.

She heard a rush of footsteps behind her, and someone grasped her shoulder.

"Our Oirish lass!" Ezra swooped in and kissed her cheek with a smacking sound. He looked triumphant.

"The meeting went well?" Dorothy said.

"Not exactly. The gentleman said, and I quote, 'It's not you, Ezra. It's the seven black phantom dogs barking and screaming around you.'" He turned back to Georgie. "It's astonishing to me too, but not everyone approves of me." He smiled at her. "I promised to leave you two alone, but I couldn't miss the chance to glimpse our lady of the flooded towers. Are you looking after our Dante?"

"I am."

Dorothy did not bring up Georgie's pregnancy, and so Georgie didn't either.

"What you are doing is ever so good for *poetry*, you know." He kissed her again and left, dodging around the tables in an exaggerated dance.

"He is—energetic."

"He isn't all that well," Dorothy said. "I think he still misses Willy, and all he can do is rail against him. He claims Willy's work has deteriorated completely, but I'm not actually sure he even believes it. I think it's more self-protection, but if I even suggest such a thing, he roars." She reached for the flask and tipped more brandy into her own cup. "He's often roaring. He says London has no intellectual life, mankind's imbecility is contagious, on it goes."

"How is your painting?"

"Oh, it's all right." Dorothy glanced off up to the ceiling and back to the cup of tea in her hands. "I get invitations to show it sometimes."

"Will you?"

For a moment she looked stubborn, almost childish. "No. I'm more interested in the work than the display of it. The display is another thing altogether. Ezra is very deep in his greatest work, his masterwork, you know. An endless poem—about everything."

"Is that any easier for you?"

"Easier?" She paused. "I don't know about that. They're not easy men."

Georgie laughed, and Dorothy smiled.

"We're planning to move to Paris."

"What? Why?"

"We've decided it will be better for us. Ezra wants to leave. I am quite happy to try something else."

"I'll miss you."

"You have Anne now. And"—she gestured—"this one."

"It can be lonely, can't it."

Dorothy looked up. "Not for Ezra, anyway. I think he's involved with other women, or at least he'd like to be."

"Are you sure?"

"It's the problem with these men."

Georgie looked at her.

"Willy will do it too."

Dorothy's face was smooth and cold as porcelain. What she said was driven by a wretchedness, and Georgie reached over and covered

Dorothy's hand with her own. She couldn't imagine Willy going off with anyone else. She wished she could tell Dorothy about Thomas of Dorlowicz, but she realised that even if she could find the right words, Dorothy would never understand it. And she couldn't risk anyone compromising the situation. No, it must remain only hers.

SIXTY-ONE

She had promised Willy that she would go and check in on Iseult,
but as she had a spare half hour after meeting Dorothy, she walked
to Berkeley Square Gardens to see the old hospital from the outside. She walked through the narrow gardens, bright green leaves
forming an arched ceiling above. She thought of all the times she
had gone into the hospital, reluctant, even resentful that it was taking time out of what she considered was her real life. She remembered the look on Mrs. Thwaite's face when they had sat together in
that cramped office and she had told Georgie about her dead sons.

Now the large house would be empty again, all those rooms for
only Mrs. Thwaite to walk around in, all the beds taken away, the
men gone home. Georgie hoped that Mrs. Thwaite wasn't alone in
there. She wondered what Anne was doing now, thought of her
soft milkiness, the filmy down of her hair, the moment where her
eyelids lifted to reveal her black eyes.

Would Thomas Pike mind that she had borrowed his voice to speak to her husband? Of course he would. She thought of the second lieutenant's lip, his lower lip, which was almost puffy, and smooth. His cheek, unshaven, the hair along his jawline soft, all the same length. The end of his jawbone almost sharp to touch. She raised her hand to hail a cab, and the car pulled in squarely at the curb. She sat back for the drive across town to the suburbs where Iseult was staying, looking out as the city unfolded out the window. Where the car finally slowed, the brick buildings, in neat lines, were identical. She paid the driver and got out of the car. When she found the address she had written in her notebook, she let herself into the building.

The apartment was on the first floor. Iseult greeted her at the door and seemed excited to see her. Georgie followed her down a narrow hallway.

"I am sorry for the tiny place," she said. "I told Willy we should meet somewhere else, but I think he wanted you to check on me. I'm not sure you'll approve, but anyhow."

They turned into a small room. A damp, moth-eaten smell mingled with old lavender. A pocked desk sat alongside a long faded couch, and here was that ugly chair from Woburn Buildings, with the stuffing falling out. Someone should have thrown that chair out years ago, but instead it had somehow made its way here. *It follows me around*, Georgie thought, and smiled.

"I know it's horrid," Iseult said quickly, "but I'm fine here, really."

Georgie peered down the hall to a dark, cramped bedroom with a single bed.

"It's not too bad," Georgie said, thinking they would get her out of this place and somewhere more suitable as soon as possible. She would arrange it as soon as she got back to Oxford. She noticed Iseult looked very thin. They both sat down on the large couch, and Iseult did not offer her tea, but looked around nervously. Georgie imagined what would have happened if Willy and Iseult had married. *Nothing would ever get done*, she thought. *They're both so hopeless.* She wondered for a moment if she should get up and make the tea herself, but decided not to bother. It would just draw this out for longer than she wanted. She knew it was unfair, but she felt repelled by Iseult's helplessness, and felt a surge of warmth for Dorothy, whom she understood so much better than this creature.

Iseult leaned down to pick up some papers from the floor, and placed them on her lap. "I'm so sorry for the mess. I've been very busy."

"What have you been doing?"

"Oh. Working at the school." They had secured her a position at the School of Oriental Languages. "And—" Iseult flung out a hand, as if to indicate the room. Georgie smiled and politely nodded. Iseult was as beautiful as ever, and this seemed to mean nobody would call her up on things that did not make much sense.

"When I hear from Willy—he seems happy. You made him happy."

"I hope that we make each other so, most of the time."

"I wish I could have an ordinary life." Iseult laughed in a way that sounded insincere. "Anne is a pretty baby. Willy sent me a photograph. Did he ever tell you how I was conceived?"

Georgie looked off down the hallway, as if to suggest that this was hardly appropriate conversation.

But Iseult went on, almost dreamily, "Mother had a lover, you know, and they had a boy who died. And they were so heartbroken, they loved the baby so much, they tried to reincarnate him. And they had intercourse on his tomb, in the crypt. And so I was born. So you see I was a failure to begin with."

"We don't get to choose our beginnings," Georgie said. She had heard the story before, and pitied her. In London, everyone referred to Iseult as Maud's cousin to pretend she wasn't illegitimate, but equally, they all knew that she was Maud's daughter. The doubleness was cruel. "But we do get to choose what comes after."

"Actually, I met someone I might marry," Iseult said. "His name is Francis."

"How wonderful," said Georgie, although she felt a sense of dread, that if this woman could not work out what she wanted, a husband could not help her. Why did she bring this up only now, and why did she look so strained when she mentioned it?

"He is a writer," she said in a quiet voice. "Willy is a great hero of his."

When Georgie left the apartment, walking down to look for a cab, she wondered what she would tell Willy. She would recommend they get Iseult out of that flat, without saying anything too terrible about what it was like. Other than that, what could she say? That Iseult looked well enough. Not sick, anyhow. That she had been working (this had been suggested even though there was little evidence of it). Had he given her that hideous chair? They could at least find her some better furniture. Georgie only now realised that she had forgotten to give Iseult the envelope with the money from Willy. She cursed and checked her wristwatch. She would rush back and drop it off. She might have to catch the later train.

She retraced her steps back to the building, tapped her way up the cold stairs, irritated with herself for forgetting. But Iseult would be grateful for the money; she would need it. She wondered if Iseult had wondered earlier if Georgie had brought something from Willy, if she had been too polite to ask.

Georgie stood outside the door of the apartment and knocked, but no one came. The door was unlocked, so she let herself back into the narrow hallway, which seemed to have tightened even since she was here before. From the windows, the afternoon was turning chalky, the air filtered through with floating dust, and she thought of the long train ride ahead, her eventual arrival home.

"Hello?" she called. As she turned into the room, the first thing she saw was a pair of long legs, laid out on the sofa, a naked torso, and Iseult's long dark hair spread out behind her like a sail. The girl leapt up silently, slim and curved, and tried to shield her body with her hands, while she rushed off into the kitchen and out of sight. But Ezra, who must have got up when he heard the door, also entirely naked, stood in front of Georgie proudly.

"Were you wanting to stay for tea?" he said coolly. He was smiling up at her. No glimmer of guilt or concern.

Georgie did not betray any surprise. She took the envelope out of her purse, with Iseult's name in Willy's handwriting on the front, and placed it on the desk. Then she turned around and walked out.

SIXTY-TWO

When she got back to Oxford late that night, everyone was already asleep. She went to the nursery first, to look in on Anne, who had her eyes closed and the blanket clasped in one pink fist. Georgie didn't wake her. She took off her shoes and walked around the house in the darkness, the floors creaking and settling under her feet.

Upstairs, she let herself into Willy's study. She wanted some more time to think through what she had seen. She knew she couldn't tell Willy or Dorothy. She could still see Ezra's defiance as he stood in that low-ceilinged room, flaunting his imperfect body, and Iseult running through to the other room. There was something joyful in the rushing about, the flurry of embarrassment for Iseult, and Ezra's pride. But as she looked out the window of the study and into the dark yard, she felt sorry for them both. It seemed to her that they were lacking something—and they were trying to find it in each other. Perhaps it was something that Ezra couldn't find in Dorothy, and something Iseult could not find in the man she spoke of marrying—but it seemed clear to Georgie that they would not find it in each other.

She saw something move in the yard, a twitching of bushes, a stray cat perhaps, but after watching for a while, she saw only bushes rumpled in the wind, revealing no creature. She wondered if she might talk to Willy about it after all, wondered what he would say. But it would likely stir up old jealousies in him, and that would mean he would bombard Thomas with more questions about his feelings for Maud and Iseult. They had been through all that already, and Thomas had already answered a hundred questions about the Gonnes. No, she would keep quiet. Outside, another twitch in the bushes resolved in a large golden cat with high haunches and a lumpy tail. The creature paraded along the line of the bushes, on display for anyone who was watching. One light paw followed another. At the edge of the lawn, it vanished again.

——— • ———

That summer they went out to Ballylee with the baby. The renovations weren't entirely finished, but Rafferty had put new green window frames in the tower, and a second cottage had been built and whitewashed, forming a cloister to grow apples and roses. The pale grey stones of the tower were interrupted by brown and gold twigs, twitching out from between the gaps. Under the bridge, the river shuffled steadily over its rocks and logs. A young moorhen tipped her head to consider the new visitors.

In the afternoon Willy was reading by the window, and Georgie was holding Anne, who was heavy in her arms. It was not yet dark, but the haze was beginning to blur the details of the land. The green was turning to brown, the brown to black; fine lines were smoothing to nothing. Georgie needed a distraction, an adult conversation, and she carried the baby over to the window seat, laid a green woollen blanket down across the seat, and placed the baby on it. Willy glanced over at them before returning to his book.

"Will you tell her a story?" Georgie said, trying to keep her voice soft.

Willy looked up again.

He stood and came over to the window seat, and stayed standing above Anne.

"Hello," Willy said to his daughter. He held out his hand above the baby and offered her his finger. She didn't take it but stared past his hand and up into her father's face, unsure if this was a game or something more serious.

"What are you reading about?" Georgie said.

"Byzantium."

The baby was still looking up at him, and he sat down beside her and spoke quietly. "In a faraway empire," he said to the baby, "at the emperor's palace, they worship monuments that never age. Inside the palace, there's an enormous gold and silver tree, which all the lords and ladies gather underneath to hear stories." More playful now, he reached over and tweaked the baby's knee with his finger and thumb. Anne reached her hand up, too slow to catch her father's fingers.

"And in that gold and silver tree," he went on, "an artificial bird sings."

The baby kicked one chubby foot into the air, then the other, and Willy caught the right foot in his hand.

"Why does it have to be artificial?" Georgie said.

Willy turned and looked surprised at her question, as if all along she had been the one telling the story.

"Because," he said, "it lasts forever."

ACKNOWLEDGMENTS AND NOTES

I can't list all the books that this novel is steeped in, but it couldn't exist without Ann Saddlemyer's wonderful biography of Georgie, *Becoming George*, as well as her edited letters between Georg(i)e and WBY. This book is also indebted to Allan Wade's edited *The Letters of W. B. Yeats*; Roy Foster's two-volume biography of WBY; James Longenbach's *Stone Cottage*; Helen Vendler's *Our Secret Discipline* and her other work on Yeats; Brenda Maddox's *George's Ghosts*; Margaret Mills Harper's *Wisdom of Two*; George Mills Harper's work on the *Vision* papers; A. Norman Jeffares et al.'s *Letters to W. B. Yeats and Ezra Pound from Iseult Gonne*; and further texts from Richard Ellmann, Warwick Gould, A. Norman Jeffares, and Deirdre Toomey. And of course, Yeats' poetry and prose was the starting point of all this. I was also lucky enough some years ago to take a class on Yeats with Jim Galvin at the Iowa Writers' Workshop. Naturally, no one is to blame for any strange corners into which I've coaxed these characters.

Many people read a draft of this book over the years and helped me to overcome several thousand anxieties about the project. They include the excellent Chelsea Wald, Katharine Dion, Laura Kaye, Keir Wotherspoon, Eirik Høyer Leivestad, Sam Gaskin, Mark Leidner, Susan Finlay, and Jeff Sissons. Bill Manhire and Ranjit Hoskote kindly wrote references along the way. Others whose friendship has carried me along over this time include Fotini Lazaridou-Hatzigoga and Steven Anthony Whiting, and many others. My gratitude is much more than it's possible to convey here.

This book owes a great deal to my wise, kind, and patient agent, Geri Thoma. I'm extremely grateful to the truly remarkable team at Tin House: Craig, Diane, Elizabeth, Alyssa, Molly, Nanci, Yash—and especially to my editor, Masie Cochran, whose intelligence, energy, and kindness is nothing short of extraordinary. Thank you, Masie.

This book was written with the support of the Akademie Schloss Solitude in Germany, as well as Creative New Zealand, the Grimshaw Sargeson Fellowship, Massey University, and the Michael King Writers Centre in New Zealand. All these institutions made this book possible.

Finally, as time muddles on I only become more and more grateful for my family, who all live on the other side of the world—especially to my parents, who gave me both love and independence, and my sisters, Polly and Zoë. While working on this book I was lucky enough to meet Eirik Høyer Leivestad, and every day since I've been grateful to him for being brilliant, playful, unfailingly supportive, and the best imaginable person to stroll through this world with.